THE
TORCHLIGHT
GAMBIT

THAD
DUPPER

The Torchlight Gambit is a work of fiction set in the near future. The premise of the novel and descriptions of naval operations and technology are grounded in fact. However, certain liberties have been taken in the interest in creating a compelling narrative. This work is fiction. Names, characters, businesses, places, events, and incidents are either the product of the author's imagination or used in a fictitious manner.

ISBN 978-0-9983476-5-3
ISBN 978-0-9983476-4-6 (ebook)

Cataloging-in-Publication Date on file with the Library of Congress
LCCN 2017-913447

Published in the United States by
Kilshaw Press LCC
    717 Golf Club Drive
    Castle Rock, CO 80801
    www.attackonack.com

Dedicated to

Captain Bradley Eugene "Joho" Johanson, USN

Commanding Officer, USS *John C. Stennis*, 2005–2008

Principal Characters

Mike "Grumpy" Bartlett: US Navy Commander, CO of VX-23

Lisa Collins: Director of the CIA

Chris Dunbar: CIA Agent and ex–Navy SEAL

Tom "Flatbush" Fraser: Rear Admiral, John C. Stennis Strike Group (COMCARGRU-3)

Chul Goh: General of North Korea Armed Services

Lauren La Rue: former Managing Director of Oasis LLC and current CIA operative

Pavo Ludovic: Leader of NetRiot cyberhacking group

Kristin McMahon: Deputy Director of the NSA

Andrew Russell: President of the United States (POTUS)

Kennedy Russell: First Lady of the United States (FLOTUS)

FOREWORD

My husband, Bradley Johanson, was the commanding officer of the USS John C. Stennis from 2005 until 2008. Thad approached me about writing this Foreword as the storyline in The Torchlight Gambit features the Stennis.

I first met Brad in 1977 at Orlando, FL where my first duty station was. Brad had several passions in his life in addition to his family – and very high on that list was being a naval aviator. He joined the Navy in April 1977 and went on to graduate from Jacksonville University in 1980 as a summa cum laude with a chemistry major.

I remember distinctly when he soloed during flight training in Pensacola in 1981, he came home with an ear to ear grin on his face. He was one happy man. It was then I knew I would not only become a Navy wife – but a Naval Aviator's wife. We then began our journey that took us across the USA numerous times and Brad traveled all over the world to many interesting places.

It wasn't long before we had our two children, Amber and John, who mostly grew up traveling with an adventure around every corner. We have many fond memories of camping across the country, going to theme parks, and experiencing the historical sights you read about in school books.

Deployments and frequent base transfers can be hard on a family. We found that staying connected to the communities that we lived in really helped with separations. By 1991 Brad had advanced to command of VS-29 Dragonflies which flew the S3-B Viking. Brad then went on to earn a master's degree in national security and strategic studies from the US Naval War College in 1995. Brad next assumed command of the USS Denver which was the precursor to achieving his ultimate goal and his next assignment.

On Friday, May 6, 2005, in Bremerton, Washington we all attended the change-of-command ceremony where Brad accepted command of the USS John C. Stennis from Captain David Buss. Commanding the Stennis, the highlight of his naval career, was a two-and-a-half-year assignment.

As planned on Friday, September 26, 2008, Brad turned command of the Stennis over to Captain Joseph Kuzmick. During the change-of-command ceremony Brad commented, "There is no finer ship and more devoted crew that I have ever served with than the John C. Stennis."

It was just a short time later that Brad retired from the Navy at the rank of Captain after a 31-year career.

We were only a few months into his retirement when Brad was diagnosed with Lou Gehrig's disease. As you can imagine, it was a devastating diagnosis for all of us but Brad faced the disease, as he did his career as an aviator with courage, a strong will and a zest for life.

As I close, I reflect on our thirty-three years of marriage as a very special time. He was a wonderful father, a caring companion and I was truly blessed to have shared this tremendous journey with him – I just wish it could have been longer. We, his children, grandchildren, sisters, parents and I, all miss him dearly. But we also are very proud – Brad spent his life in service to his country and in that all the Johansons take great pride.

To close, I will add if you have the wherewithal please consider donating to the Muscular Dystrophy Association to aid in ALS research. My brave warrior and I would greatly appreciate it.

Junay Johanson
Bremerton, WA

PROLOGUE

This morning found President Paek, the leader of North Korea, on the phone with the son of the late sheik Abdul Er Rahman.

"Good morning, my friend," said Paek warmly to Salman Rahman, the twenty-two-year-old son of the sheik whose untimely demise was believed to be the result of a secret attack by the Americans.

Getting right to the point, Salman replied, "Yes, good morning. Mr. President, I am calling to enlist your help."

"Of course. What is it you require, Salman?" Paek asked the young sheik, who had inherited his father's immense wealth as well as his hatred for the United States.

"My father's managing director, Lauren La Rue, the one who defected to America—I need your help to find her. We almost caught her in Dubai last year but she escaped," said Salman Rahman.

Seeing an opportunity to help himself, Paek replied, "Salman, I think we can be of service in that endeavor."

"Mr. President, she is being protected by the CIA, so it will not be easy. Plus—and this is important—I want her captured alive," said Salman, his voice evoking the vengeance that was one of the hallmarks of the megawealthy in the Middle East.

"No doubt, it will be very difficult," said Paek, positioning for something he wanted.

"That's why I called you, Mr. President. With your resources, I am certain my search for her will be greatly accelerated."

Paek, barely thirty years old, had not yet developed the gravitas of his deceased father. As a result, his words often came off like a collection of plagiarized lines rather than sophisticated oratory.

"Salman, I knew your father. I did business with your father; I considered your father a friend. If you say this woman is your enemy, then she is my enemy as well," said Paek. "I'll have my intelligence chief contact you to assist in your task," he continued.

"Mr. President, last year my government in Riyadh obtained missile technology from the Chinese," said Salman.

"Yes, we are aware that King Abudallah procured some new anti-ship ballistic missile technology," said Paek.

"President Paek, I have come into possession of three of those missiles, the Dong-Feng 21D missiles. I would like to offer them as a sign of my gratitude. Would they be of interest to you, sir?"

Paek was pleased at the offer. He guessed the missiles had cost Salman many millions of dollars to obtain, but the cost was immaterial, as he was driven by his desire to capture La Rue.

"Yes, they would be of value to us, Salman. I will have our people work out the details for their transport," said Paek.

"I am happy to help in any way I can," replied Salman.

"Clearly the gesture of a friend, Salman, thank you," said Paek as he terminated the call.

The call had greatly exceeded Paek's expectations. Obtaining the Chinese-made DF-26 anti-ship missiles would give Paek an important advantage in his escalating conflict with the

Americans, whom he despised and was determined to fight at every turn.

It was January 6, a crisp, sunny Saturday morning in New York at Pier 88 at the foot of Forty-Eighth Street on Manhattan's West Side.

Pier 86, the home of the Intrepid Sea, Air and Space Museum, usually commanded the attention of this portion of the waterfront, but not today.

Today at Pier 88, in full dress ship with flags flying from mast to mast, the newly refurbished SS *United States* was being put back into service by President Andrew Russell, the forty-sixth president of the United States.

A reviewing stand at the foot of the pier covered with bunting for the occasion set off the podium from which the Seal of the President of the United States hung.

First to speak was the mayor of New York, who welcomed the president and the large collection of VIPs on hand for the festive event. At the conclusion of his remarks, the mayor introduced the next speaker, Tim Cook, CEO of Apple.

Cook began, "Thank you Mr. Mayor. I would like to begin by acknowledging President Russell, Senators Schumer and Gillibrand, Cardinal Gotimer, members of Congress, and the members of the armed forces here today. I would also like to thank the New York Police Department for their support in arranging this grand event.

"Five years ago, an Apple systems engineer, who is with us today, sent me an email with an extraordinary idea. He suggested that Apple purchase the historic ocean liner the *United States*, which was rusting away in Philadelphia. His vision was to refurbish and modernize the

United States to make it a floating venue that would cruise the world hosting Apple events and providing classes for young people all over the world.

"Today, that idea becomes a reality. After four years and an investment of $4 billion, we are ready to put this landmark of American ingenuity and design back in service. And she's never looked better," said Cook, turning to admire the towering liner behind him with its funnels painted in the familiar red, white, and blue.

At 990 feet and now sixty-five thousand tons, the *United States* had been completely gutted and renovated, courtesy of Apple. In addition to accommodating up to two thousand passengers and a crew of eleven hundred, the ship possessed the latest in technology. It was a floating data center, innovation lab, training facility, and hotel all in one.

After highlighting the technical innovations of the ship and recounting Apple's goal of rescuing this amazing part of American nautical history, Cook finished strong: "As you know, my predecessor at Apple loved good design. It was his passion. And when you look at the design of this magnificent liner, you can tell it was ahead of its time, and for that reason its design is enduring. Apple is pleased and humbled to have been able to repurpose this great ship as an innovation lab that will travel the world educating and informing the next generation of engineers, gadflies, and geniuses. And let me close by saying, Steve would have loved what we're doing today." At this point Cook introduced President Andrew Russell.

President Russell, mindful of the time, kept his remarks brief while still recognizing the historical significance of the event. "On this brilliant January morning, we welcome back to the Port of New York one of its finest liners. Designed and built in the 1950s, the

United States represented the state of the art in terms of shipbuilding, engineering, and innovation. And today it takes that place again, thanks to the vision and resources of Apple. But now the *United States* has an expanded mission of bringing technology and education to the next generations of the world's youth."

The president continued for a few more minutes before closing. He then walked over to the prow of the ship along with his wife, Kennedy Russell, who exclaimed, "I rechristen thee SS *United States*. May God bless her and all who sail on her." And with those words, she swung the ceremonial bottle of champagne, which exploded on the bow of the sleek liner as the US Marine Band played "The Stars and Stripes Forever" followed by "New York, New York."

Apple had had many internal debates about whether to change the name of the ship. While being civic-minded and proud of its US roots, it worried that the name *United States* would not be in keeping with the new ship's mission as a lab for the youth of the world. In the end, Tim Cook went with tradition and kept the original name, knowing that it was "bad luck" to change the name of a ship.

It was a great event—great for the country, for the city, and for Apple. Clearly Apple had made the right decision. It had taken only a fraction of its $256 billion cash hoard and put it toward the *United States* project, but the amount of goodwill Apple would realize from the *United States* would be enormous.

With the festivities out of the way, there was real business to discuss.

Under the guise of a tour of the ship, Tim Cook welcomed President Russell, Sterling Spencer, the president's chief of staff, and Lisa Collins, the director of the CIA, to the William Francis Gibbs Suite, named for the naval architect who originally designed the *United States*.

"Thank you again for attending today's event, Mr. President," said Cook.

"It was a great event and you and Apple should be proud of this achievement," replied Russell.

As they sat down, Spencer took over. "Tim, we would like your assistance for a mission we have in mind for the *United States*," he said.

This caught Cook a little off guard. After all, they'd just put the ship in service forty-five minutes earlier.

"We think for its inaugural cruise the *United States* should go to South Korea and then visit North Korea," Spencer said dryly, which befit his personality.

"North Korea?" was Cook's only response.

"Yes, we think it will be in keeping with the role you just laid out for the ship. The US government won't condone the visit, but we won't prevent or criticize it either. Furthermore, going to North Korea will advance your narrative of how Apple technology can help bring the world together," added Spencer.

Cook said, "We were planning to bring the *United States* to San Francisco for an Apple company event as its first port of call."

President Russell replied, "You have the opportunity for the first voyage of your ship to make history. No other company has ever been in a position like this. Apple will be at the forefront not only in technology but in global outreach as well. Think of the PR opportunities for you."

"While I am intrigued by the idea, what's this really about?" asked Cook.

This was the cue for Lisa Collins to join the conversation. "Mr. Cook, when the *United States* makes port in Busan, South Korea, we are going to need cabins for one hundred. We will be putting a team of security personnel on board. That's all you need to know other than the mission in North Korea is important to our national security and that of the world."

Cook wasn't surprised at her reply, but he was clearly annoyed and shot back at Collins, "Director Collins, we don't know each other that well, but let me share with you my opinion of the CIA and the other US intelligence agencies. You harass us endlessly about our encryption. Your agents make comments almost daily that portray Apple as unwilling to cooperate with the CIA, and frankly, your *cyberexperts* are a team of engineers who couldn't cut it in Silicon Valley so they had to take government jobs."

Any hope President Russell had of keeping the discussion friendly went out the window with Cook's last remark. But before Collins could respond, the president stepped in. "There's no need for this to get personal. Tim, this is what we need you to do—it's what *I* need you to do. We need the first visit of the *United States* to occur in Busan, South Korea, on April eleventh. We want you to reach out personally to President Paek of North Korea and suggest the *United States* visit Namp'o, North Korea. Tell him you think it would be history making if you can be part of their Day of the Sun celebrations on April fifteenth. Tell him you don't care what I or the US government thinks and that you are looking to make history with your ship's first voyage. I think he will accept your offer as another way to embarrass the US government, which is just fine with us."

After a pause, and in a cooler tone, Cook responded, "I understand, Mr. President. Give me a few days and you will have my answer, sir."

As the meeting finished, President Russell asked for a minute alone with Cook.

"Tim, clearly you aren't aware, but there's a strong possibility, if not a likelihood, that Lisa Collins will succeed me as president. And her influence will only grow leading up to that election. It would do you and Apple well to get on her good side. In addition, I didn't appreciate your comment about our cyberanalysts."

"I apologize, Mr. President," said Cook, "It was an inappropriate comment. You know how much I think of you and your leadership."

Russell nodded and continued. "Tim, I'm counting on your support in this matter. It's very important. I wouldn't ask you if this were just some sort of political maneuver."

Cook nodded that he understood.

The president closed with, "I look forward to your response, but I expect it to be positive."

As they left the suite, the president said, loud enough for Cook's staff to hear, "Congratulations, Tim. It was a great event today—for Apple and the world. You and your team should be very proud." The president paused for a few minutes to take pictures with the executives of Apple, and then he was gone.

A week later the president's chief of staff came into the Oval Office saying, "Mr. President, I heard from Tim Cook. The *United States* will be making its first trip to South Korea and he is going to reach out to Paek about visiting the North as well."

"Good, good," was all the president said as they moved on to other business.

CHAPTER ONE

Deep inside Cheyenne Mountain in Colorado at NORAD Headquarters, the screen on First Lieutenant Camila Alvarez's screen started to flash.

"Sir, we have a possible missile launch from Shampoo."

Shampoo was the code name for Namp'o, North Korea, a known missile site located on the Yellow Sea, or what today is more commonly called the East China Sea.

The on-duty officer, Major Brian Sloan, toggled over to the missile-tracking screen on his MIDS display. MIDS was the US Air Force's new Missile Information Defense System.

Alvarez zoomed her display to the East China Sea area and added, "Sir, we have confirmation. We are tracking a Korean missile launch. Confidence is high. I repeat, confidence is high."

As he administered instructions on his keyboard, Major Sloan picked up his handset and pressed the P1 button. "This is Giant Killer on alert. Giant Killer is issuing a P1 missile launch warning for the East China Sea. POO"—point of origin—"is Namp'o, North Korea."

With the P1 Alert, activity in Cheyenne Mountain, located near the Air Force Academy in Colorado Springs, dramatically increased. Sloan got on the phone with his commanding officer, Colonel Tim

Raftery. "Yes, sir, we are tracking a launch of a ballistic missile from North Korea."

When a P1 Alert is issued, all commands of the US Navy, US Air Force, Army, and Coast Guard, as well as the NSA, CIA, and White House, must be notified.

Before Colonel Raftery hung up he barked, "I'm coming down"; then the line went dead.

Sloan turned his attention back to his MIDS screen. "Alvarez, what's MIDS telling us about the missile?" Just as the US Navy tracks and tapes all enemy submarines to document their acoustic signatures, MIDS was now analyzing the heat signature, speed, and track of the North Korean launch to determine what type of missile it was.

"Sir, MIDS is classing the missile as a Chinese DF-26. It's a 'carrier killer,' sir." Alvarez used the colloquial name for the DF-26 because it was thought that this anti-ship ballistic missile, or ASBM, if nuclear armed, could destroy a US Navy aircraft carrier.

Sloan shot back, "Lieutenant, how can the North Koreans be firing a DF-26 missile? Rerun your analysis."

"Sir, I did," she quickly replied. "MIDS is indicating the missile has the heat signature and performance characteristics of a Dong-Feng 21D."

The Dong-Feng 21D was an improved variant of a standard ballistic missile modified to be an anti-ship missile specifically for use against US aircraft carriers. With a range of fifteen hundred nautical miles and traveling at a reported speed of up to Mach 10, or seventy-six hundred miles per hour, the DF-26 could be armed with either a conventional or a nuclear warhead, reportedly up to 150 kilotons. To put that in perspective, the Hiroshima bomb was fifteen kilotons and the Nagasaki bomb twenty-one kilotons. A nuclear-armed DF-26 would be up to ten times as powerful.

Major Sloan yelled to an airman to bring up the tactical plot for the East China Sea. "Who do we have out there?"

The airman put the tactical plot on one of the four ten-by-ten-foot displays that overlooked the entire control room. "Sir, Carrier Strike Group 3—the *John C. Stennis* Strike Group—is in the East China Sea."

Hearing the news, Sloan picked up his handset and issued the following priority alert: "Giant Killer is going to battle stations. All stations confirm and authenticate. Alert the *Stennis* Strike Group. Giant Killer has picked up a launch of what we are classing as a Dong-Feng 21D in their AOR"—area of responsibility—"priority 1."

Going to battle stations is the highest level of alert Giant Killer can set, and it is the customary alert level for a missile attack on either the US homeland or a base. Over the last twenty years, going to battle stations has been utilized only a handful of times. One was on 9/11 and another was when President Andrew Russell's family was attacked on Nantucket the year before.

The USS *John C. Stennis* (CVN-74), one of the United States' supercarriers, along with the escort ships that formed Carrier Strike Group 3 (CARGRU-3), had put to sea from the newly reopened naval base in Subic Bay, Philippines. The US Navy almost always deployed one of its carrier groups to provide a military presence in the East China Sea.

The local time on the *Stennis* was 7:30 p.m. when the Giant Killer call was received.

In the *Stennis's* Combat Direction Center (CDC), screens started blinking as the Giant Killer alert was received.

Lieutenant Commander Larry Stone, the *Stennis*'s CDC duty officer, picked up the handset and pressed the button for the bridge. "Captain, Giant Killer has just gone to battle stations. They are tracking a DF-26 'carrier killer' fired from North Korea heading to the East China Sea."

Traveling at seven thousand miles an hour, the inbound DF-26 could cover the approximately fifteen hundred miles from its launch in Namp'o to the location of CARGRU-3 in barely fifteen minutes.

The captain responded, "On my way. Alert the admiral."
On the admiral's bridge of the *John C. Stennis*, sitting in his command chair, was newly flagged rear admiral Tom "Flatbush" Fraser, commander, Carrier Strike Group 3—in short, COMCARGRU-3. Upon being notified of the ASBM, Admiral Fraser also headed to the CDC.

Captain Ryan of the *Stennis* arrived first and asked, "Did our Tall Boy pick up the launch?"

He was asking whether the Aegis cruiser of the carrier group had detected the missile launch. It was the task of the Ticonderoga-class Aegis cruiser to provide air defense to US carrier groups using its state-of-the-art missile systems.

Just as the captain spoke, on board the USS *Mobile Bay* (CG-53), the Ticonderoga-class cruiser, the BMD (ballistic missile defense) screens started lighting up.

Adhering to procedures and without waiting for a confirmation, the BMD operator on the *Mobile Bay* issued an alert to all ships in CARGRU-3. "This is Red Crown on Guard." Red Crown was the call sign for cruisers assigned to US carrier groups. "Vampire, vam-pire, vampire, Red Crown is tracking an inbound vampire BRAA, 015, 1,200, 3.3, beam east." The BRAA call indicated bearing, range, altitude, and aspect of the inbound missile, designated as a vampire, which indicated that the BMD classed it as an enemy missile.

In a matter of seconds, every ship in CARGRU-3 went to battle stations, missile.

That meant three Arleigh Burke destroyers and the cruiser USS *Mobile Bay*, as well as the *Stennis* and their accompanying fast-combat support ship, USS *Rainier* (AOR-7), were all in the process of manning battle stations to repel a possible incoming anti-ship missile attack.

In addition, underwater the USS *Washington* (SSN-787), a Virginia-class attack submarine attached to the strike group, was manning battle stations, which included rising to the depth of one hundred feet in order to be ready to launch its defensive anti-ship missiles.

Rear Admiral Tom Fraser was now in the CDC along with his staff.

"Execute Group Order Baker Foxtrot Zulu," commanded the rear admiral. This was the order for his carrier group to disperse the group at maximum speed, go active on all tracking systems, and implement what is called a SP-JASHO condition on all ships.

SP-JASHO was a defense condition specifically designed to defend against an inbound missile attack. It stood for spoof, jam, and shoot, which included (1) spoofing, which sends false images to the incoming missile, (2) jamming the inbound missile's tracking system in order to confuse it, and (3) all the ships in the group employing their BMD—ballistic missile defense systems—and firing a variety of missiles intended to intercept and destroy the inbound missile.

The missile had already been in the air for five minutes. That meant a potentially nuclear-armed anti-ship ballistic missile traveling at a speed of two miles per second was headed toward the USS John C. Stennis Strike Group. Tensions were high all around. Captain Ryan pressed the button on his handset for the bridge and ordered the officer of the deck, "Execute Baker Foxtrot Zulu ahead flank."

Ryan then pushed the button for the chief engineer. "CE, it's the CO. Pull out the rods; I want flank speed—give us all you can."

The chief engineer responded, "Aye, aye, ahead flank, indicating 125 rpms."

With that, the vibrations on the USS *John C. Stennis*, all hun-dred thousand tons of it, started to increase as the ship accelerated past its official to p sp eed of th irty-three kn ots. Li kewise, th e Arleigh Burke destroyers of the group were all nearing thirty-six knots as every ship in the group ran from the incoming North Korean missile.

With Giant Killer going to battle stations, the US Secret Service needed to notify and secure the president. That meant interrupting the president, who was at the White House hosting a breakfast meet-ing with the Republican opposition leaders.

Dan Nicols, the president's US Secret Service detail chief, came into the West Wing's Roosevelt Room and whispered the words no president wanted to hear: "Sir, we have a situation."

President Russell stood up, saying, "Ladies and gentlemen, something has come up. We'll need to continue this discussion at another time."

The president was quickly ushered into the elevator that would take him to the Situation Room, which was housed under the West Wing. When the Secret Service informed him that Giant Killer had gone to battle stations, Russell demanded, "My family?"

"Yes, sir, the first lady and the children are being secured.

Your children haven't left for school yet, sir." The president greeted the hastily convened staff in the Sit Room by immediately asking, "What do we have?"

"Sir, we have picked up the launch of what appears to be a Dong-Feng 'carrier killer' missile from North Korea. The missile is six minutes out from the *Stennis* Carrier Group, which is in the East China Sea coming out of Subic," said the vice chairman of the Joint Chiefs of Staff, Admiral Brad Johnson.

"Can the group shoot it down?" asked the president.
"Unclear at this point, sir. They are spoofing and jamming but it is only a matter of minutes before the missile will hit."

"The USS *Washington* is firing its Harpoon missiles as fast as she can get them off."
"We don't know if the DF-26 is armed, sir. We have made no overt act of aggression, so this attack is unprovoked," added Johnson.
"What the hell are the North Koreans doing with a Dong-Feng?" was the president's next question.

"Sir, we don't know where the North Koreans would have gotten it but we know it was launched from Namp'o and our systems are classing it as a Dong-Feng with confidence high," said Admiral Johnson.

On the bridges of every ship in CARGRU-3, everyone was bracing for the flash of the detonation.

As the seconds ticked off, the D F-21D s tarted t o veer o ff course. At first the deviation was slight, but then it became more erratic and pronounced. The missile fell into the sea eighty miles from the *Stennis* Carrier Group without detonating. It wasn't clear whether their jamming and spoofing h ad proven successful, o r the missile had suffered an internal failure, or even if it had been issued a self-destruct order. That would a ll b e discovered later, but for now Admiral Fraser asked the CDC officer, "Are there any other threats on the board?"

"Sir, the scope is clear. There are no airborne or ballistic threats. We are only tracking some small fishing boats approximately twenty-five miles from Home Plate," said the CDC lieutenant, using the code name for the flagship, the John C. Stennis.

The admiral's chief of staff sent out a message to the group to stand down from general quarters and to re-form into a tactical formation. He then ordered that all ships in the group continue to remain on alert with their surface-to-air weapons and radars. Fraser turned to his chief of staff and said, "Send the *Kidd* to see if they can find any of the debris from the missile. Also, have the *Hamilton* get those fishing boats out of here." COMCARGRU-3 was referring to the USS *Kidd* (DDG-100) and USS *Paul Hamilton* (DDG-60), both Arleigh Burke destroyers of DESRON-21—Destroyer Squadron 21—attached to his carrier group.

"Copy, Admiral," replied the captain.

Minutes later, Admiral Fraser convened his staff. "Gentlemen, why do I feel like we were caught with our pants around our ankles?"

The admiral was referring to the inability of USS *Mobile Bay*, whose job it was to defend the carrier group, to fire any of its interceptor missiles. The BMD system, made up of the AN/SPY-1D radar and Aegis Combat System, had detected the incoming enemy missile but wasn't able to track or paint the Dong-Feng to get launch coordinates.

"Yes, our jamming and spoofing worked, but other than the *Washington* we didn't get a single shot off. If that missile had detonated a nuclear warhead, the group would have sustained significant damage. We were lucky this time, gentlemen, and we don't rely on luck, do you read me? Get on it." With that the admiral departed to brief the commander, US Pacific Fleet, known as COMPACFLT, who in turn would brief the CNO, the chief of naval operations. The staff remained in the conference room, continuing to review the actions taken during the attack.

In the Sit Room President Russell turned to his chairman of the Joint Chiefs, who also had joined the conference bridge, saying, "Take us to DEFCON 4—find out if there are other hostile actions under way anywhere else. Also, have the South Koreans raise their alert posture."

Acknowledging Lisa Collins, the director the CIA, who had conferenced in, the president said, "Lisa, verify this was launched by the government of North Korea."

"Will do, Mr. President," responded Collins.

George Riordan, the director of the NSA, was also on the bridge. "George," the president said, "what does the NSA know?"

"Sir, not much at the moment. If this was a DF-26, we know North Korea doesn't have that technology. Recall the Chinese did sell some DF-26s to KSA"—the Kingdom of Saudi Arabia —"but they weren't specials"—in other words, nukes. "My bet is if this was a 26 and it was indeed fired by North Korea, then they got it from the Saudis."

The president shook his head. "The Saudis again."

Not waiting for a reply, the president turned to Admiral Brad Johnson and asked, "What assets do we have in the area in addition to the *Stennis* Group?"

"Sir, we have the *Michael Mansoor*, the new Zumwalt destroyer, off Vietnam. We have the submarines USS *Florida* and USS *Connecticut* at Pearl. And there's the *North Carolina* escorting the

United States, per your orders, but it won't arrive in the area for about a week."

The president knew what Johnson was suggesting when he mentioned the USS *Florida*. The USS *Florida* was an Ohio-class ballistic submarine that had been modified to house the top secret Torchlight technology. Very few knew of this development, and for the moment Russell needed to keep it that way.

Soon after being sworn in as the forty-sixth president, Andrew Russell was given a top secret briefing on Torchlight by the program director, Jim Hartel.

"Mr. President, Torchlight is a laser-based technology specifically designed to defeat ballistic missiles," he began. "By using an extremely powerful and focused laser beam, Torchlight has the ability to destroy incoming missiles.

"That said," continued Hartel," the challenges of the Torchlight technology are many. First, the weapon requires a tremendous amount of power. We use the next-generation nuclear reactors configured in a series. But that alone is not enough. We also employ EDFAs, or an erbium-doped fiber accelerator, which allows us to amplify the power of the laser beam by a factor of ten. With the EDFA technology, we take the one million megawatts generated from the reactors and increase it to ten million megawatts to power the laser weapon systems."

The president asked Hartel, "What about the targeting system?"

"That's the other challenge of the Torchlight program—tracking and steering. For tracking, we have integrated Torchlight with the new S-band radar the Navy is developing—the SPY-6." Hartel was referring to the next-generation state-of-the-art radar system that was being developed by Raytheon and would provide a new search capability for air and ballistic missile defense.

"As for steering," said Hartel, "we have adapted technology from our latest-generation fighter jets and incorporated it into Torchlight. We have taken the fast-steering mirror from the F-35 Lightning, a technology from Ball Aerospace in Boulder, Colorado, and adapted it to allow the laser beam to track at extremely fast intervals—at the microsecond level. We also added a photon detector and a quad cell to provide added steering accuracy.

"In addition, we have added antiroll gyros to the laser-targeting systems, anticipating that Torchlight will be deployed at sea as well as on land."

The president went on the offensive. "Mr. Hartel, we are spending in excess of $8 billion on the Terminal High Altitude Area Defense (THAAD) missile system this year. Why is that not money well spent?"

Hartel was expecting a question along those lines and replied, "Mr. President, there are four main reasons why Torchlight is superior to THAAD. First, as you no doubt know, the kill rate for THAAD is sixty percent. Torchlight's is in excess of ninety percent so far. THAAD has a range of a hundred and twenty miles. Torchlight's range is more than twice that. And from a cost perspective, every time we fire Torchlight it costs us practically zero. We are generating a laser beam made up of highly concentrated photons. The latest budget numbers for THAAD indicate that each missile costs us $75 million."

The president replied, "I don't doubt your facts, Mr. Hartel, but I have mobile THAAD launchers in South Korea, Hawaii, Guam, and on the West Coast. They are operational at this point. Torchlight isn't."

"Mr. President, when THAAD was envisioned, twenty years ago, it was a very formidable defense system, but Torchlight is the next-generation solution in virtually every dimension," said Hartel. Just for emphasis he added, "Torchlight is more accurate, has a longer range, is faster, has a lower cost, and can be mounted on our submarines."

President Russell had already decided that Torchlight held the promise to eclipse THAAD, but he wanted to hear Hartel's defense, which made him even more committed to the program.

The president pivoted and asked, "Jim, what's the plan to get this technology into the fleet for testing?"

"Mr. President, we are deploying land-based Torchlights at our bases in South Korea, the Philippines, Vietnam, Hawaii, and Guam, as well as on the coasts of the US, but none of those installations are complete yet. Estimated time to get them online is late next year, sir. In terms of the Fleet Readiness program, our plan is to test the SPY-6 radar with Torchlight together on our first sea-based platform on the USS *Florida*."

The president interjected, "The *Florida*? Isn't that an Ohio-class boomer?"

Hartel nodded. "Correct, sir. The *Florida* was a ballistic submarine, or 'boomer,' but we recently converted it to a special mission under the Torchlight Program and redesignated it as SSGN-728. Sir, the *Florida* was chosen because at 560 feet in length and more than eighteen thousand tons she had the room needed to install the reactors required to power Torchlight. We removed the twenty ICBM missile silos and in their place installed six of the new Bechtel A1B nuclear reactors from the new *Ford* class of aircraft carriers, the SPY-6 system, the EDFAs, and, of course, the laser."

Hartel concluded his briefing by saying, "Mr. President, Torchlight has the potential to be a game-changer, but it has some technical hurdles before it can become operational. Not to mention, sir, the impact it might have on the atmosphere. Some of our scientists at the Jet Propulsion Labs in Pasadena worry that such a powerful laser could 'tear' a hole in the atmosphere, causing unfiltered gamma rays from the sun to bombard the earth, possibly compromising the planet's core. We have been conducting tests on that and we believe those concerns are unfounded. Sir, once the *Florida* is fitted out, it will sail out of Pearl in Hawaii to conduct fleet testing. We call it the Death Star of the Fleet, sir."

The president had approved the next phase of the Torchlight project, which included field-testing the technology on the USS *Florida*.

Of course, all of this was fifteen months ago. Since then, the *Florida* had completed its installation and begun its testing of Torchlight. The results were very promising, but it was still expected to be another year before Torchlight completed its fleet readiness testing and would be ready for official deployment by the Navy.

The president, bringing his attention back to the situation at hand, addressed his Sit Room team. "Brad," he said, addressing the vice chairman of the Joint Chiefs, "move the *Florida* and *Connecticut* into the East China Sea ASAP."

Admiral Johnson responded, "Copy, sir."

Pavo Ludovic was the leader of a cyberhacking group based in the Brasina area of Dubrovnik, Croatia. He and his team, known in the hacking world as NetRiot, occupied a small house in view of the Adriatic Sea on the old French Road. It was a cadastral plot of land that in an earlier time had been cultivated for agriculture.

Today just a few olive trees remained. The only thing that could have given away that this was no longer a simple country house was the multiple satellite dishes set up in the yard. But to see them you would have to gain access to the property, which was shielded by an eight-foot-high wooden fence and guarded by two Rottweilers.

Ludovic and NetRiot were part of the black underworld of cyberterrorism. Their particular expertise was penetrating the financial system known as SWIFT.

The Society for Worldwide Interbank Financial Telecommunication, or SWIFT, provides a network that enables financial institutions across the globe to send and receive information about financial transactions in a secure, standardized, and reliable environment.

Today, SWIFT links more than nine thousand financial institutions in more than two hundred countries, which exchange an average of fifteen million messages per day.

NetRiot had been syphoning off millions from the SWIFT accounts of its less technically astute members. Easy pickings were the accounts of Bangladesh, Thailand, and many of the African countries. And it was for that reason that NetRiot was hired by a company out of North Korea with the nondescript name of Imperial Imports LLC.

Pavo reminded his team leader, "Antonija, make sure you keep the lifts under US$10,000 so as not to raise any red flags."

Antonija, an expert in hacking bank systems, understood Pavo's order and nodded. By keeping the amount they stole in each transaction small, the Brasina team had accumulated almost $100 million in pilfered funds. That, plus the fees they charged their clients, including Imperial Imports LLC, a front for the North Korean government, made them all wealthy. Of course, they did not consider themselves criminals but rather cyber–freedom fighters.

Other cyberterrorist groups were focusing on stealing and leaking confidential information. This included state secrets, as in the case of Edward Snowden, but increasingly included, as was witnessed in the 2016 US election, the hacking of personal information such as emails, text messages, and photos. These were the areas that had propelled WikiLeaks to its current vilified position of power, influence, and fear around the world.

Beyond the theft of personal data, the other risk from cyberterrorism was the disruption of society and the spread of anarchy. Cyberattacks on airlines, air traffic control systems, hospitals, the electric grid, and banking systems all represented high-profile targets for the various hacking groups.

The US intelligence agencies—the NSA, CIA, and FBI—all have cyberoperations, as do the intelligence organizations of every first-line country today. The US military apparatus provides both defensive and offensive cyber capabilities. The United States Cyber Command, known as USCYBERCOM, located in Fort Meade, Maryland, is the centralized command of cyberoperations. USCYBERCOM is the coordination point for elements of the US Army Cyber Command, the US Navy's Fleet Cyber Command/ Tenth Fleet, the US Air Force's Twenty-Fourth Air Force – Air Forces Cyber and the Marine Forces Cyberspace Command.

In addition to these formidable assets, governments would often employ cyber attack groups like NetRiot and Guccifer with the benefit of removing themselves from the groups' predatory activities.

To defend against those threats, governments, businesses, and powerful people were investing millions of dollars to deploy electronic messaging systems (text and email) that were hackproof. But the notion of a hackproof system was a fallacy. To that end, some people, most notably Saudi sheiks and Russian oligarchs, had stopped using electronic communications altogether, electing to have proxies do their communicating for them.

It was for these reasons that cyberterrorism had joined radical Islamic terrorism and North Korea as one of the top three threats facing the security and safety of the United States. Pavo Ludovic and his team at NetRiot were considered one of the best hacking groups, and as a result, their services were in high demand.

Kristin McMahon, deputy director of the NSA, was a rising star whose reputation had only grown after she'd been involved in the analysis that contributed to the rescue of the Russell children when they were kidnapped on Nantucket.

In addition to a promising career at the NSA, McMahon was in the final stages of planning her April 28 wedding to US Navy pilot Commander Mike "Grumpy" Bartlett. Commander Bartlett was the newly promoted commanding officer of VX-23, the Salty Dogs, based in Patuxent River, Maryland. VX-23 was the Navy's premier Test and Evaluation squadron. In addition, Bartlett had worked closely with President Russell on the plan to exact justice from the man responsible for last year's attack on the president's family—the late Sheik Abdul Er Rahman of Saudi Arabia.

As a couple, it was nice for McMahon and Bartlett to, on occasion, escape the sphere of the Washington intelligence and military worlds. Tonight found McMahon and Bartlett on their way to dinner with friends at a Georgetown bistro.

As Bartlett navigated his 1985 Porsche 911 through the neighborhood streets of Georgetown, McMahon said, "I'm looking forward to seeing Pam and Dave."

Bartlett replied, "Me too. It'll be nice to have a dinner where we aren't talking shop with your spy friends."

McMahon, who was now expert in picking up on Bartlett's sarcasm, responded, "Or spending a night with your fighter pilot buddies and their supersized egos."

"Who are you referring to? Do you mean the best of the best?" came Bartlett's reply.

"Exactly," responded McMahon with a smile. She actually liked Bartlett's aviator friends, even if the discussions always included a heavy dose of squadron reminiscing, with some of it bordering on a cross between a frat party and a ready-room technical briefing.

But tonight's dinner with David and Pam Weaver would include none of that. David was a European history professor at Georgetown and Pam was a pharmaceutical scientist expert in transdermal transfer systems.

It made for an interesting foursome. But tonight, a lot of the conversation would be about the upcoming McMahon-Bartlett nuptials.

Once seated, Kristin and Pam immediately started talking about the wedding while Mike and David talked sports and cars. David Weaver was a transplanted New Yorker, so of course he followed the New York teams, but it being early April, it was too soon for baseball. With that in mind, the topic moved to cars, given that the commander was restoring a 1967 Mustang with plans to build a re-creation of the car from the movie *Bullitt*.

David said to Mike, "My advice, get the project done quickly, because once you and Kristin are married and start a family, time for things like restoring a car will evaporate." David spoke from firsthand knowledge. He and Pam had a two-and-a-half-year-old son and were working on their second child.

Bartlett nodded as he responded, "I hear you. My goal is to get the car completed this year. Plus, my career rotation calls for an at-sea assignment next year."

David's eyes rolled as he said, "Well, you better make the honeymoon and the next few months count, then."

Bartlett nodded and said, "Kristin tells me you're headed to Europe?"

"I am. I'm going to Munich for a conference on the history of the Austrian and Ottoman Empires and their impact on today's Balkan ethnic strains."

Bartlett looked quizzical. Weaver continued, "The history of the Balkans and their religious conflict goes back over a thousand years and to a large extent continues today. We will be discussing some of the historic and even anthropologic reasons for the discord. But really it all boils down to economics and religion. The Turks and the Germans have fundamentally different approaches to life, business, and religion. On one hand, you have the people of Germany, Switzerland, and Austria, who prize order and discipline in their societies and have a strong separation of church and state. Then you have the Turks, who are a very emotional people and make religion and family the center of every aspect of their lives. Those two cultures collide in the geographic area of the Balkans. It's a combustible mix—then and now. The only real solution is separation."

Bartlett asked, "Can't all conflicts be reduced to that—differences in religion and economics?"

"Perhaps, at a high level, but what's interesting—or disturbing— about the Serbian-Croat conflict is how it has resisted evolving. At Georgetown, one of my colleagues, a biologist, likes to say that a virus must mutate in order to survive. However, here, the lack of mutation hasn't threatened their survival. They're locked in a two-thousand-year cycle, they've made very little progress, they haven't evolved, yet it hasn't burned itself out yet either."

Bartlett was puzzled and asked, "So if the society hasn't mutated, why has it continued to survive?"

"Well, that isn't the substance of my paper, but to answer your question—everything needs to mutate in order to survive. Every society, every religion, even relationships. Mutation and adaptation are key to longevity.

"In order for an ethnic conflict to mutate to a new state, it requires a period of two to three generations, or about eighty years, in order to break the current cycle. That's the mutation. Without mutating, peace or progress cannot occur. Look at Northern Ireland, which is now completing the second generation of peace. One more generation without violence and Northern Ireland will have broken their cycle. Ditto with civil rights in the US, apartheid in South Africa, and the India-Pakistan conflict. But today's hot spots of Serbia and the Middle East—none have had even one generation of peace to start the cycle. At least not yet."

"So what's the meeting in Munich about? To recommend the start of an eighty-year stretch of peace in Croatia and Serbia to break the cycle? Certainly it's not that easy," said Bartlett.

"Well, that would be an abbreviated way to describe it, but, yes, we are suggesting a formula for change to begin the mutation cycle," said Weaver. "As you know, historians study the past as a way to predict the future," he added.

David paused, saw he was dominating the conversation, and said, "But enough of solving the world's problems—how's the wedding planning going?"

Bartlett responded by rolling his eyes, but it was a good cue for them to join the other conversation that was under way between the two women.

Kristin said, "It's getting hectic as the date approaches, especially with the president and first lady attending—it just adds to the complexity."

Pam added, "I think it's so romantic to be having your wedding at Annapolis, and it's got to be incredibly exciting that the president and first lady are attending."

"It is amazing, but with their attendance we run the risk of losing some control over the wedding," said McMahon.

Bartlett added, "If you want I'll call Andrew Russell and tell him we're eloping to Vegas."

Kristin deadpanned, "I'm sure our parents would be thrilled with that suggestion."

Bartlett added, "Other than the metal detectors and the Secret Service snipers, it'll be your run-of-the-mill wedding."

Not missing a beat, Kristin fired back, "It's not the Secret Service or snipers I worry about. It's your squadron buddies. I don't want the reception to turn into a toga party."

Bartlett replied in a more reflective tone, "Ten years ago that would have been a valid concern, but in the 'new Navy' that sort of behavior isn't tolerated. I mean it, I've seen COs and captains get relieved for behavior that ten years ago wouldn't have even raised an eyebrow. It's all for the best, but on occasion there's a career officer who falls victim unfairly to the new policy."

Bartlett realized he had entered lecture mode. He quickly regrouped and added, "But besides that, I'm afraid Father Time is catching up with the members of my class from Annapolis and even with the members of my first squadron VFA-143."

"Hmm," replied McMahon with a smile. "VFA-143, remind me again, what's that squadron's name?"

Bartlett quickly responded with the squadron's Latin motto, "Sans Reproache, baby—what's wrong with that?" He added the "baby" to get a smile out of Kristin, which it did, but also because in the fighter community you always ended a squadron motto with the term "baby."

Pam now joined in, "'Baby,' maybe the 'new Navy' needs some more work?"

But Bartlett already knew what was coming. "The Pukin Dogs," stated McMahon flatly, looking at Pam.

Pam blinked. "The what?"

"That's right," said McMahon, "the name of VFA-143 is the Pukin Dogs. And remember to leave off the *g*—that's very important."

Pam laughed and said, "I'm sure that will go over great with the first lady."

"Ha," quickly responded Bartlett, "you probably didn't know but Andrew Russell flew with VFA-143. You'd be fighting a losing battle if you try to enlist the support of POTUS."

Glancing at Pam and David, McMahon said, "And you wonder why I worry about the reception?"

Bartlett added, "Well, honey, we'll be mixing the Pukin Dogs with the Salty Dogs," referring to Bartlett's current billet as CO of the Test and Evaluation squadron based out of the Naval Air Station Pax River, where Bartlett and VX-23 were certifying the new F-35C Lightning II fighter jet for fleet duty.

"That's too many 'dogs' for any wedding, if you ask me. Just make sure they behave themselves," McMahon said with a laugh.

Pam injected, "Well, we're looking forward to the wedding. And seeing all those pilots in their uniforms—yay."

CHAPTER TWO

L auren La Rue, who a year ago had been on the CIA's most wanted list, was now working for the US.

La Rue had worked last year with Sheik Abdul Er Rahman, the mastermind behind the Al Qaeda–funded mission to kidnap President Andrew Russell's family as they vacationed on Nantucket. La Rue, as the sheik's financial manager, had unknowingly arranged the financing for the mission.

However, La Rue had been captured as part of defeating the operation.

Subsequently, La Rue cut a deal with the Justice Department by agreeing to work for the CIA to help penetrate networks similar to the sheik's. And that is how Lauren La Rue found herself on this cold April morning headed to the CIA headquarters in Langley, Virginia.

Prior to La Rue's arrival, a meeting was under way with the director of the CIA, Lisa Collins, the deputy director of the NSA, Kristin McMahon, and key members of their staffs.

"In order for us to advance Operation Deadeye, we need to make contact with NetRiot in Croatia. Our intelligence tells us that NetRiot can provide us with a Chinese missile operating system hack, which is critical to the overall success of Deadeye," said Collins.

"And our best avenue into NetRiot is La Rue," added McMahon.

"Can we trust her at this point? She's only been with us for five months now," remarked Collins.

A staff member spoke up. "Zoran Kordic is the key. He knows La Rue and trusts her from their past dealings with the sheik. We need La Rue to get us access to NetRiot through Kordic. Given the high priority of Deadeye, I don't see we have a choice."

Everyone in the room knew that last statement was one hundred percent correct, but still concerns were great.

"I don't disagree, but we know the sheik's people are still after La Rue. I give her only a fifty-fifty chance of coming back alive," said McMahon.

McMahon was referring to the bounty on La Rue's head. The bounty was not to kill La Rue but rather to capture her. Killing La Rue would be too kind in the eyes of the sheik's family and associates. No, they wanted her captured so she could be tortured and made an example for all to see.

"It's imperative that we make contact with NetRiot, and we need to do it at once to maintain our timeline. In order to protect La Rue, we'll send one of our best agents with her. Plus, we'll have a ready evacuation plan in place in case things fall apart," Collins said.

Reading the reluctance in the room, she added, "Look, we'll send her over there and try to get her back here ASAP. Frankly, it's a risk that we must take."

Thirty minutes later, Lauren La Rue joined Director Lisa Collins and Deputy Director Kristin McMahon in the fifth-floor conference room. It was noteworthy that the attendees of this meeting, where the country's most secret covert operations were being discussed, were all women. It was a remarkable image and represented the progress that had occurred in the intelligence community and American society overall—with more still needed.

Collins began, "As you were briefed, Lauren, we believe the North Koreans have obtained some sophisticated Chinese anti-ship ballistic missile technology. We don't think it came directly from the Chinese. Our intelligence indicates it was obtained from Saudi Arabia, to whom the Chinese sold their technology last year. Four days ago, the North Koreans fired one of these missiles, unarmed, at the *John C. Stennis* Carrier Group, operating in the East China Sea."

La Rue listened attentively despite being familiar with the information from having read the briefing paper that was distributed prior to the meeting.

Collins continued with intel that was not in the briefing paper, "We have identified a cyberterrorist group that goes by the name NetRiot operating in Dubrovnik that we believe helped the North Koreans finance the purchase of the Chinese missile technology."

La Rue asked, "Have we been able to identify the flow of funds?"

Collins replied, "Yes, but as you can imagine it's a very complex flow. Most of the funds, we believe, originated in the Bangladesh SWIFT hack."

Both McMahon and La Rue nodded, knowing that hacked funds were often used to fund arms purchases and, indirectly, terrorist activity.

McMahon spoke: "The NSA has been surveilling groups within KSA, Croatia, and North Korea. What we don't know is if the government of Saudi Arabia knew of the missile sale or if it was just a black-market transaction."

La Rue grimaced. "You're not thinking of sending me to KSA, are you?"

Collins replied, "No, Lauren, we don't want you to go to KSA. But we do want you to go to Croatia and meet with Zoran Kordic. I believe you know him. Kordic can introduce you to NetRiot and their leader, Pavo Ludovic." As Collins spoke, photos of Kordic and Ludovic came up on the large flat-screen in the windowless conference room.

"Tell us about your relationship with Kordic," requested McMahon.

"Relationship?" said La Rue. "There is no relationship. I know Zoran from prior dealings I had with him for Sheik Rahman. I believe he trusts me. We transacted hundreds of millions of dollars of business while I was in Dubai."

"Good," replied Collins. "Lauren, we need to leverage your experience with Kordic and convince him to introduce you to Ludovic. Ludovic is doing business with a North Korean front called Imperial Imports LLC. We want to learn everything we can about them and who funded the purchase of the Chinese missile technology."

La Rue responded, "That's all fine, but I'm not a field operative. Plus, you know there's a price on my head from the sheik's family."

"We completely understand, Lauren," said Collins, "but this falls in your area of expertise—international banking. Plus, you're the only one who knows Kordic. We'll put a thorough security plan in place for you. Plus we'll send one of our best field agents with you."

"And when were you thinking I would go?"

"Tomorrow. The plan has you flying Dulles to Frankfurt and then to Montenegro, where you'll make contact with Kordic. From there you'll go by car to Croatia."

"I see. I'd like to meet the field agent you're thinking of sending with me first before I commit," requested La Rue.

"We can make that happen. His name is Chris Dunbar. He is an ex–Navy SEAL who joined the Agency five years ago. He's one of our best field operatives," Collins stated as she closed her folder, the indication to McMahon and La Rue that the meeting was over. It was cold, rainy, and gray in P'yŏngyang, North Korea, as was typical this time of year. The black limousine carrying General Chul Goh stopped at the entrance to the General Committee building. A soldier quickly opened the door to his car and escorted the general in silence to the office of the president of North Korea.

There President Paek w a s sitting w i t h h i s t w o trusted advisers. To his left was the head of North Korea's secret police, the State Security Department (SSD), and to his right the head of North Korea's version of the CIA.

General Chul Goh, general of the Missile Command Services of North Korea, saluted the president, who nodded and demanded, "General, what's the operational status of the DF-26 missiles?"

"Mr. President, we have two missiles remaining after our test. Our teams are preparing to arm one with a fifty-kiloton warhead. We believe we will have it ready for service within two weeks."

Paek nodded and leaned over to have a private conversation with the head of the North Korean spy agency.

Looking back at Goh, he said, "General, you are to continue your work to make both missiles operational—both the unarmed missile as well as the missile with the warhead. I want to be kept apprised of the progress on both. I want the launch of our next missile test to coincide with our Day of the Sun celebration on the fifteenth; Secretary Lui will provide you with the targeting coordinates."

General Goh spoke carefully. "Mr. President, the

Americans are on heightened alert as a result of our last missile. We know they are moving additional assets into the area. Should we fire a test another DF-26 at their carrier group we must expect some form of retaliation."

The president, who did not tolerate opinions and commentary, shot back, "General Goh, your job is to prepare the missiles and follow orders. That is all. Get the missiles operational and report back. Dismissed."

With that the general saluted and quickly exited the room. After Goh departed, the head of North Korean intelligence asked Paek, "Can we count on Goh when the time comes to carry out his mission? I have my doubts."

President Paek sat in silence for a minute before replying. "I do not share your concerns about Goh. He has proven himself to be reliable and trustworthy, but put a backup plan in place just in case."

That was the North Korean way—no matter what position one attained in the military, society, or government, no one was bigger than the institution itself and backup plans were common.

"We have another matter to discuss," said Paek, turning to his heads of security and intelligence. "We have received an offer from the CEO of Apple. They are bringing their newly outfitted ship of technology for a visit to the South and he offered to also visit us in the North," said Paek.

"The Apple ship visiting us?" asked his intelligence chief. "Sir, it is a spy mission."

"Possibly," said Paek. "They have offered to participate in the Day of the Sun festivities. It could be a very good thing to show our people how we are willing to interact with outside influences such as Apple. Plus, I think the visit would very much annoy the

American government; at least, that is what the Apple CEO indicated. But more importantly, it would give us another American bargaining chip. The Americans will not attack us if we have their cruise ship in our harbor. It will give us tremendous leverage when we fire our next DF-26. I am going to agree to let them visit us."

As General Goh rode back to his base in Namp'o, about twenty-five miles south of P'yŏngyang, the thought of firing another missile—armed or unarmed—at the US carrier group weighed heavily on him. For the first time in his career he disagreed with the direction the president was pursuing. Yes, he had been a strong sup-porter of North Korea developing a nuclear arsenal. He had worked countless hours implementing their Hwasong-14 ICBM capability. He had always believed it to be a deterrent and safeguard against an attack from the South. But now Paek's aggression against the US and his escalation of firing at the US carrier group was taking the North down an increasingly confrontational path, one that Goh did not think would end well for his country

The next day at 3:30 p.m., a black suburban pulled up to Lauren La Rue's Georgetown town house. Even though she now worked on a CIA salary, she had made millions in her previous assignment as the financial manager for Sheik Abdul Er Rahman. Part of her negotiation with the Justice Department was to keep the wealth she had accumulated working for the sheik. An agreement was reached that La Rue would donate $18 million to the dependents of those who died in the Attack on Nantucket and she could keep the rest.

The black suburban drove La Rue to Dulles International Airport, where she avoided all security using her CIA credentials, then boarded United Airlines Flight 989 to Frankfurt. Once on board the 777 airliner, she settled into seat 12H in business class. A few minutes later a man in his late twenties sat next to her. He was tall, at six foot three, with very short dark hair and chiseled features. Dressed all in black, he also sported a five-day beard. As he sat he turned to La Rue and nodded. They had met the day before at CIA headquarters.

She nodded and said, "Good afternoon, Chris."
"Lauren," the agent acknowledged with a slight nod. Their cover was as a sales team on their way to a meeting with the T-Mobile wireless carrier in Montenegro. Chris Dunbar would be the technical support and La Rue the salesperson.

As they prepared for takeoff on the eight-hour evening flight to Frankfurt, Chris Dunbar stood and took out his headphones and a hooded sweatshirt from his carry-on tote, surveying the passengers around him.

As the flight attendant came down the aisle, Dunbar said, "I'll be back in a minute."

He made his way to the restroom after walking through the first-class cabin. He then stopped in the galley to ask about the time of departure, allowing him the opportunity to size up the flight attendants.

La Rue watched Dunbar as he made his way back to his seat. As he reached his seat he put on his sweatshirt, pulling the hood over his head. La Rue thought it would be very hard to identify him with the hood pulled down and his headphones on. But an eye skilled in the art could see he was ex-military and that he knew how to handle himself. Commander Mike Bartlett was sitting in his office at Pax River, Maryland, going over a flight plan for the afternoon's flight, when his yeoman came hurriedly into his office. "Sir, I have a call for you from the White House—on line one."

"Commander Bartlett, this is Alice Ahern, the president's personal sec- retary. The president would like to meet with you tomorrow at 10 a.m., if that's convenient."

The commander chuckled to himself. He knew when the commander in chief wanted to meet with you, you became immediately available whether it was "convenient" or not.

"Yes, of course, Ms. Ahern."

"Thank you, Commander. I will notify security to have a pass ready for you. Please arrive thirty minutes early to clear security. Good day." With that she hung up.

That left Commander Bartlett to sit in his office wondering what POTUS wanted to discuss with him. But any further thought about that would have to wait. Bartlett was scheduled for a hop in the F-35C Lightning II, which meant he had a briefing session for the flight. After that he would suit up, and preflight his

Bartlett was developing a fondness for the F-35C Lightning II—the C indicating it was the carrier version of the F-35. Which wasn't a surprise—what fighter pilot wouldn't want to fly the latest, newest fighter? The things he could do with the Lightning he could only dream of doing in the F/A-18 Hornet. And Bartlett knew how to fly the Hornet very well.

As Bartlett approached the flight line his plane captain saluted.

Bartlett, returning the salute, said, "LaTroy, is everything checked out?"

"Yes, sir, you're good to go. She looks fine, doesn't she, Commander?"

Walking around the jet checking the various control surfaces, Bartlett replied, "She does look good. And she flies even better than she looks."

After climbing into the cockpit of his $120 million fighter, he put on his $400,000 Gen III Helmet Mounted Display System or HMD, plugging the umbilical into the fighter's console so the avionics could sync with the heads-up display of his helmet. The HMD was a breakthough in technology and was fitted to each pilot by a laser scan of the pilot's head which was used to create a 3-D custom helmet liner. Bartlett was fully aware of the money that was needed to create the fighter in which he was sitting. Building, flying, and maintaining jet fighters was an expensive proposition, and one of the main reasons why so many in Congress were keen to fund the X-47B unmanned combat air vehicle program—a fancy name for unmanned Navy drones.

But that was all in the future. Today, Commander Mike "Grumpy" Bartlett would be flying the most advanced fighter in the world, along with his squadron mates of VX-23, out over the Chesapeake Bay on their way to open air over the Atlantic.

Bartlett called the tower for clearance for takeoff: "Lightning 73, ready to depart runway 6."

Five hours later, after a successful mission, Mike Bartlett turned his Porsche into the driveway of the home he shared with his fiancée in Potomac, Maryland. It was just after 6 p.m. as the garage door opened. Bartlett noticed the empty spot on Kristin's side of the garage and figured he had time to get in a run before she got home. After changing and stretching he started down their street, heading toward the track at the Bullis School, not far from their home. Bartlett liked running on quarter-mile tracks so he could check his times. Pilots were competitive in almost every aspect of their lives.

Back at home, with his run over, he was getting out of the shower when he heard the beep of their alarm system, which told him Kristin was home.

As he entered the family room he saw McMahon looking over the mail.

"Hi, Kris, how was your day?"

"Fine, how was yours?" She gave him a quick kiss.

"Good, I had an eval hop with the squadron. The F-35 continues to check out. It's one sweet bird. Also, I got a call from the White House."

That got her attention.

"The White House? So how's the president?"

"Not sure, but he wants to meet with me tomorrow morning."

"Maybe he wants to talk to you about your bachelor party," said McMahon with a straight face.

"No doubt." Bartlett chuckled.

McMahon laughed in return and said, "I'm going to change."

Bartlett settled onto their sectional couch, putting his legs up on the ottoman as he reached for the TV remote control.

A few minutes later Kristin was back downstairs, now wearing a pair of capris and one of Bartlett's too-large Navy T-shirts. She grabbed a Vitaminwater from the fridge and plopped down on the couch next to Bartlett, where she immediately reached for the remote and changed the channel to CNN.

"Hey, McFly, I was watching that," chided Bartlett. He always called her McFly instead of McMahon anytime she did something that annoyed him, referencing the old *Back to the Future* movie.

"We have a lot of TVs in this house. I want to watch Anderson Cooper."

"Anderson Cooper, are you kidding me?" repeated Bartlett.

"Yes." Now it was McMahon's turn to goad Bartlett. "He's sexy."

"Anderson Cooper?"

With that Bartlett leaned over and grabbed McMahon as she squirmed, trying to get away. "Yes, yes, yes, he's sexy, he is."

"You say you're attracted to Anderson Cooper with this specimen of masculinity sitting right next to you?" Bartlett demanded as he continued to tickle McMahon.

Through the laughter all McMahon could get out was, "Yes, yes, yes."

As the laughter subsided they fell into a long kiss.

McMahon eventually pulled back and said, "Fly-boy, are you interested in dinner?"

She knew how to get to Bartlett.

He leaned back onto the couch, stretching, and said, "How about Chinese?"

That worked for McMahon. After all, she was deputy director of the NSA and had put in a long day. She got up, grabbed the phone, and hit the speed dial to the local Chinese take-out place they liked.

Forty-five minutes later they were seated at the table eating take-out when McMahon brought up the White House meeting. "So, what do you think the president wants to talk about?"

"I don't have a clue. You know how he likes to keep abreast with what's going on in naval aviation. Maybe he wants to ask me about how the F-35 is checking out."

McMahon frowned. "The leader of the free world? He could do that with a phone call or just ask for a briefing paper."

She was right and had more experience than Bartlett on how Washington worked.

"I bet he wants to talk to you about a position in his administration," stated McMahon.

Bartlett didn't respond. He knew he wasn't ready to leave the Navy yet. Besides, he was confident he would be soon be selected for promotion to captain. He was on a fast track career-wise, with a goal to command an aircraft carrier. But with his marriage in four weeks and now at thirty-five, Bartlett was ready to start thinking about the next phase of his life, including a family.

Bartlett knew firsthand how tough sea deployments were and the enormous strain and sacrifice they put on Navy families.

He just replied, "Well, we'll know soon enough. My meeting's tomorrow at ten."

At 9:30 a.m. sharp, Commander Mike Bartlett approached the White House visitor check-in security office. He handed his military ID to the White House security officer, who verified that Bartlett was on the access list.

The security officer handed back the ID, saying, "Sir, please step through the metal detector." Once he was through the detector, another security officer then checked Bartlett with a wand. After completing the security check, Bartlett was approached by a young assistant, who was clearly expecting his arrival. She began, "Good morning, Commander. Please come with me."

Bartlett nodded, not used to not being saluted, and followed the aide through the halls of the White House, eventually arriving at the West Wing. There she transferred him to the waiting area outside the office of Ms. Alice Ahern, the personal secretary of the president of the United States.

The aide let Ahern know the commander had arrived. The time was 9:45 a.m. Bartlett sat in the antechamber wearing his service dress blue uniform with three gold stripes on his cuffs, a pair of gold wings on his left breast, and his service ribbons and Command

Ashore pin – a trident and a star. He held his hat with its gold braid on its visor on his lap with both hands as he observed the activity around him. This was his first visit to the Oval Office, and it didn't matter who you were, a visit to the Oval Office was always an impressive and somewhat intimidating experience.

Commander Bartlett, used to flying high-performance jets and dealing with stressful situations, like all pilots, had developed certain mental exercises to maintain his composure and concentration. As Bartlett sat waiting, he monitored his breathing and worked to slow his heart rate.

At exactly 9:58 a.m. the aide returned and brought the commander to Alice Ahern's office.

"Good morning, Commander Bartlett. I'm Alice Ahern." The commander held his hand out to shake hers.

"The president will be with you in a minute. Is this your first visit to the White House?" she asked.

"Yes, ma'am," replied Bartlett.

On Ahern's computer screen a light came on, indicating that the president was now ready for his visitor. Ahern first went into the Oval Office to confirm that the president was ready. This was standard protocol for the White House—only Ahern, the president's chief of staff, Spencer Sterling, his personal aide, and his wife, Kennedy, had "walk-in" privileges to the Oval.

Coming out of the Oval Office, Ms. Ahern stated, "Commander, the president will see you."

With that the commander placed his hat under his left arm and entered the office razor straight. Once inside he stepped toward the desk, came to attention, and saluted.

The president looked up from his desk and returned the salute, saying, "Commander, how have you been?" He closed a folder and came around his desk to extend his hand to Bartlett. "Mike, please take a seat," he said as he waved his hand for Bartlett to join him on the couch, to his left.

The president, always a gracious host, asked, "How's Kristin and how are the plans for the wedding progressing?"

"She's fine, Mr. President. Frankly, Kristin is taking care of most of the details."

"That's the right move," replied the president with a smile. "Mrs. Russell and I are looking forward to it. It's been a while since we attended a wedding, no less a Navy wedding."

"Thank you, sir," was all Bartlett could think to say.

Bartlett had spent many hours with the president, getting him requalified on the Super Hornet only six months earlier, after which he and the president flew on the mission that shot down Sheik Abdul Er Rahman's private jet. But that had all occurred in flight suits, briefing rooms, and cockpits. Now meeting with the president in the Oval Office, he felt the full weight and magnitude of it all.

Just then Spencer Sterling entered the office and sat down on the couch to the president's right.

"Sterls, this is Commander Mike Bartlett. I believe you remember him from Operation Warlord," the president said, using the code name for the mission where the president shot down the sheik's private jet.

Sterling replied, "Indeed I do, Mr. President. Commander, two weeks ago the North Koreans launched a Dong-Feng 21D at the *Stennis* Carrier Group operating in the East China Sea. It didn't have a warhead, but as you can imagine it got our attention."

"The North Koreans launched a Chinese missile? How's that?" asked Bartlett.

"We believe North Korea got the DF-26 from Saudi Arabia. Last year China sold a few DF-26s to the Saudis. We've been after them to give us one so we can see how it works, but as of yet the Saudis aren't cooperating. We believe the Saudis sold a few DF-26s to North Korea."

Spencer continued. "Commander, we're concerned about this link between the Saudis and the North Koreans. So are the Russians and the Chinese. The fact that North Korea obtained missile technology from the Saudis and then fired it at the *Stennis* is of grave concern.

"Commander, we have a new weapons technology code-named Torchlight. Let me emphasize this is *top secret* information."

Bartlett nodded that he understood.

"Torchlight is an ultra-high-powered laser weapon system intended to shoot down ICBMs as well as ASBMs like the Dong-Feng. We're in the process of deploying Torchlight here in the US, South Korea, Guam, and Hawaii, but it won't be operational until late next year. We also have installed a version on board the USS *Florida*, which is ready for fleet testing. The feedback we received so far is all very positive," concluded Spencer.

The president looked at Bartlett. "Which brings us to the point of our meeting. Commander, I'd like you to assess the Torchlight installation on the *Florida* and report back to me in terms of its readiness and effectiveness. I want you to work with Rear Admiral Tom Fraser, in command of the *Stennis* Strike Group. Commander, we have intelligence that indicates that North Korea will fire another DF-26 at the *Stennis* in as little as two weeks. If they do I want to use Torchlight to shoot it down."

Spencer added, "Commander, you'll head out to the *Stennis* first and then to the *Florida*. Immediately following this meeting you will get an in-depth technical briefing on Torchlight. It will be conducted by the program director, Jim Hartel, who will accompany you into theater."

"Commander Bartlett, Tom Fraser flew with me with VFA-32 off the *Truman* as a nugget. Flatbush knows you're coming and will cooperate with you fully," said the president, using the rear admiral's call sign. The president then stood, signaling the end of the meeting.

"Commander, if Torchlight isn't ready, we'll need to move our ships out of the area in a hell of a hurry," said the president dryly. "And that's something I don't want to do. I don't want to run from the North Koreans."

Bartlett stood as well at this point and said, "Understood, Mr. President. Your confidence in me means a lot. I won't let you down, sir."

"You never have, Mike. Give my best to Kristin and I hope she won't be too upset with you traveling so soon before the wedding."

"I'm sure she'll understand, Mr. President."

The president just shook his head.

"Miss Ahern will have the information about your next meeting," said Sterling.

Bartlett saluted and exited the Oval Office. As he paused at Ms. Ahern's desk, he let out a big exhale. She handed Commander Bartlett a package marked "TOP SECRET," which contained the background information on Torchlight and the logistics about his next meeting with the program director, Jim Hartel. Bartlett reflected on what he had just heard and what he said to the president about Kristin understanding his having to fly to South Korea tomorrow. This was a conversation he was not looking forward to having.

CHAPTER THREE

Lauren La Rue and Chris Dunbar landed in Montenegro on an Austrian Air flight connecting through Frankfurt. After passing customs, they were met by Zoran Kordic, who immediately recognized La Rue.

Greeting La Rue and Dunbar with excellent English, he said, "Welcome to Montenegro," then kissed La Rue on each cheek.

"Zoran, it is good to see you. You look well. This is my associate Ted Yates."

Dunbar shook hands with Kordic.

"My car is not far; can I help you with your bags?"

Dunbar shook his head and followed La Rue and Kordic as they made their way to the car, with Dunbar surveying the perimeter as they walked.

Arriving at the car, Dunbar placed their bags in the trunk of the modest Skoda. Zoran said, "Lauren, I received your message and made contact with the party you asked to meet. We need to travel to Dubrovnik. It will take about three hours to get there tonight. It isn't far, but we'll be traveling through the mountains and the roads are not good in some parts. I have water bottles for your refreshment in the car."

Once they were inside the car, Zoran's demeanor became more businesslike. He added, "I have arranged a meeting tomorrow with

Pavo Ludovic of NetRiot. Your cover is that you are representing an American political group looking to collect personal information about potential opposition candidates for your next election."

La Rue nodded, as Kordic's story comported with the mission brief.

As they drove through the mountains and small villages outside of Montenegro's capital city of Podgorica, La Rue was taken by how time and technology seemed to have passed this region by. Yes, everyone had cell phones, but as dusk descended there were very few lights on, nothing like you would see in a typical Western city. It was clear the region was still dealing with the aftermath of the sectarian violence of the 1990s.

Dunbar asked Kordic, "How did Ludovic become a computer expert living in Dubrovnik? It looks like there is minimal electricity in the region. Did he study abroad?"

Kordic replied, "He did. If a student here shows an aptitude for math or science, the state sends them to Russia for technical training. Once there, if they display an ability for computers, the Russian Interior Ministry provides them with advanced training. Eventually they are conscripted to serve five years with the ministry's cyberunit. Pavo Ludovic completed his service and after agreeing to do independent work for the ministry was allowed to leave Moscow. He returned to Dubrovnik to be closer to his family. Family ties are very important here. And, of course, there was a girl.

"Drawing on contacts made while in Moscow, he formed a team of hackers. Over the last four years he and his team have completely assimilated into the dark web of cyberterrorism. The upshot—he and the members of NetRiot are all wealthy and now offer their services to the highest bidders," added Kordic.

Dunbar listened intently, with his favorable impression of Kordic increasing with each additional fact he shared with them.

The blue Skoda slowed as they approached the border crossing between Montenegro and Croatia. Kordic handed the three passports to the Croatian soldiers, who were little more than Croatia's version of TSA agents. After a short conversation, stamps were applied to the ersatz passports and they continued their drive to Dubrovnik, a picturesque city situated on the Adriatic just across from Italy.

Kordic had made reservations for them at a midrange seaside hotel mostly frequented by locals and Europeans. After checking in, the three decided to go to dinner.

Kordic recommended a local restaurant run by the same family who owned the inn. As they ate, the conversation kept strictly to talk of the history of Dubrovnik and sightseeing attractions. Becoming more familiar with field operations, La Rue expected they were under surveillance from either the waiter, the people at nearby tables, or a powerful directional microphone—a technology that surely Ludovic would know about and probably employ.

Once dinner finished, the three said good night and turned in. This suited La Rue just fine, as it had been a long trip to Dubrovnik and she looked forward to sleeping in a real bed.

Dunbar was up early the next morning and went for a run around the area. At the agreed time, he met La Rue and Kordic in the hotel lobby.

Kordic said, "Our meeting isn't until 11 at a café along the waterfront. Until then I will give you a tour of Dubrovnik."

After walking through the town and touring the Stradun bell tower, St. Blaise's Church, and the Walls of Dubrovnik, it was time to meet with Pavo Ludovic, leader of the notorious NetRiot cyberteam.

Kordic led La Rue and Dunbar into the small seafront café, where he quickly recognized Ludovic sitting at a table in the rear of the café with two other men.

Kordic began, "Pavo, you look well."

Pavo Ludovic reacted with much less exuberance and simply nodded, saying, "Zoran, I received your message."

La Rue, a self-confident and accomplished businesswoman, knew her part well. "Mr. Ludovic, I am Amy Anderson. Thank you for agreeing to meet with us. This is my colleague Ted Yates."

Ludovic shook hands and replied with more energy, "Welcome to Dubrovnik, Miss Anderson."

He introduced his two partners using only their first names. "This is Antonija and Frano." They nodded, and all six sat at the table as the waitress came up to take their orders.

La Rue, wanting to play up her American role, ordered a Coca-Cola Light instead of coffee, which was what she would have preferred and what everyone else ordered.

With the pleasantries out of the way, La Rue began, "Mr. Ludovic—"

He interrupted and said, "Please, call me Pavo."

"Very well, Pavo," she started again. "Please call me Amy. I represent a group interested in hiring your team for an important and highly confidential project."

"Miss Anderson, all of my clients' projects are highly confidential. People don't come all the way to Dubrovnik because they want us to hack into someone's Facebook account," he said with a smile that generated a soft chuckle from his partners. You could tell it wasn't the first time his team had heard Ludovic use that line.

La Rue continued. "The next US presidential election will take place in two and half years. We're looking for someone to help us collect information on the top three Republican opposition candidates who we believe are the most likely ones to challenge the sitting president. We believe Senator Stephen Krone of Texas, Governor Ricardo Rengifo of Florida, and Governor Ann Longley of Ohio will be the top contenders. My client would like as much information as you can collect on each."

She knew Pavo had heard these sorts of requests before. In today's world of hacking, the business could be distilled into two main areas: hacking banks or businesses and collecting the personal data of powerful people. Although planting false stories was now accounting for an increasing part of his business.

Ludovic replied, "Three such powerful people, Amy. They'll have many firewalls and advanced encryption. It will be very difficult."

"No doubt, Pavo, but that's why I'm in Dubrovnik this morning and not in an Internet café in Austin, Texas, or Palo Alto." Her response caused Pavo to smile.

She went on, "In addition, it's critical the data not be shared with anyone else, unless, of course, we request that to happen."

La Rue was indirectly referring to Julian Assange, the leader of WikiLeaks and the scourge of intelligence communities and governments everywhere.

It was now time for Ludovic to get a dig in. "The land of the free and the home of the brave, eh, Amy. You Americans, you talk of your democracy and your freedoms, but I get more business from America these days than I do from Moscow."

La Rue was forceful in her response. "Listen, Pavo, if you're interested in debating politics or world history, we can do that some other time. Right now, I'm here to transact business."

"How long are you looking for this surveillance and data collection to last?" asked Ludovic.

"We'd like it to begin right away with weekly drops and run right up to the primary in June. Obviously, once the Republican candidate is chosen we would drop the surveillance on the other two individuals and add the VP candidate."

Ludovic spoke to his team in Croatian, and after a little back-and-forth he said, "The cost will be $60 million. Half up front, the other half in three payments as we deliver the information. Also, I will want a third in US dollars, a third in euros, and a third in Swiss francs."

La Rue knew she had to negotiate.

"Chaos Club, Darkhole, Guccifer—NetRiot isn't the only game in town," said La Rue, naming the other powerful hacker groups as a feint.

Ludovic smiled. "Miss Anderson, do you think you're buying a BMW? Why do Americans always think they can negotiate?"

"Because everything is negotiable, Pavo," said La Rue calmly.

Ludovic brought both hands to his forehead and closed his eyes in thought.

After a minute he said, "You Americans always wear me out. Fifty million, thirty up front, twenty on the back end in three currencies."

La Rue looked at Dunbar and Kordic and knew the time had come to close the deal.

She held her hand out, saying, "Agreed. Pavo, we have a deal."

As the meeting broke up, Ludovic stood—then paused and, looking straight at La Rue, said, "Glad we could do business together, Lauren."

With a shocked expression on her face, La Rue didn't say a word.

Leaning closer, Ludovic added, "Lauren, I suggest you leave Croatia at once. If I know you're here, no doubt so do the Saudis."

With that, Pavo Ludovic, the leader of the notorious NetRiot hacking group, and his team exited the café and were gone.

Dunbar was first to speak. "Our cover's blown. We need to leave right now. Kordic, get the car."

On the other side of the world, in Namp'o, North Korea, General Goh was reviewing the progress on installing the fifty-ki-loton warhead on one of the two remaining DF-26 "carrier killer" missiles. The work was taking place in a lab that was three stories underground but was protected by a twelve-foot-thick concrete lid, making it practically impenetrable to an attack by air. Most of North Korea's military command and control and ammunition stores were underground.

General Goh was full of misgivings about this assignment— ones that he could not share with anyone—not even his wife.

He was becoming increasingly concerned that his leader was taking the country down an exceedingly dangerous path. The place-ment of a fifty-ton warhead on the Chinese missile was just the latest and most reckless action to come from P'yŏngyang.

General Goh was also thinking about an incident that had occurred in the fall. He was at a park with his children when a ball from another family rolled toward them. The father ran toward Goh to retrieve it and apologized. As he picked up the ball, the father placed a scrap of paper on the ground at Goh's feet and said, pointing to the paper, "Oh, that must be yours."

Goh quickly walked away and kept playing with his children. A few minutes later Goh walked over to the paper while checking something on his phone. When finished, he went to slip the phone into his pants pocket but missed and the phone fell on the ground. As he retrieved the phone he picked up the note, all in the same motion. On the paper was a message, "If you ever want to talk about your nation's future call this number 218 0193 466."

Once home he wrote the number on the inside of a pair of old shoes he rarely wore and shredded the paper.

He had never thought of actually using the number—but at the same time he kept it, so somewhere in his subconscious he must have known this day would come.

Tonight, after dinner with his family, he went up to his closet and copied the number from the shoe. Tomorrow, he decided, he would buy a prepaid cell phone and call the number.

For Goh, the decision to buy a prepaid phone was easier said than done. The general had a driver who picked him up every morning and a staff lieutenant who waited on his every need. Plus, in the par-anoid state that was North Korea, everyone was under surveillance, something General Goh knew well. The general couldn't ask his aide to buy the SIM, nor could he buy it himself —that was too risky. Instead, he decided he would ask his son to buy it. The general didn't like involving his child, but he thought the action was benign enough not to raise any concerns. Teenagers in North Korea, like teenagers everywhere, were addicted to mobile phones, so buying a new phone or SIM was unlikely to raise any suspicions.

Returning home that night, the general went to talk to his eldest son, who was thirteen.

"Hwan, how was your day, son?"

"Fine, sir. We're working on a science project that uses dry ice," replied Hwan with some enthusiasm.

The father nodded and added, "Ah, sublimation—the process of going from a solid to a gas, bypassing the fluid stage." His sonnodded and expanded on the general's point to explain how they would measure the process.

After discussing the project, Goh casually asked, "Oh, were you able to pick up the phone?" His son nodded and handed him the bag with the new phone and prepaid SIM in it.

After dinner Goh went into his backyard to have a cigarette. The general then inserted the SIM into the new phone, powered it up, and answered a few questions on the screen. Once the phone was activated a few seconds later, he dialed the number he had been given six months earlier.

In a secret communication center in South Korea outside of Seoul, a light started to flash on the screen indicating an incoming call from one of the seed numbers the CIA had planted with the KCIA, or Korean Central Intelligence Agency. The operator pressed a few buttons, transferring the call to the on-duty KCIA agent, who saw the number had been assigned to General Goh.

Speaking in Korean, the agent said, "Yes."

General Goh anxiously said, "Are you available? I was given this number some time ago." The general's heart was pounding, as he knew he was about to cross a line over which he could never return. "Yes, but I need assurances for my family and personal safety."

"Of course, we can guarantee that. It's important for us to meet in person and limit this transmission. We need you to develop a toothache. Have your staff call your dentist to schedule an appointment. We will intercept the call and indicate your dentist is on vacation and have you see the covering dentist. We will meet you at that office. Start complaining about a toothache to your staff over the next two days. We will meet you on Wednesday or Thursday, whenever they schedule the appointment. Do not call this number again."

Once the general hung up, he took the SIM card out of his phone and walked over to the corner of his yard. He used his shoe to dig into the soil next to his favorite Oyama magnolia tree and dropped the SIM into the hole and spread the dirt over it.

Unbeknownst to General Goh, North Korea's Reconnaissance General Bureau, or RGB, which was responsible for the clandestine and cyberintelligence operations for North Korea, had noted that a call was made near the general's house using an unofficial phone. That, in and of itself, was not enough to raise a red flag, as it could be that one of the general's children or friends was using a new cell phone in the house. The agent logged the event and then went on monitoring the other eight screens in front of him.

The next morning, while reviewing his schedule for the day with his flag lieutenant, the general stopped midsentence and rubbed his jaw. "Ah," he moaned.

His flag lieutenant picked up on it right away and asked, "General, is something disturbing you?"

"Yong, it's one of my teeth."

"General, would you like me to make an appointment with your dentist for later today?"

"No, Yong, I'm sure it will go away."

The general then quickly changed the subject. "Yong, tell the driver to pick up the pace. I don't want to be late for the staff meeting."

"Yes, General." Yong tapped on the bulletproof divider that separated the passenger compartment from the driver and waved his finger in a rotation, signaling for the driver to speed up.

In response, the driver hit the grill lights and siren so that they could navigate through the morning P'yŏngyang traffic.

Ms. Ahern had just shown Mark Holloway, the secretary of state, into the Oval Office. "Good morning, Mr. President," Holloway said.

President Russell was already sitting and talking with Sterling Spencer, and he nodded to Holloway as he entered.

"Mark, I want to bring you up to date on Torchlight."

"Mr. President, I was briefed on Torchlight just last month."

The president smiled. "Mark, a month without intel on a project like Torchlight makes you antiquated." Without waiting for a response, the president continued. "As you know, North Korea fired an unarmed Dong-Feng at the *Stennis* two weeks ago."

"Yes, Mr. President."

"Our plan for Torchlight is akin to Israel's Iron Dome. Only, our iron dome will cover all the US, with a second dome covering Vietnam, the Philippines, Japan, and South Korea. Beyond that, we'll have sea-based Torchlight platforms that we can deploy as needed. This will not only create a dome that will protect us from a missile launched from North Korea but also encompasses the new Chinese base on the Spratly Islands."

"Mr. President, there's no doubt the Torchlight technology is very promising. Has it continued to progress?"

"A sea-based version will be operational within ten days. And that's why I wanted to speak with you."

Spencer Sterling then chimed in. "Mark, there are less than twenty people who know Torchlight is going operational so soon. We need that information treated as ultra–top secret."

"Of course," replied Holloway.

The president continued. "The NSA believes that in just a matter of weeks the North Koreans will fire another DF-26 missile at us. We believe the target will again be the *Stennis* Carrier Group."

Holloway, one of the most astute of President Russell's cabinet members, said, "Mr. President, using a US carrier as bait sounds very risky to me."

"I agree. That's why I am sending a special team to assess the status of Torchlight. They'll be in theatre tomorrow. If the team says Torchlight is ready, I plan to use it to shoot down any missile fired at us. Not only will it defend the *Stennis* but it will serve as a demonstration that will let everyone from Iran to Russia know that we can shoot down any missile fired at us. We will have demonstrated our own Iron Dome."

"Mr. President, how can I be of service?"

"Mark, first, I wanted you to be in the loop so when the event happens you can brief the Brits, French, Germans, and Japanese—they'll have detected the launch and will be on edge. But more importantly, we aren't going to let the North Koreans fire another missile at one of our carriers without retaliating. We plan to use their launch as a catalyst to force a regime change in North Korea."

President Russell paused to let those words sink in. "We plan to give President Paek an ultimatum. He must step down and leave the country within twenty-four hours or face retaliation by the United States. We'll threaten to hit every one of his military and government facilities. It's time to reunify the Korean peninsula."

Holloway didn't miss a beat. "Sir, China is on board with this?"

"One hundred percent," replied the president. "However, there's a catch. In order to get the Chinese buy-in, we had to agree togradually withdraw our military presence from the peninsula. It will happen over a seven-year period once reunification has begun."

"Mr. President, just to continue, sir. How convinced are you about China's motivation to support this plan?" Holloway rejoined.

"I understand your reservations, Mark," said the president. "China's motivation is twofold. First, they, like us, get rid of the threat of an unstable Paek with nuclear weapons. Second—and this is very strategic to them—they get the US to eventually withdraw from the Korean Peninsula."

"Losing our bases in the South and with China's new bases on the Spratley Islands, do you think it is wise for us to reduce our military presence in the region?" added Holloway.

"No, I don't, but that is specifically why we have reopened our base in the Philippines, expanded Guam, and created our joint NATO base in Vietnam. Those bases, along with Torchlight, will give us the assets we need to maintain a strong presence in the region," said the president with conviction.

"Mr. President, understood. Getting back to the regime change—what's the time frame for that to occur?" asked Holloway.

Spencer replied, "Our intelligence indicates they're only weeks away from their next missile launch. We think it's likely they'll fire at us on April fifteenth, during their Day of the Sun holiday."

"Mr. President, what about Paek? What is your plan for him?"

"He and his family will be exiled to an island he owns in the northern Philippines. He will agree to this or he'll find his time on this earth cut short," said the president without remorse.

"And South Korean president Young-woo, is she prepared for

this—and is she up to it?" asked Holloway."Yes, to the first question and only time will tell on the second. It will take a lot of support from us in the form of financial aid."

"It's an ambitious plan, Mr. President. Torchlight will undoubt-edly set off an arms race with China and to a lesser extent Russia," replied Holloway.

"Perhaps, but they don't represent a threat to us like North Korea does. The threat to our safety is North Korea, Iran, and ISIS, and none of them will be able to defeat Torchlight for at least a decade. In that time we'll be able to instigate even more changes," stated the president.

It was clear to all three men that history was being made. Of course, to achieve this—Torchlight had to work.

CHAPTER FOUR

Dunbar was already on his satellite phone as they got into their car. He was given two encryption keys to use to establish secure links on their laptop. Dunbar entered the keys and started a secure chat with the European CIA Center (ECC).

Dunbar sent, "CB. IER." *Cover blown, immediate extraction requested.*

ECC replied, "Copy. Ext DBV." *Extraction to come from the Dubrovnik Airport.*

Dunbar again: "What's the ETD?"

ECC: "DTF. Shift key 10." *Details to follow.* That last part instructed Dunbar to terminate the chat session and reestablish it in ten minutes using his other encryption key. The interval, no doubt, was to give the ECC time to work through the details of arranging their extraction from Dubrovnik.

Dunbar informed La Rue and Kordic, "We need to get back to them in ten minutes. In the meantime, let's get out of here and start going dark."

Going dark was the colloquial term for going EMCON, or emission control, where they would not emit any electronic signals.

As Kordic steered the car out of the center of town and headed south on Jadranska Cesta, La Rue took the SIM cards out of their iPhones and handed both the phones and the SIMs to Dunbar, who threw the iPhones as far as he could from the speeding car. After scratching and bending the SIM cards, Dunbar put them in his pocket as Kordic pulled into Orsula Park, where he felt they could wait in safety.

Dunbar reconnected via their laptop and sat phone using the other encryption key Kordic had obtained earlier.

ECC came online with a short transmission: "DBV, 3:15 D-ABOG."

The message indicated they would leave at 3:15 p.m. from the Dubrovnik airport and their ride was a German-registered plane with the tail number D-ABOG.

Dunbar simply replied, "C," indicating that he copied the message, and quickly disconnected.

Kordic, Dunbar, and La Rue then followed a similar procedure to dismantle, destroy, and dispose of their laptop and sat phone, scattering the components in various locations in the park. Dunbar went into a nearby porto-san and threw the SIM cards he was carrying down the hole. He muttered under his breath, "Be my guest and try to fish them out of there."

When he returned to the car, Kordic said, "I need to get rid of the car." Kordic knew his car probably had a tracking device on it or at the very least had been identified as the car they were using.

Dunbar simply nodded. Kordic was speaking only to Dunbar and barely acknowledged La Rue, since the mission had moved into an operational phase.

Kordic added, "I'm going to leave you here. It'll be easier for me to get another car on my own. If I'm not back in forty-five minutes, you're on your own." Kordic then handed Dunbar a map of the area and pointed out where they were and where the airport was.

After reviewing the map, Dunbar responded, "Roger, we leave in forty-five if you're not here."

Dunbar had set what is known as a DCON. If Kordic didn't return in forty-five minutes, Dunbar and La Rue would assume something had happened to him. It was standard procedure to set a DCON which stood for departure condition.

After Kordic left, La Rue said to Dunbar, "What now? We just wait?"

Dunbar replied, "Correct. That's the plan until Kordic returns. For now, we're a couple enjoying an afternoon in the park. Let's walk toward the water so we aren't visible from the road."

As they headed toward the ocean, the path became steeper and Dunbar reached out to offer his hand to La Rue.

Kordic slowed as he entered the Srda exit's sharp curve. That's when the shot rang out. A second later Kordic was dead, his Skoda careening into the guardrail. Kordic had been killed from a shot from a sniper using a high-powered rifle with a scope.

Salman Rahman, the son of the now departed Sheik Abdul Er Rahman, who had led the Islamic Front, had learned from President Paek of La Rue's expected presence in Dubrovnik.

Salman had dispatched his security team to capture La Rue and terminate her companions. Kordic's car had indeed been tracked. Now the task was to find La Rue and the CIA agent with her.

Ludovic had been paid $5 million by Paek via Imperial Imports LLC for the information that La Rue would be in Dubrovnik. That's how the dark world worked—no one could be trusted and everything was for sale.

Commander Mike Bartlett was escorted out of the West Wing and was brought to the Green Room on the second floor of the main section of the White House.

As he entered the room, another man walked toward him.

"Commander, I'm Jim Hartel, the PM for Torchlight," said Hartel, exhibiting a certain confidence.

Bartlett shook Hartel's hand and added, "Please, call me Mike."

"Very good, Mike. Torchlight has entered its final phase of field-testing. As you know, we have installations being built on US soil as well as at sites in South Korea, the Philippines, Guam, and Vietnam, but none of them will come online until late next year. Our most advanced implementation is on a submarine, the USS *Florida*, where Torchlight has successfully shot down drones and test missiles."

Bartlett interrupted. "Jim, what was the performance envelope of the shoot downs?"

"First, we conducted test shots against dummy Tomahawk cruise missiles with a one hundred percent intercept success rate."

"A Tomahawk is subsonic and flies at, what, five hundred and fifty knots? Any Sidewinder launched from an F/A-18 could shoot down a Tomahawk."

Ignoring the comment, Hartel continued, "We then tested Torchlight against a series of unarmed LGM-30 Minuteman III missiles fired from Vandenberg Air Force Base in California. As you know, the LGM-30 can attain speeds over fifteen thousand miles per hour and has a range of eighty-one hundred miles. The *Florida* shot it down about a thousand miles off the California coast. We had a ninety percent success rate on those tests. No Sidewinder could knock down a Minuteman." The last point was intended as Hartel's response to Bartlett's Sidewinder crack.

Bartlett was now impressed. "Torchlight was able to shoot down a Minuteman traveling at well over Mach 10? What's holding you back from getting a higher kill rate than ninety percent, Jim?"

"We're still debugging the guidance system on Torchlight. The switching speed of the chips is more than fast enough to deal with a target traveling at fifteen thousand miles per hour—or thirteen thousand knots—but the optical sensors sometimes get confused by other targets in the kill zone, such as a commercial airliner or a satellite. The time it takes to discern friend from foe is what's leading to the ninety percent kill rate."

Bartlett asked, "Are the ground stations more accurate than the sea-based Torchlights?"

"They will be once they're operational. At least that's what our modeling indicates. That said, the sea-based Torchlights *are* expected to perform within plus or minus three percent of the land-based units. The reason our submarine-based Torchlight is ahead of the land installations is because of SPY-6," said Hartel.

SPY-6 was the Navy's new radar system, which was nothing short of amazing.

"SPY-6 is so good that we made integrating it with Torchlight a priority. Hence, the sub-based Torchlight deployment is ahead of the land units," added Hartel. "Where we do have some concerns is with the power plants. The new Bechtel A1B nuclear reactors are powerful enough, but sometimes we get a phasing issue that causes one of the units to drop offline. We designed Torchlight to fire with only four of the six reactors online, so if we have a scram it will still leave us with one reactor for redundancy. We've thought about using seven reactors, but we just don't have the real estate in the sub for that many."

As they continued the session, a knock came on the door and a White House security guard handed Bartlett a note.

Bartlett read it, then turned to Hartel. "Jim, we take off tomorrow for Seoul from Andrews at 05:00. We'll stop in North Island, San Diego, for fuel and then continue to Midway and then on to Seoul. We'll have a lot of time in the air to continue the briefing, so let's plan to wrap this up in the next hour or so, so we can go home, pack, and take care of any family details."

They discussed the mission brief that Bartlett had received from the president—that the North Koreans were expected to fire another DF-26 at the *John C. Stennis* Strike Group.

Bartlett added, "Jim, we can't run a ninety percent confidence level where the *Stennis* and its crew safety are concerned. If we can't get a higher kill rate, we are going to have to move our assets out of the East China Sea, and that's something the president explicitly said he did not want to do."

"Copy," said Hartel. "Our design team is just about finished with their latest software build. Not to get too detailed, but the subroutine that gets called when a reactor scrams right now is inefficient and we're tightening it up so a scram won't interfere with Torchlight's performance and tracking. The new version of the software should be available by the time we land in Seoul."

Bartlett nodded; he liked the command of the details that Hartel exhibited. He knew the other man would make a good partner.

As they were finishing, the door to the Green Room opened and in walked Brad Johnson, vice chairman of the Joint Chiefs of Staff, a four-star Navy admiral.

Bartlett immediately pushed his chair back, stood at attention, and saluted.

Hartel also stood but without the military edge and with no salute.

The admiral started, "As you were."

Bartlett and Hartel sat down, with Admiral Johnson also taking a seat.

"I wanted to talk to you both before you left for Seoul," said Admiral Johnson. "Gentlemen, I wanted to add my support to your mission and stress its importance. It's critical that Torchlight is mission ready and mission capable. As you know, we expect the North Koreans to fire another Dong-Feng at the *Stennis*. And while the *Stennis* can defend herself, the DF-26 is something we don't have a lot of experience with yet. So, it's imperative for Torchlight to work. If it doesn't it will embolden both North Korea and China and any regime with enough money to buy a DF-26."

Admiral Johnson, with gold wings on his dress blue uniform, had made his career in naval aviation, and he had an agenda. "And not to get either of you too caught up in Pentagon politics, but there is also a lot at stake here. Politically, if we are forced to move our carrier out of the area, it will send a message that we no longer can exert maritime control over the region with our carrier strike groups. And believe me, that message will not be lost on Congress. It'll indicate to some that the day of aircraft carrier dominance is over. It will arm the advocates of the new Columbia-class subs—the program to replace the old Ohio-class submarines—with a potent argument to shift funding from naval aviation to the submarine force. So, gentlemen, you see the stakes are very high, both strategically and politically. Torchlight must work. Do you read me?"

Both men replied, "Yes, sir."

"What I have shared with you is TOP SECRET. You tell no one. Not your wives, not your girlfriends, not your priest, not your rabbi, not the rubber duck in your shower—no one. Are we clear?"

Again, both men replied, "Crystal clear, sir."

"Good. Good luck, gentlemen." Then Admiral Johnson closed with the line he had used many times throughout his career. "Take the fight to the enemy. Complete your mission. Stay safe."

With that Admiral Johnson left the Green Room. Neither Bartlett nor Hartel spoke for a minute after he left. Instead they just processed the information they had been given.

It was particularly impactful to Bartlett, who was a naval aviator and aspired to someday command a carrier strike group of his own.

"First a meeting with the president in the Oval and now this visit from Admiral Johnson. I would say a mission doesn't get any higher profile than this one," said Bartlett. "Jim, what's the backup plan in case Torchlight doesn't work?"

"There's really only one option—THAAD, the Terminal High Altitude Area Defense. It's the current antiballistic missile defense system designed to shoot down short-, medium-, and intermediate-range ballistic missiles. But THAAD only has a 120-mile range and a sixty percent kill rating. Other than THAAD, the *Stennis* will have to rely on what they used during the first DF-26 attack. They'll have to SP-JASHO their asses off," said Hartel, referring to the carrier group's ability to jam and spoof any incoming missiles.

"Jim, how much work was it when you conducted the LGM-30 Minutemen III tests?"

"A hell of a lot," replied Hartel.

"I'd like to run some additional tests with LGM-30s using your new code and do it while Torchlight is only running with four reactors. What would it take to make that happen?" asked Bartlett.

"What would it take? An act of God and a ton of work, not to mention a gigantic push from the brass and DoD. That's what it would take."

Bartlett picked up the phone on the table and said, "Admiral Johnson, please."

Bartlett and Hartel worked out the details of a plan with Admiral Johnson's staff to conduct two more LGM-30 missile tests while Bartlett and Hartel were on board the *Florida*. The staff would finalize the details while Bartlett and Hartel were in transit to Seoul.

General Goh was having lunch in his office when he let out with another moan. It was loud enough for his secretary to hear. It had been the third time today that Goh had made a similar complaint.

Taking the bait, his secretary called the general's flag lieutenant, Yong, and said, "I think the general needs to see his dentist. He has an opening tomorrow morning. I am going to schedule an appointment."

Nothing happens in North Korea without approval. Yong immediately entered the general's office to gain the general's permission to make the appointment.

Goh agreed, saying, "I think you're right, Yong. I was hoping this would just go away, but it seems to be getting worse."

The secretary made a call to the general's dentist's office. As planned, the call was intercepted by the South Korean intelligence agency and the CIA. Steps were put in motion for the general to go to the office of the "covering dentist" the next day at 10 a.m.

That night the general did not sleep well. He kept running through the details of tomorrow's ersatz dentist meeting and what he would ask and what he would say. After thirty-seven years of service and rising to his current rank, which made him the number three flag officer in terms of seniority and responsibility, Goh was about to embark on a path that could lead him to be convicted of treason and put to death. And the risk was not just his. If he was convicted, disgrace and hardship would fall on his family as well. He spent the night tossing and turning with anxiety.

At the scheduled time, Goh was ushered into the "dentist's office" by a hygienist while Flag Lieutenant Yong sat in the waiting room. There, dressed in dental garb, was a South Korean agent, who discussed with Goh the possibility of participating in a coup to overthrow President Paek.

While they talked, another man, also dressed in dental clothes, told the general that he was going to give him a shot of novocaine and put a filling in one of his teeth to provide a complete cover. Forty-five minutes later Goh exited the examination room thanking the doctor and his staff. He nodded to Yong, who got on his cell phone to alert the general's driver they would be coming down shortly.

"Do you feel better, General?" asked Yong.

"Yes, Yong. It appears they were able to address the issue before it became an abscess. When we get in the car I want to review the briefing book for my meeting with Admiral Kim," said Goh, moving to more pressing matters as they headed for the elevators.

As they drove back to North Korean military headquarters in Namp'o, Goh was processing what he had just heard in the "dentist's office." He learned that the situation was far more serious than he'd thought. The South Korean agent told him that the South was ready to reunite with the North and that steps were under way to destabilize Paek's leadership. Goh was offered a leadership position in the reunification efforts once Paek was in exile. While Goh did not give a response or indication as to whether he would cooperate, he had agreed to meet with these foreign agents. There was no gray area here. Goh had crossed a line—a line that could put him in front of a firing squad.

A united Korean Peninsula. His thoughts lingered on that idea. Was this the opportunity that he had waited for his entire adult life? Goh knew that if North and South Korea could take the dollars they each spent on defense—especially those dollars spent on maintaining the DMZ—they could do much to help the underprivileged of both countries. He was a warrior and had spent his entire career in the military, but over the last few years he increasingly had come to the realization that both countries spent too much of their GDP on the military. Goh was looking at the world from a broader perspective, and he believed a unified Korea would benefit both countries and their people. In addition, he was worried that Paek was taking his country down a destructive path that would lead to the suffering and death of many of his countrymen.

When Goh's meeting with Admiral Kim concluded, Goh had more time to reflect on his meeting at the dentist's office. Goh asked himself, *So, they want to exile Paek and his inner circle. Do they think Paek and his people will just "go gentle into that good night"?*

No, thought Goh, *there is no way Paek will accept exile. The Americans surely have to know that. They will need to deal with Paek in a permanent manner. In a way that will ensure he can never be a threat to the reunified Korea.*

Part of the proposal called for Goh's family to be relocated to the South or to the US and assume new identities. Goh thought his family, especially his two sons, would welcome such a move, but his wife would resist leaving. Goh knew his wife would not leave him, especially knowing the risk he would be undertaking. That said, Goh was also confident she would ultimately follow his wishes.

For now, Goh decided he would not tell his wife anything until the plans were finalized.

CHAPTER FIVE

Dunbar said to La Rue, "It's been forty-five minutes and Kordic isn't back. We need to start moving to the airport."

"How will we get there?" she asked.

Dunbar motioned to the parking area. "We'll steal a car or hike there."

La Rue shot back, "Wasn't that Kordic's plan? And who knows where it got him?"

As Dunbar glanced at her he saw several small boats moored in the small bay off Orsula Park.

Dunbar said, "Let me see that map again." La Rue handed it to him, and they both paused as Dunbar surveyed the coastline.

"You're right. We aren't going by car. We're going by boat," said Dunbar.

They both looked out on the bay toward the collection of small dinghies.

They scaled the steep path until they reached the rocky seashore.

Dunbar said, "I'll get a boat and bring it to shore for you."

La Rue smiled. "Chris, I was a swimmer in college and still do twenty-lap workouts daily. Just try to keep up." She sat down to take off her shoes and rearrange her bag so it would fit over her shoulders like a backpack.

On the empty beach, La Rue next stripped down to just her underwear.

Dunbar just stared as La Rue, now wearing only a black bra and thong, folded her clothes and placed them in her bag.

Dunbar sat as he took off his shoes and stuffed them into his shirt. He then handed his Glock G43 and a few magazines to La Rue, saying, "See if there's room in your bag for these."

With their possessions secured in La Rue's bag, they both made their way into the cold April waters of the Adriatic.

"Jesus," let out Dunbar. The water was freezing. He knew he could make the quarter-mile swim, but he needed to do it as quickly as possible so as not to risk hypothermia. He wasn't sure about La Rue, but if she struggled he could pick her up with the boat.

La Rue dove into the cresting wave, exiting on the other side of it, and started her efficient strokes toward the boat without looking back at Dunbar. For the first one hundred or so yards, La Rue was faster than Dunbar.

But the water was so cold that La Rue saw purple clouds roll over her closed eyelids as she tried to maintain her pace, taking in air on every third stroke. La Rue was a well-conditioned swimmer and could cover the quarter mile in just over six minutes, but that was before the frigid waters took their toll.

Dunbar, on the other hand, who had been subjected to freezing water temps during BUD/S training, needed almost seven minutes to make it to the dinghy. The muscle mass on his two-hundred-plus-pound frame became harder to propel the colder he got.

Dunbar reached the dinghy first. He reached his hand out to La Rue to help her into the boat.

As La Rue pulled her dry clothes from her bag, she watched a shivering Dunbar, who had swum in his street clothes.

"Here," she said, handing him a tarp that was on the boat.

Dunbar immediately wrapped himself in it as he focused on the outboard engine.

"Damn," he exclaimed, "there's no battery."

But there was a paddle.

La Rue asked, "Can we paddle?"

"We can, but it's seven miles and it'll be hard work and take a long time. Let's check out the other boats. Maybe we'll get lucky."

On their fifth boat they got lucky. Using the tools on their boat (every boat has a small toolbox), Dunbar transferred the battery to their boat.

After a few minutes of fiddling, the outboard motor coughed to life.

Gas was his next concern. He took a gas can from the third boat they had inspected and headed at a moderate speed on a south-south-west course to the small harbor town of Cavtat, which would leave them only two miles from the Dubrovnik airport.

La Rue couldn't help but notice Dunbar's shivering, so she reached her arm over Dunbar and leaned her body into his, sharing whatever body heat she had with him.

Under the power of the motor it didn't take long for them to cover the seven miles. Dunbar surveyed the wharves as they entered the small fishing village and chose a dock away from the larger wharves, pulling into an empty slip. He quickly jumped onto the dock and tied up his skiff and then extended his hand to help La Rue out of the boat.

As they walked down the dock, Dunbar was surveying the seafront for a good place to lay low. They still had about two hours before their charter would be ready at DBV.

They were both still very cold, so Dunbar's priority was to find someplace indoors and warm.

He saw a seaside hotel but knew if someone was looking for them, they would likely check local hotels for an American couple. There were, of course, a handful of bars they could go to, but there, too, they would probably attract unwanted attention.

That's when he saw a sign for a spa.

Five minutes later both he and La Rue, wearing only towels, entered the hundred-degree sauna. They just sat there for ten minutes without talking, letting the hot air warm their frozen bodies. When a rivulet of sweat ran down Dunbar's forehead, he spoke. "We can stay here for about another half hour or so, but then we'll need to move out."

La Rue just nodded with her eyes closed as she continued to bask in the luxurious heat of the sauna.

A minute later she opened her eyes and took note of her partner's shirtless chest.

She said, "Huh, I would have figured you for the tattoo kind."

Dunbar smiled and said, "Any I may have had are long gone. It goes with the job. It wouldn't be helpful to have a 'semper fi' tattoo right here," he said as he pointed to his flexed biceps.

La Rue just nodded.

A few minutes later Dunbar said, "Time."

As they left the spa Dunbar said, "I'll pick up some supplies from that convenience store and then we'll make our way to the airport. What would you like?"

Coming out of the store, Dunbar handed La Rue a can of Coca-Cola Light and a bag of pierogis, which La Rue hungrily ate as they walked toward the edge of the town, toward the airport.

Dunbar said, "We're flying on a German charter. The tail code is D-ABOG. We aren't going into the passenger terminal. We'll approach via the private jet hangars and make our way out to the tarmac. It'll be parked away from the other jets."

Meanwhile, the sheik's security force that had taken out Kordic was stationed at DBV.

La Rue and Dunbar were now on the perimeter of the airport. They watched as vehicles approached the checkpoint to enter the passenger terminal, the private terminal, and the freight area.

Dunbar saw a DHL van approach one of the buildings outside the security perimeter. The driver got out and carried three packages into the building.

Dunbar exclaimed, "That's our ride, come on."

With that they made their way to the van. Dunbar pulled up on the unlocked rear door and they both got in.

Dunbar rearranged the boxes in the back so he and La Rue would be shielded if the driver had picked up any packages from the office building.

Fortunately, he had none. The driver got in and made his way to the security checkpoint. The guards knew the driver well, so they just waved him through and did not ask to open the back of the van.

The van proceeded to the freight area, where it was backed into the loading dock. The driver got out and went into the freight office to complete some paperwork.

As he did, Dunbar and La Rue exited the van, slinked their way past the freight buildings, and approached the private hangars.

That's when Dunbar saw it: Not far from the private passenger terminal was a white Gulfstream with red, black, and gold on its vertical stabilizer and the tail code D-ABOG. The door was open. Dunbar could see movement through the cockpit windows, indicating the pilots were on board. It was still twenty minutes before departure time but Dunbar was eager to get onto the jet and airborne.

Another thing Dunbar noted was that there were no blocks around the landing gear. Aircraft, once landed, got their wheels chocked so as to prevent the aircraft from rolling while on the ground. But in this case the Gulfstream sat on the tarmac with unchocked wheels. The informed observer would know that this was atypical and indicated a quick egress.

Just then Dunbar saw a canvas cargo cart at the side of the terminal building.

"Stay here," he said to La Rue as he quickly walked over to the cart.

Upon his return he said, "Your ride, madam."

Dunbar helped La Rue into the cart and then placed some cardboard on top of her.

"Stay down as I push you to the jet. Hunch over some," said Dunbar as he looked around.

Dunbar looked back into the DHL van and grabbed a hat that was lying on the passenger seat.

He checked his Glock in his waist holster.

"Okay, time to go. If anything goes bad, just run to the jet. Don't look back; don't worry about me. Just get on that plane," directed Dunbar.

The tension was too high for La Rue to say anything, so she just nodded.

As they made their way along the forty yards or so to the Gulfstream, the copilot came down the stairway and approached Dunbar to help him with the cart while the pilot started the engines.

The copilot then held the cardboard up to obstruct the view as Dunbar helped La Rue out of the cart and she scooted up the stairs. The jet engines were now spinning.

Dunbar grabbed the cart and pushed it hard to get it out of the way.

That's when the first shot rang out. Instinctively, Dunbar ran to the cart for cover as more shots rang out. The Gulfstream pilots, observing the situation, swung the jet around on the taxiway to position themselves for takeoff. The downside of this maneuver was that it put the door on the opposite side from where Dunbar was crouched behind the cargo cart.

Dunbar saw a luggage tug and made a break for it.

He jumped on the tug and started it up, steering toward the door side of the jet. By now the airport police had been alerted to the gunfire and were returning fire. The upshot was that Dunbar had a small window to get onto the Gulfstream while the sheik's people were returning fire at the airport security force.

Dunbar jumped off the moving tug, rolled along the tarmac, and then clambered up the jet stairs, pulling the doorway shut as the Gulfstream accelerated down the taxiway.

The Gulfstream took off from the taxiway, not waiting for controller clearance. It was a maneuver that would surely get the pilots' licenses pulled—that is, if anyone could ever ascertain who the pilots were.

Inside the cabin, the wind whistled from where two bullets had penetrated the fuselage. Dunbar and the copilot applied what amounted to a high-tech version of silly putty to the bullet holes and covered them with duct tape, which would allow the cabin to pres-surize. The patches were temporary but should last for the flight. As a precaution, the command pilot wore an oxygen mask for the entire flight and flew at an altitude between ten thousand and twelve thousand feet.

The original flight plan had them flying fifteen hundred kilometers to the US base in Ramstein, Germany, but with the damage sustained to the Gulfstream IV the pilots decided instead to divert to Naples, shortening their flight to 475 kilometers.

As the flight went "feet wet" over the Adriatic, the pilots turned off their transponder and flew the approach to the US naval base in Naples via radio transmissions only.

As they sat together in the Gulfstream, La Rue asked Dunbar, "Do you think Kordic is okay?"

The look on Dunbar's face said it all.

"We were lucky. The moment Ludovic called you by your real name, it was touch and go. We're going to have to review our US-based security plan for you, not to mention we still have to get out of Europe safely."

"Where do we go from Naples?" asked La Rue.

"The Company is working on that right now," said Dunbar.

Dunbar went to the cockpit to get an update on the flight and when they would be landing in Naples as well as what security precautions were being taken.

Coming back from the cockpit, Dunbar turned to La Rue and said, "Hey, for someone with no field experience you handled yourself really well today."

It was the first nice thing Dunbar had said to her. La Rue replied, smiling, "And imagine what your SEAL buddies would say if they heard you were outswum by 'someone with no field experience.'"

"Outswum?" replied Dunbar. "What are you talking about?"

"The first hundred yards, I completely beat you," said La Rue.

"Who helped who into the boat?" said Dunbar.

"I guess we're just going to have to settle this in a pool when we get back," challenged La Rue.

Dunbar shook his head and said with a confident smile, "There's nothing to settle, but if you want, when we get back to Langley we can go to the pool, where your demise will be complete."

It was 4 p.m. when Kristin McMahon was escorted into the first lady's office.

"Kris, it's so nice to see you again," said Kennedy Russell.

"Thank you, ma'am," replied McMahon.

"Ma'am. You're going to 'ma'am' me?" said Kennedy with a warm smile. "Please call me Kennedy. It'll add some sense of normalcy to this place."

McMahon just smiled and nodded, still somewhat intimidated by the surroundings.

"Kristin, the reason I wanted to meet with you is to make sure you're fine with our attending your wedding."

Kristin thought for a second before replying. "Mrs. Russell, Mike and I are honored that you and the president are even considering coming."

"Well, I wanted to ask you in person. My biggest concern was to make sure the president's attendance doesn't do anything to take away from your day."

"We're delighted that you'll be attending."

"Well, good. We're looking forward to it," said the first lady. She added, "If the wedding were in May, the president said he was going to have the Blue Angels do a flyover."

Kristin blinked and then asked, "Does the fighter pilot thing *ever* go away?"

"No, never! I expect there'll be a lot of aviators attending."

Kristin replied, "A ton, and I told Mike I didn't want the reception to devolve into a frat party."

"Well, that might be one of the biggest benefits of having us at the wedding."

"I bet it will help. Mike's best man, Lieutenant Commander Zack 'Roaring' Rohrbach, is known for his partying. He's the one who came up with the idea for ImAFighterPilot.com," said Kristin.

She could tell by the look on the first lady's face that she wasn't familiar with the website, which was confirmed when she stated, "I don't know what ImAFighterPilot.com is."

Kristin regretted bringing up the topic but had no option but to explain it.

"ImAFighterPilot.com is a website only for fighter pilots and, to put it politely, it's a dating site."

"Really," said the first lady, thinking out loud. "I wouldn't think Navy pilots needed a website to help them find dates."

Kristin remarked, "Well, ma'am, some of these 'dates' are very short in duration."

"Oh," said the first lady. That was followed by a longer "Ohhh," once she grasped the meaning of what Kristin had just said.

"And this website was the brainchild of Mike's best man?" asked Kennedy Russell.

"It was, and apparently he's making a small fortune from it. To be fair, Zack's a great guy and Mike says he is a gifted pilot, but he has the testosterone level of a high school boy. I warned all my bridesmaids about him, but you know what it's like when they put on those dress white uniforms." Having both fallen for naval aviators, they knew firsthand the point Kristin was making.

"I'm just glad ImaFighterPilot.com didn't exist when Andy was flying," Kennedy said, laughing, as she made a mental note to tell her husband about it.

Just then an aide to the first lady came in and handed her a note.

"I shouldn't keep you, Mrs. Russell," said Kristin, still not comfortable calling the first lady by her first name.

"Kristin, we are so looking forward to attending, and please let me know if any of the security issues become too much of a burden. We'll completely understand."

"Mrs. Russell, Mike and I are just so honored that you and the president will be attending." Kristin got up and shook the first lady's hand as she exited her opulent office.

Kristin texted Mike that she had just wrapped up with the first lady.

The response she got back surprised her. "I'm still at the White House in the Green Room. Why don't you stop by?"

McMahon asked the first lady's secretary to arrange for an escort to take her to the Green Room on the first floor of the main building of the White House.

An aide knocked on the door and opened it. Sitting in the room was her fiancé with Jim Hartel, program director of the Torchlight project, whom Kristin knew from her dealings with the DoD.

"Hi," said Mike, standing to give her a quick kiss. Turning to Hartel, he said, "Jim, this is my fiancée, Kristin McMahon, DDI for the NSA."

Jim Hartel responded, "Yes, we've met. We worked together on the WikiLeaks Vault 7 investigation last year."

Kristin replied, "Jim, it's so nice to see you. I didn't know you were working with Mike."

"Well, neither did I until about three hours ago." She thought that might explain why the president wanted to meet with Mike earlier this morning.

McMahon knew Hartel was a senior program manager who worked on weapons systems for the DoD. McMahon also knew better than to ask anything more about what they were working on—at least not until she was home with Mike.

Jim excused himself, saying he needed to call his office, which would give Bartlett and McMahon some privacy.

After Hartel left the Green Room, Kristin asked, "So how did your meeting go with the president?"

"Good," replied Bartlett. "Due to my work on the F-35 project, he asked me to assess the status of another weapons system."

Kristin could read Bartlett well and just said, "And . . ."

"And," added Bartlett with a pause between his words, "it's going to require me to travel some."

"When and for how long?"

"I fly to Seoul tomorrow. I don't know exactly for how long. I would say a week or two."

And with that a silence fell over the room.

Clearly, Kristin understood whatever the president had discussed with Mike had to be important. She also knew they both were senior professionals in the service of the government and duty came before personal issues—but it was their wedding.

"We'll talk more about it tonight, but the short answer is—go, complete your mission, and get back here ASAP. Do you read me, Commander?"

Bartlett smiled, thinking how closely Kristin's words mirrored those of Admiral Johnson. He simply responded with a quick salute and an "Aye, aye, ma'am."

By then Hartel was reentering the room.

Kristin regrouped and said, "Okay, then, I'll see you tonight."

She turned to Hartel. "Jim, so nice seeing you again. Best of luck on your assignment. Make sure you get my fighter jock back here in time for our wedding." Hartel nodded and McMahon left.

It was later that afternoon when Pavo Ludovic, the leader of NetRiot, returned to his office after the meeting with Lauren La Rue.

He was scheduled to get on a Skype call with another hacking group, Guccifer 2.0, which had become infamous for its hacking on behalf of the Russian government of the Democratic National Committee in the US's previous election.

Pavo began, "My friend, what's going on in your world?"

The leader of Guccifer, who used the pseudonym Het, responded, "Busier than ever. If we were a start-up, our valuation would no doubt rival Palantir's." Het was referring to the secretive tech start-up that had a pre-IPO valuation of $9 billion. Palantir, whose expertise involved big data and data analytics, was contracted by all three US intelligence departments—the FBI, CIA, and NSA—to assist them with their data analysis needs.

"It is funny you mention Palantir. I just met with some Americans this morning," said Ludovic.

"What did they want?"

"What do they all want? Power, control, influence over their adversaries—a competitive edge. The names change but the game remains the same, just with different releases of software to hack," said Ludovic.

"I'll share with you something interesting. One of my teams has penetrated the Chinese cruise missile operating system. We believe we will be able to hack into them very soon. Would that be of interest to you or one of your clients?"

Ludovic knew that Guccifer had pivoted their core competency from hacking banks to hacking weapons systems, which was different from NetRiot, whose focus was still on banking, email, and power grids. Pavo responded, "Yes, I would be interested. How much?"

Het replied, "Let me get back to you on that once we have succeeded, but for you, my friend, I would think US $20 million would be a fair price. Or what about a swap? How about you trade me your latest SWIFT hack and I'll give you the cruise missile hack."

Ludovic thought and said, "Done, but you agree not to sell the Chinese code to anyone else for three months."

"One month," said Het.

"Het, you have a deal. Call me when the code is finished. Good day."

As Ludovic hung up he thought about what had just happened. This transaction could be his exit. He could sell this hack to the Americans, Europeans, and Japanese for an amount large enough to allow him to retire. All major hacking teams had a half-life that was usually measured in a single-digit number of years. And Ludovic had been at it for more than four years. He knew his time in the business was coming to an end and he wanted to get out before he became victim to the same violence that had befallen Kordic earlier in the day.

Just like any exceptionally talented entrepreneur, Ludovic didn't know if he would be satisfied with "retirement"—especially at just twenty-eight years of age. But he figured his couple hundred million of tax-free dollars would ease his stress.

Ludovic called to his team leader, "How's the SWIFT hack of Panama proceeding?" Ludovic was referring to a hack they were performing for their North Korean client Imperial Imports LLC.

"Good, Pavo. We are lifting $1 million to $1.5 million a day from Panama's SWIFT transactions. Panama's volume is so high that they don't even notice it."

Ludovic patted his team leader on the shoulder and said, "Good, but no more than $10,000 per transfer. I don't want to trip any of their circuit breakers." Ludovic was referring to the software and AI tools banks and other financial organizations were implementing on an almost weekly basis to combat fraud and malicious cyberintrusions.

Ludovic noticed the Ferrari brochure next to his team leader's keyboard. "Doing some shopping, Antonija?"

"I just bought a 488 GTB," he said, referring to the latest Ferrari model.

"Clean, I assume?" asked Ludovic.

"Of course. I paid cash via one of my LLCs. The car is at my villa in Tuscany. There's no footprints back to us," the team leader assured him.

"Make sure of it," was all Ludovic said. Ludovic didn't like his people spending large or flashy amounts of money. It attracted attention, and attention invited the curious. But his people were young and worked incredible hours, so he couldn't prohibit the occasional indulgence.

Ludovic went to his den, where he'd had a high-tech sleep pod installed, the same model used on the Google campus in California. Recently Ludovic had taken to spending an hour every day in the pod in deep deliberation. With thoughts of retirement now gone, he considered the Guccifer hack and how he could most effectively market it. He also was thinking about how he would need to test it to ensure that it worked.

CHAPTER SIX

General Goh was due to give his weekly update to President Paek.

"Mr. President, we have succeeded in installing the warhead on the DF-26. We are now beginning component testing. We expect that testing to be completed within five days; then we will move on to system testing."

Paek just nodded.

Goh continued, "Our plan has us finished with all testing by April eighth. Then we will move the missiles onto their mobile launchers and repeat the system tests. Barring any problems, we will be operational by mid-April."

Paek spoke. "Excellent, in time for our Day of the Sun celebration." The president was referring to the North Korean public holiday that celebrated the birthday of Kim Il Sung, which occurred every year on April fifteenth. "General, which sites have you selected?"

"Mr. President, as you know, the DF-26 is launched from a mobile launcher, but it needs a solid surface like a road to fire. If we don't use a concrete pad we run the risk of debris damaging the missile's engines during liftoff. We have identified ten sites around Namp'o and Kwail that are suitable."

Paek nodded and then said, "General, make sure all sites are ready and capable of firing the missiles. We'll select the final locations once system testing has completed. Also, I want you to prepare decoy missiles that we can position at other sites. We need to keep the prying Americans from knowing the exact locations of our real missiles."

"Of course, Mr. President," replied Goh, knowing that North Korea made extensive use of decoy missiles that were made of wood but painted to look like the real thing and indistinguishable from a live missile when viewed from a satellite. The meeting continued, with Paek's second and third in command pressing Goh for more details on the missile testing.

Before Goh was dismissed, Paek said, "General Goh, you have two sons, no? Isn't the oldest getting to the age where he'll soon be submitting his application to the Technical Institute?"

The Technical Institute was North Korea's most prestigious engineering school; admission was highly selective.

"Yes, Mr. President. He'll be applying this summer," responded Goh.

"I'll make sure his application is received favorably. I'm sure he'll be a credit to our great nation, just as his father has been."

With that, General Goh just nodded and added, "That is very kind of you, sir."

Goh then saluted and sharply left the room.

But Goh's head was spinning. Never had the president ever mentioned his family, not once in all his years of service. The comment, while received as a great compliment by all in attendance, set off alarm bells for Goh.

It could be that Goh was just being paranoid given his recent interaction with the South, but his paranoia had served him well throughout his career. Goh was now suspicious and would have to take more care in any interactions he had going forward. In addition, he now needed to formulate a more extensive escape plan for his family. If the occasion arose, it would need to be implemented at a moment's notice.

Later that night, a plumbing service van pulled up to the Goh residence.

With a knock on the door, the serviceman and his apprentice entered the home. Once in the basement, they turned on the tap to the basin to mask any eavesdropping technology.

"General Goh, we need to know when the missile test will take place. In order to implement our plan, we need an act of provocation from your government," said the CIA agent dressed as a plumber.

"Before we get to that, what about my family?"

"We will secretly evacuate them to China the day of the launch."

"What makes you think they will be safe in China?

The other CIA agent jotted down a note as Goh spoke. He alternated between taking notes and replacing a valve to the water heater. Every aspect of this mission had been considered, and if the general's house was ever inspected by the SSD, it would show the new valve.

"General, we guarantee your family's safety. Once the mission is completed you will be offered options. You can head up the new North Korean government with an eye toward unification with the South. You will have the support of the US, China, and South Korea in this endeavor. Or you and your family can relocate to China or the US with new identities. General, you can make history and set a new path of prosperity for your people. In time, you will be hailed as a hero."

That last line lingered in Goh's mind . . . *in time.*

Would he be given the time?

"Paek won't go quietly—you realize that."

"Of course, General. We will deal with Paek and his senior advisers."

Goh nodded and said stoically, "The launch will take place on the Day of the Sun celebration, on April fifteenth."

"General, we will be in contact with you next week. Schedule a massage Wednesday evening at the Eden Club at 7 p.m." The agents took the next few minutes to finish replacing the water heater valve and then departed the residence. The entire event took just forty-five minutes.

Goh went outside to his meditation garden and smoked three cigarettes while he processed what he had just heard.

La Rue and Dunbar had landed safely in Naples and were met by two CIA agents at the Navy base known as Naval Support Activity Naples.

As they drove, the lead agent briefed Dunbar and La Rue. "We need to get you back to the US pronto. We have a C-130 on the tarmac that'll take you to Heathrow."

Dunbar glanced out the window and saw the car was approaching a matte gray US Air Force C-130 with its engines already spun up.

"Once at Heathrow, MI-5 will get you on a flight to New York. You aren't going back to DC. You'll stay in New York at a safe house until we're certain the sheik's people have lost your trail."

Dunbar said, "I know people like the sheik's security force. They won't give up. The only way to deal with them is to take them out."

No one responded, but they knew he was right.

Minutes later the C-130 was airborne on a heading of 315 degrees on a direct approach into LHR (the airport code for Heathrow). Two hours and forty-five minutes later, Heathrow, one of the busiest airports in the world, had cleared the C-130 for a straight-in approach, something practically unheard of at LHR. Once the plane landed, their flight taxied to a remote part of Heathrow, where the plane was met by two unassuming black London taxis. These cars looked identical to the ubiquitous TX4 purpose-built London taxicabs. But these cars were different. They were equipped with run-flat tires and bulletproof windows, plus the drivers were MI-5 agents trained in evasive-driving techniques.

The agents greeted Dunbar and La Rue. "Good evening and welcome to the UK," said the lead MI-5 agent. It was going on 8 p.m.

"I'm afraid you won't be with us long. We've booked you on an American Airlines flight to JFK, which leaves within the hour."

The MI-5 agent handed La Rue and Dunbar their tickets, adding, "You'll be boarded last. We have American Airlines uniforms for you. Your cover will be airline employees deadheading back to New York."

La Rue entered the second taxi, where she quickly changed into the AA flight attendant uniform. Next Dunbar jumped into the cab and moments later exited wearing the uniform of a three-stripe copilot. The MI-5 agent then handed Dunbar an electric razor so he could shave his seven-day beard, which would not have fit with his cover of an airline pilot.

"Your flight will land at JFK, where you'll be met by the Company."

They all got into the first cab for the short drive to the stand where the American Airlines triple seven was parked.

When the car stopped, the MI-5 agent handed a phone to Dunbar so he could speak with the US CIA country head for the UK to discuss the details of the New York part of the plan.

The CIA UK lead agent told Dunbar that once they landed they would be transported to a safe house in the Rockaway section of Queens, not far from JFK. There they would be debriefed on their Dubrovnik mission.

"You should know," added the CIA agent, "we confirmed that Croatian police found your contact Zoran Kordic shot in his car."

At the conclusion of the call, Dunbar handed the phone back to the MI-5 agent so he could dispose of it.

"Best of luck to you both," said the MI-5 agent as he opened the car door to direct La Rue and Dunbar to the stairs that would lead them up to the Jetway.

"I hope next time you will come to London for a longer visit," said the MI-5 agent.

As Dunbar and La Rue entered the cabin, the lead purser on the flight greeted them with a knowing look and escorted them to two adjourning business-class seats, adding, "Captain, let me know if we can provide anything."

Dunbar thanked her and settled into his seat. A moment later he went to the restroom, where he checked his Glock G43 mini 9mm pistol and three six-bullet magazines. Dunbar loaded the Glock, put it into a jacket pocket, and put the three spare magazines in the other pocket and headed back to his seat. But before sitting he made his way up to the first-class cabin and then circled the entire business-class cabin, checking out other passengers. The only passenger he thought could possibly be a problem was in seat 4F of first class. Dunbar didn't even bother with coach. No agent of any country ever flew in coach, especially on transatlantic flights.

Dunbar would keep an eye on the passenger in 4F as the flight progressed.

Within minutes the flight was airborne, and it was only a few minutes later that Lauren La Rue reclined her business-class seat and drifted off to a much-needed sleep. She wasn't used to fieldwork, and the activities of the day plus the heightened stress had wiped her out—the meeting with Ludovic, their narrow escape from Dubrovnik, their flight to Naples and then to London, all of it had exhausted and frightened her.

La Rue slept under the watchful eye of CIA agent and ex–Navy SEAL Chris Dunbar.

As Commander Mike Bartlett pulled into the garage of their Potomac home, he saw that Kristin's Audi S5 was already in its spot. He had hoped to make it home before Kristin so he could get a run in and think through what he was going to say to her about his trip to Seoul.

As he entered the house he chuckled as he heard the treadmill motor going. Kristin obviously had the same thought—that a run would help her put her thoughts in order.

He entered the exercise room and waved to Kristin, who had her earbuds in and just nodded to him.

Good, he thought, *I'll go for a run outside.*

A minute later Bartlett was on their driveway stretching before he took off on his four-mile run. His playlist for today's run was Gaslight Anthem, the Killers, and the soundtrack from *Hamilton*.

He returned to their driveway in under thirty-two minutes and then walked down his street to cool down before entering their house.

Kristin, who had just finished a quick shower, was preparing dinner as Bartlett took his earbuds out. "Hey, hon," he said.

She said, "Hi," but it wasn't in her normal bubbly tone.

Bartlett headed to their master bathroom and took a shower before donning an academy T-shirt and some cargo shorts; then he returned to the kitchen.

"So how was your meeting with the first lady?" asked Bartlett.

"We can talk about that later. Let's first talk about your meeting with the president."

Direct and to the point, thought Bartlett. Kristin wanted to get to the bad news right away.

"He asked me to go on a mission for him to Seoul. It should take ten days, maybe two weeks. I leave in the morning with Jim Hartel."

"Mike, the wedding?" Kristin said with a sigh.

"I know, I know. But it's only two weeks. I'll be back home by the fifteenth, in plenty of time," he said, referring to April 28, the date of their wedding.

"That's if everything goes to plan, and it never does," shot back McMahon. "What sort of mission is this? Will you be flying?"

"No, no flying. We're going to be testing a new weapons system. And that's about all I can say about it."

Bartlett could tell his last line did not go over well.

"I realize it doesn't matter that I am deputy director of the NSA and hold a TOP SECRET clearance. It's okay," Kristin said sarcastically.

"Okay, the mission is an offshoot of the Terminal High Altitude Area Defense program but with newer laser technology. We know the North Koreans have some Chinese Dong-Feng 21 'carrier killer' missiles. We'll be testing this new variant of THAAD, which is capable of taking out the Dong-Feng as well as their Hwasong-14 ICBMs."

"North Korea. The president couldn't send you to a more tense area," a worried Kristin McMahon responded.

"I'll only be in Seoul for a day before embarking on the *Stennis* and then on a submarine as we conduct our tests."

"You on a sub? Why did the president think you were the best person for that duty?"

"I don't know exactly. I think it's a combination of my test work at Pax and my work with him on Warlord after the Attack on Nantucket. He wanted a trusted person to assess the readiness of this new weapons system."

"As I said at the White House, complete your mission and make sure you are back here—safe and sound—by the twenty-eighth, mister." McMahon finished her preparation and said, "Dinner's ready."

As they sat down to eat, McMahon made a note to do some checking at the NSA about a new laser-based antimissile weapons system.

"So now tell me about your meeting with the first lady," Bartlett said.

"It was fine. She wanted to make sure that their attendance wouldn't overshadow the ceremony."

"That was nice of her. What do you think about that? Is it a concern?" asked Bartlett.

"No, I'm fine with it. I think it's a great honor. You agree, don't you?"

"Are you kidding? Of course I agree. Besides, do you really think anyone ever says no to this president—especially on a request like this?" opined Bartlett.

"With the president and first lady in the room, your squadron buddies will have to behave. That's one upside, I guess," added McMahon.

Bartlett paused and looked directly into McMahon's eyes. "Kris, it's our wedding—you're the bride. Whatever you want, we'll do.

Don't let yourself get manipulated. The most important person in that room won't be the president, first lady, or any of the admirals—it'll be you."

She smiled at his show of support and affection, then leaned over and kissed him.

When dinner was over, Mike cleaned up the dishes and Kristin went into her office to write a few notes she would slip into his shaving kit and the pockets of the uniform shirts he would take with him on his trip.

As she wrote the notes, she thought about all the risks of being a fighter and test pilot and now these missions for the president. She loved that Mike was held in such high esteem and admired his drive for important work, but she was beginning to feel the stress of being the spouse of someone whose career carried him into harm's way. She thought, *I guess I will be running a lot on the treadmill while he's away. That will be good for my fittings.*

"Mr. President, the vice president is here to see you," said Alice Ahern.

Jack McMasters was Andrew Russell's running mate and good friend. Just how good a friend had been demonstrated during last summer's attack on the president's family while they were vacationing on Nantucket. Vice President McMasters had proven himself under very trying circumstances, and as a result their friendship was rock solid.

"Thank you for seeing me, Mr. President," said the VP as he entered the Oval Office.

"Of course, Jack," replied the president, and they made their way to the opposing couches in the Oval near the fireplace.

"How are Kennedy and the kids?" next asked McMasters.

"Good, Jack. And Helen and your children?"

"Fine, sir. Mr. President, I am afraid I have some bad news to share with you," the VP said next.

Andrew Russell just paused and looked directly into the eyes of his friend.

"Andy, I've been diagnosed with acute lymphocytic leukemia."

There was just silence, as there always is, whenever that word is mentioned.

The VP continued, "They found it during my routine annual physical. Can you imagine?"

Jack McMasters, who had played football in the SEC for Ole Miss, was a large man, at six foot four and a hefty weight, and always looked in good heath.

"Jack, Jack, I'm literally at a loss for words. I'm stunned," said the president.

"I know, it's a real kick in the head, isn't it. They say I have phase three leukemia and they want me to start radiation and chemo at once."

The president just nodded and listened as McMasters continued to relay the details of his condition and his treatment.

"Andy, I should be able to keep up with my duties, but I will need to take the weeks off during my chemo, as they say I will not have much energy. Plus, I want to spend time with my family."

"Jack, you take off as much time as you need. As a matter of fact, I don't want to see you working. Focus on your health and your family. I assume you have talked to the doctors at the Mayo Clinic and at Sloan Kettering?"

"I have. I'm going to be getting my treatments in New York at Sloan."

"They're the best," said Andrew Russell.

"Mr. President, about the second term. I don't think I can commit to that at this point, and I know the activities are about to kick off."

"Jack, there is one thing I want you to focus on, and that is getting better. You're my friend and my partner. Don't let anything distract you from focusing on your health. That is what matters."

McMasters nodded. "I would like to keep this information confidential, Mr. President, until we have a better handle on what exactly the prognosis will be."

"Of course, Jack." The president nodded. The president knew at some point not too far off they would need to share this information with the public, but for now they would handle it as a private matter.

After a few more minutes of conversation, the vice president stood to leave, saying, "Thank you, Mr. President. I wish I had better news for you this morning."

Andrew Russell then approached his friend, and they embraced, each of them supporting the other, as they had throughtout their political careers.

It was a beautiful early April day in Hawaii as the *United States* rode at the pier of the Honolulu cruise port.

The captain of the *United States* was an ex-Cunard captain, Nigel Clifford.

The yeoman welcomed the liner captain with, "Good morning, Captain. The admiral will be right with you."

A moment later the yeoman picked up the phone on her desk and replied, "Yes, Admiral."

Captain Nigel Clifford was then escorted into the office of Admiral William F. Sauer, the Commander, U.S. Pacific Fleet, or COMPACFLT.

"Captain Clifford, thank you for coming. It's a pleasure to meet you," said the four-star US Navy admiral.

"Of course, Admiral," said the newly appointed master of the *United States*.

"Captain, let me introduce Commander Carver. He'll be conducting the briefing."

"Thank you, Admiral, Captain Clifford," began Commander Carver. "Sir, we want to go over some of the details for your planned port call in Namp'o, North Korea."

The ex-Cunard captain nodded.

"Upon entering the Port of Namp'o you will pick up one of their harbor pilots, as is the norm. The pilot will assist you in navigating the waterway and your docking."

Again, Clifford just nodded.

"Once docked, our security forces will disembark your ship and get picked up by sightseeing vans that will be provided by our team on the ground there. That will occur on the morning of the fourteenth. But it is the fifteenth, your departure, we want to talk to you about, sir.

"Sir, we want you to be ready to leave Namp'o on the fifteenth sometime between 11:30 a.m. and noon, at a moment's notice. The challenge is that you will not have the benefit of any harbor tugs or a pilot. You'll need to leave under your own power and sail out of Namp'o harbor at high speed, possibly taking evasive action."

"So, let me understand," said the ex-Cunarder. "Once we receive your order, we are to immediately put to sea and leave Namp'o and head for the open waters of the Yellow Sea at best possible speed. Is that correct?" said Clifford.

"Yes, sir. It is imperative that once word is received, you immediately put to sea at flank speed," said the commander.

Admiral Sauer joined the conversation. "Captain, we have a Chinese national, a merchantman captain who is very familiar with Namp'o harbor, who will board your ship here in Pearl. He'll be able to answer any of your questions and can help you practice the maneuver you'll need to execute to leave Namp'o."

"I look forward to meeting him, Admiral," said the captain of the liner. "During our refit, we had bow thrusters installed that will help us immensely with our pier-side maneuvering, Admiral. If I can be given clearance by the Honolulu harbormaster, I would like to schedule some practice drills with my bridge and engineering officers."

"We'll make sure you get all the cooperation you need from the harbormaster," said Admiral Sauer.

After a few more minutes of discussion, Clifford closed by saying, "Admiral, my grandfather was an officer in the Royal Navy. During World War II he captained the Nelson-class battleship HMS *Rodney*. He spent most of the war dodging German U-boats as he escorted convoys from America to Britain. He also played a major role in hunting down and sinking the *Bismarck*. I've always wanted the opportunity to know what it's like to command a ship in harm's way. I am quite confident my officers, crew, and I can handle this mission, sir."

With that, Clifford stood and smartly saluted COMPACFLT. He exited with Commander Carver, who would introduce the Chinese captain to Captain Clifford.

The *United States* spent the next thirty-six hours practicing the corkscrew maneuver from their Honolulu dock without the aid of any tugs or pilots, much to the dismay of the Honolulu harbormaster. On the evening of April 5, the *United States* departed

Honolulu at high speed, headed to Busan, South Korea, for their next port of call.

After landing in Seoul, Commander Mike Bartlett and Jim Hartel had a few hours to clean up in the Busan officers' quarters before boarding an aging and somewhat graceless but dependable C-2A Greyhound of VRC-30, the Providers, for their flight out to the USS *John C. Stennis*, located somewhere in the East China Sea.

Later that morning the C-2A Greyhound caught the three wire on the USS *John C. Stennis*, where a safety officer promptly escorted Hartel and Bartlett to the captain's outboard cabin. There they were met by Rear Admiral Tom "Flatbush" Fraser, COMCARGRU-3, his staff, and the captain of the *Stennis*, Craig "Chaser" Ryan. After introductions and with a Marine standing guard at the door, Hartel began his presentation. His first slide was entitled "Operation Baem," *baem* being the Korean word for "snake." The plan called for an increased tempo for testing Torchlight, with the goal that it would be operational in the next two weeks, should the North Koreans fire another DF-26 at the *Stennis* Carrier Group.

You could feel the unease in the room as Hartel finished his presentation and paused.

Captain Ryan was the first to speak. "Mr. Hartel, what assurance can you provide us that Torchlight will be able to intercept the Dong-Feng?"

Jim Hartel nodded, expecting the question.

"Captain, that's exactly what Commander Bartlett and I will be doing over the next ten days. We'll be testing the Torchlight installation on the *Florida*. If we have any doubts about Torchlight's readiness, then the mission will be scrubbed and the *Stennis* will depart the AOR," said Hartel, using the Navy's acronym for "area of responsibility."

Captain Ryan asked, "Admiral, what do you think about using the *Stennis* as the bait for this trap?"

It was the question that was on everyone's mind.

Newly flagged rear admiral Fraser paused before responding, then said, "Captain, in order to catch a big fish, you need some big bait. We're the bait. We're going to be in harm's way, and only everyone's extreme focus, concentration, and training will keep us safe. You all have my assurance that if Torchlight doesn't test out to my satisfaction, I will contact the president directly about canceling the mission."

Captain Ryan added, "So, if the North Koreans fire another DF-26, your ray gun will shoot it down. Is that correct, Mr. Hartel?"

Jim Hartel replied, "Yes, Captain, we'll position the *Florida* twenty miles off the coast of North Korea so we'll be able to pick up their launch as it happens. Torchlight should be able to knock down the DF-26 before it's within five hundred miles of the *Stennis*."

"That sounds good, Mr. Hartel, but at seven thousand knots, if the *Florida* misses we'll have only five minutes before it is on us. Five minutes," said Captain Ryan.

"Copy that, Captain," was all Hartel said in reply.
For the officers of the *John C. Stennis* present, their unease remained unabated.

As the meeting broke, Rear Admiral Fraser asked Commander Bartlett to remain behind.

"Commander, if you detect any problems or shortcomings with Torchlight—any—you are to report back to me. That is a direct order, Commander. I will not put my five thousand sailors or this ship at risk. This idea of a carrier group playing possum while North Korea takes potshots at us is not my idea of a proper use of a US Navy carrier group."

"Understood, Admiral. I can tell you I met personally with the president and he said almost the exact same words. Admiral, it's the reason I'm here. If Torchlight is not ready, he told me he'll move your group out of the Yellow Sea."

"Commander, I served with Andrew Russell with VFA-32 on the *Harry Truman*. And I agree there's no way he'll put the *Stennis* at risk. I would bet my life on it. That said, if there's an iota of risk with Torchlight, you will inform me. Are we clear?"

"Yes, sir, Admiral, crystal clear," responded Commander Bartlett. "Tomorrow a helo will take you out to the *Florida*. Until then, work with my staff on the details of the testing." Rear Admiral Fraser, COMCARGRU-3, exited the outboard cabin, but not before Commander Bartlett saluted the two-star admiral.

Jim Hartel and Mike Bartlett spent the rest of the afternoon with the admiral's staff going over various test plans. Being operationally focused, the staff of CARGRU-3 wanted an option added that did not rely on Torchlight. The admiral's chief of staff, a captain, said, "Mr. Hartel, Commander Bartlett, the *JCS* Carrier Group will not rely on an unproven Torchlight for our safety. *JCS* will rely on our SP-JASHO as well as our air wing."

Jim Hartel felt the frustration of being constantly challenged. "Captain, you will recall when the North Koreans fired the DF-26 at the *Stennis* a few weeks ago, the *Mobile Bay* was unable to get off a single shot. Captain, nothing has changed since then. So you can SP-JASHO to your heart's content, but without Torchlight, your carrier and its group will be at risk. And by the way, if you're thinking

THAAD will help, keep in mind it has an operational range of only one hundred twenty miles, which the North Koreans are well aware of—so I anticipate they'll program a flight path for their DF-26 that keeps them out of the range of THAAD. I understand and appreciate your concerns, but Torchlight is your best option other than turning tail and running."

Bartlett winced when he heard that last line and interjected before anyone could react, "Jim, thank you for that. I suggest we take a five-minute bio break." He knew the operational focus of deployed officers was so sharp that every detail of every mission was heavily scrutinized and debated. And Operation Baem certainly wasn't the *Stennis's* typical mission.

After another thirty minutes of discussion the briefing concluded and Hartel and Bartlett went to their cabins to relax before dinner with the admiral and his staff, where they expected they would get another round of grilling about Torchlight. Bartlett couldn't blame them. Their duty was to carry out their mission and protect their crew.

Hartel and Bartlett had individual staterooms that shared a common bathroom. Bartlett knocked on Hartel's stateroom door.

"Jim, you need to understand the stress and the operational tempo that the *JCS* officers are under and bear that in mind when you answer them," said Bartlett.

"I understand. I was just getting defensive after an entire afternoon of constantly being challenged and in some cases lectured. That plus we've been traveling for the last thirty hours and I could use some shut-eye. But I get your point. I'll keep that in mind during tonight's dinner.

"Not to throw kerosene on the fire, but just how confident are you in Torchlight, and are you right about THAAD, or is that just competitive disdain?"

"Mike, I've spent the last five years of my life working on this project. The technology is proven. The testing has either met or exceeded its goals. It's a game-changer weapon system that'll make the Israelis' Iron Dome and THAAD look like flip-phone technology compared to the iPhone."

"Tell me more about why you seem to be so down on THAAD."

"It was a good idea when it was first conceived over twenty years ago. But it has a low kill rating and limited range. It's basically a Sidewinder on steroids," said Hartel, referring to the US Navy's venerable and loved heat-seeking missile, which had been equipped on every Navy fighter since the F-4 Phantoms in Vietnam.

"A Sidewinder on steroids," said Bartlett, echoing Hartel's words. "I know you're sold on the value of Torchlight, and I am too, but what I'm asking is, what keeps you up at night about Torchlight and will it shoot down an armed DF-26 in the next two to three weeks?"

"Well that's the sixty-four-thousand-dollar question, isn't it? We'll know better after our tests on the *Florida*. But I believe Torchlight will be able to shoot down anything the North Koreans can throw at it—period."

With that Bartlett left to visit the ready room of Carrier Air Wing 9's (CVW-9) fighter squadron, VFA-41, the Black Aces, whose CO he knew from his days at the academy.

As Jim Hartel sat in his stateroom, Bartlett's question weighed heavily on him. His worry for Torchlight wasn't the hardware. That was rock solid. It was the software—that was his concern. Would the Torchlight software work as advertised, especially in a mission situation?

Tonight, President Andrew Russell would be having dinner with his family, which was an increasingly rare occurrence.

"So, what happened at school today?" the president asked his children.

Katie, his eleven-year-old daughter, was first to answer. "We're getting ready for our play."

The president knew they were performing *Guys and Dolls* and both Katie and his thirteen-year-old son, Andrew, had leading parts. "After dinner, maybe the forty-sixth president of the United States can get a sneak preview," he said in a way he knew the children could not resist.

The kids quickly ate dinner and then asked to be excused to prepare for their mini performance.

With Andrew and Kennedy Russell at the table alone, the conversation turned to the Bartlett wedding.

"I met with Kristin the other day. I wanted to make sure our attendance wouldn't be a burden to them."

"What did she say?"

"She said all the right things. I think they're happy to have us attend.

"You know, she asked an interesting question. She asked if the 'fighter pilot thing' ever goes away."

"And what did you say?" asked the president, clearly interested in her answer.

"I told her the truth—that *no*, it never goes away."

The president didn't really have an answer to that. "On that note," he said as he got up from the table, "I think we're ready for a little preview of *Guys and Dolls*."

At the conclusion of the impromptu performance, Kennedy and Andrew Russell both clapped, with the president standing and saying, "It isn't often you get a standing ovation from the president, but in this case it's merited."

The kids went off to do their homework with big grins on their faces, which left the president and first lady with some time alone.

Their conversation turned to their summer vacation.

"So where would you like to go this summer?" started the president.

"Somewhere safe. Does that exist?" replied Kennedy.

Since last summer's terrorist attack on their family, Kennedy had become more and more protective, almost to the point of a recluse. The president thought that over time it would subside some, but it seemed to be getting more intense. To be fair, it had only been seven months since the attack, which had resulted in his wife and children being kidnapped for a short time by Al Qaeda.

"Ken, the kids have never been safer. You know we increased their Secret Service detail from four to twenty agents. And they never take the same route to school," stated the president.

The president was referring to their route to the Sidwell School which was only four miles from the White House. The Secret Service had plotted ten different routes they could take to the school, and every day a randomly generated number known only to the children's Secret Service detail was used to select the route.

"I appreciate the increased security for the kids, but at the same time I worry what it's doing to them. Andy, if the kids want to go to a Starbucks with their friends, it needs to be planned days in advance so the store and its staff can be background checked. Imagine what that does to them!"

"Ken, it comes with the job. You know that."

"That's just it, Andy. I'm beginning to wonder whether it's worth it."

"What are you saying? Are you suggesting that I shouldn't run for a second term?"

There was an uneasy pause in the room.

"No, I am not saying that, but, Andy, you need to work with me on this. The kids come first—we always said that."

"Of course, and they do," he said. "So what are your thoughts about our vacation? I know Nantucket is out."

"I'm not sure. My staff is coming up with some ideas we can review. I think probably Colorado or maybe Jackson Hole, Wyoming," said Kennedy.

The president nodded, pretty much expecting that suggestion. He said, "I need to take a call, but when I get back, how about we catch up on *Game of Thrones*? We're a few episodes behind."

Kennedy just nodded.

As the president left he saw his daughter and started singing, "I feel my heart is leapin'! I'm having trouble sleepin'! 'Cause I love you, a bushel and a peck. You bet your pretty neck I do!"

CHAPTER SEVEN

I t was late in the evening when La Rue and Dunbar landed at JFK. They were met by the local CIA team and driven in a black Chevrolet Suburban the short drive to the Rockaway Beach safe house.

The house was a good choice, because right next to it was an open lot that provided added privacy.

Once inside, the local CIA team briefed Dunbar and La Rue on how long they thought they would be staying—a week, maybe two. That wouldn't be a problem, as the house was fitted with the latest secure communications systems. So even though they were in an out-of-the-way location in Queens, New York, they would have instant access to Langley and CIA headquarters.

The first priority for La Rue was to get out of the American Airlines flight attendant outfit that the MI-5 had given her and take a shower.

Dunbar, being Dunbar, first wanted to check the perimeter and then assess the view from every window of the house, as well as check the arsenal of weapons that every safe house maintained.

With her shower finished, La Rue entered the kitchen wearing a running suit that she'd found in her room.

"Don't you want to take a shower?" she asked Dunbar.

"I will in a minute, but I wanted to secure the location first."

"Well, it looks pretty secure to me. I'm going to log on and see what's going on."

And with that Dunbar left for a shower and to change into clean clothes.

La Rue logged into Langley and checked her inbox, which was full of mainly standard briefing emails. She then checked her several Gmail accounts, along with her ersatz FB, Instagram, and Twitter accounts.

In one of her Gmail accounts was an email from Pavo Ludovic.

Lauren,

I have something that I think you will be very interested in. I suggest we Skype Saturday at GMT 20:00.

By the way, I hope you enjoy New York. It's nice this time of year.

Pavo

La Rue shook her head. Hopefully he didn't know where in New York they were.

Dunbar entered the kitchen reinvigorated from his shower and in clean clothes. He was hungry and made his way over to the completely stocked fridge.

"What's up?" he asked, seeing La Rue was logged on to the network.

"Not much, other than an email from Ludovic welcoming us to New York."

"You serious?" Dunbar asked, pausing from drinking milk from the carton.

"Take a look."

Dunbar leaned over La Rue's shoulder and read the brief email, saying, "Twelve o'clock GMT, that's 8 a.m. our time. So, you'll speak with him tomorrow morning. He doesn't know where we are other than New York, but I am going to alert Langley anyway. There's no way he could know about our safe houses—or which one we are in. But just to be sure, I'll let the local team know about this."

Dunbar went into the other room and called Langley to share with them Ludovic's email.

When Dunbar came back into the family room, La Rue said, "It's late. I'm going to turn in. See you in the morning."

Dunbar simply said, "Good night." It was unlikely that Dunbar would get much sleep tonight, given the Ludovic email.

As the sun broke on Saturday, April 7, both Dunbar and La Rue were up, showered, and in the kitchen.

"Good morning," said La Rue, looking refreshed after the night's sleep and feeling better about being back on US soil.

"Morning. Can I fix you something to eat?" asked Dunbar.

"You cook?" asked an incredulous La Rue.

"I do. What's so surprising about that?"

"Nothing, but it's not what I would expect from an ex-SEAL."

"There's such a thing as an ex-SEAL? And to answer your question, I learned to cook while in college. I had a job as a short-order cook. That's before I dropped out to go to BUD/S training in Coronado."

La Rue nodded. "What college did you attend?"

"I was an Iowa State Cyclone—a gymnast, a ring man."

"Really? ISU? I went to Wisconsin in Madison."

"Oh, one of those."

"What does that mean?"

"You know what they say about University of Wisconsin—beer, brats, and badgers. I bet you were in a sorority too."

"Sorry to ruin your fantasy, but no sorority, although I did find time for the occasional beer and brat. And what are you giving me a hard time about? What was life like at Iowa State as a gymnast?"

"Life was fine."

"I bet your SEAL buddies would love to see a photo of you in your leotard."

"You know what looked good in that *leotard*? These guns," said Dunbar flexing his large biceps.

"Imagine, all that muscle and I still was faster in the water than you were. I outswam a SEAL."

"What reality do you live in?"

"The one in which I swam faster than you." La Rue smiled.

"Anyway, we were talking about food. What would you like?"

"An omelet?"

"Coming right up. What do you want in it?"

"What do we have?"

"Just about everything. Let's see—peppers, cheese, ham?"

"How about all three?"

A few minutes later Chris Dunbar slid a plate in front of Lauren La Rue and one for himself, adding, "Dig in."

She took a mouthful and a second later said, "Hey, this is good."

"I told you I could cook."

"You did. Do you do laundry too? Because if you do I might have to marry you."

Which brought on an awkward silence.

After a moment Dunbar said, "No, no laundry, just cooking." He smiled to ease the mood. "Anyway, now you know about me. What about you? How does a Badger wind up in the Middle East working for Al Qaeda?"

"Well, like most things in life, it was by chance. After graduating from Wisconsin, I got an MBA from the NYU Stern School. That led to a lot of interviews with investment banks—Goldman, J.P. Morgan, and some consulting companies like Allen & Co. and McKinsey. But I also took an interview with an organization that was very secretive."

Dunbar nodded as he dug into his food.

"At first, I thought it was for a London skunkworks handling high-speed trading. That intrigued me, but before I knew it, I was in Dubai being wined and dined the likes of which I had never seen, let alone imaged. And the rest I guess you read in my file."

"I did, but that still doesn't explain why you would work for a man like Sheik Abdul Er Rahman. He was well-known as the leader of the Islamic Front in the intelligence community."

"Well, I can tell you I never picked up any hint of terrorism. Yes, he was a ruthless businessman and someone you didn't want to cross. And he did some questionable financial transactions, but tell me, doesn't that describe half the investment bankers on Wall Street? It was only the last couple of months that I started to question his dealings, and by then I was already planning my exit. The operation on Nantucket was the final straw."

"The operation on Nantucket—you mean when the sheik bankrolled the kidnapping of the president's family. That was the last straw for you," Dunbar added sarcastically.

"Everything in hindsight looks crystal clear to you and the NSA, CIA, and FBI, doesn't it? But I'll tell you, when you are in the middle of it, it isn't that obvious. I can promise you that."

As Dunbar listened, he thought La Rue's words were exactly the sort of thing a Navy SEAL team leader would say during a post-op debrief. He understood what she meant and, as a matter of fact, was developing a growing respect for her.

Changing the topic and lightening the mood, Dunbar added, "Well, I'm glad you liked the omelet."

"I did. Now let's prep for the Ludovic call. I wonder what he wants to speak to us about."

"Don't know. Maybe he wants to follow up on the offer we made him while in Dubrovnik."

"No, he knows that was just a ruse. I'll bet it's either a new hack or some personal information on someone powerful. Maybe he wants to sell us his back door into the SWIFT system. We know he's been lifting millions off unsuspecting wire transfers."

"We'll find out soon enough," said Dunbar, ending the topic.

Before they initiated the Skype call with Ludovic, La Rue started a program on her laptop known as an "IP address bouncer," which would defeat anyone trying to obtain the IP address of her laptop, which could in turn be used to determine their location. With the program running, Dunbar and La Rue put on headsets as they waited for Ludovic to initiate the Skype call.

A minute later the familiar tone of the Skype ring sounded on La Rue's laptop, and a second later the video image appeared. She toggled her keyboard to bring the image up on the large screen in their media room.

"Good morning, Amy Anderson," said Pavo Ludovic, utilizing the fake name La Rue had used during the meeting in Dubrovnik.

"Well, Pavo, you said you had something of interest to discuss," returned La Rue.

"Getting right to the point as usual. Are there no Americans who value politeness?"

"We do. We would just prefer to keep this conversation as short as possible so someone doesn't decide to launch a cruise missile at your location."

"Touché," said Ludovic." All right, then, what would your client be willing to pay for a hack of the Chinese missile operating system?"

La Rue couldn't believe what she was hearing. Trying to keep her composure, she responded, "We may be interested in that."

"Oh, you may be interested in that? Is that right?" came Ludovic's sarcastic response. "I want $100 million, cash paid in advance. And if you try to negotiate, I'll double it. You know it's worth it. You have twelve hours to make your decision before I offer it to my next buyer. Contact me tonight at 011 385 20 916 2376 via WhatsApp with your answer. Good day."

La Rue finished writing down the number Ludovic dictated and then turned to Dunbar. "We need to talk to the director immediately."

"Hold on, Gunga Din. It's Saturday morning, and by the way, how do we know this is legit?" questioned Dunbar.

"It's legit. The one thing about Ludovic—he doesn't play tricks or waste time. I'm calling Director Collins."

Lisa Collins picked up her phone. "Hello, Lauren, I was meaning to call you to get a firsthand debrief on how things went in Dubrovnik with NetRiot."

"Our cover was blown almost immediately," said La Rue.

"Yes, I was made aware of that," Collins replied.

"But that's not why I am calling you on a Saturday morning, Director. I just got off a Skype call with the leader of NetRiot, and he says he can get us a hack of the Chinese missile operating system."

"Do you think he's legit?" asked the director.

"Totally. Ludovic doesn't waste time. If he says he can get us the code, I believe him."

"What does he want for it?" was the next question.

"A hundred million," La Rue answered.

"We're going to have to verify the hack first," returned Collins.

"Of course. I would make that a condition, but we need to move fast. Ludovic says we only have twelve hours before he shops it to someone else," replied La Rue.

"If you feel this is legit, I'll get the ball rolling ASAP. Let's code word this," said the director.

"How about 'Badger'?" said La Rue, smiling at Dunbar as she said it.

"'Badger' it is. I'll get back to you." And with that Collins was off the line.

"Mr. President," said Sterling Spencer, "here are the latest figures on the DNC fund-raising for our second-term campaign."

"It looks like we are well ahead of our plan," said the president.

The president had not shared the news about the vice president's leukemia with anyone yet. Not with the people in the room—or with his wife.

Ron Kirby, the president's campaign manager, nodded and added, "Yes, Mr. President, we are. I've put together a list of campaign events for you and the first lady for the coming months."

The president glanced at the list and told him, "This is fine for me, Ron, but we aren't going to be involving the first lady to this level."

Kirby looked at Spencer and then added, "Of course, Mr. President. Just let me know which events she can make."

"She'll give a speech at the convention as well as accompany me when I accept the nomination, she'll attend the Al Smith dinner in New York, and, of course, she'll be with us on election night. But that's it."

"Mr. President, the press loves her. Such a limited schedule for her is going to raise questions," replied Kirby with a tinge of alarm.

"Ron, in the aftermath of last year's kidnapping, we are going to strictly limit her appearances."

"Mr. President," added Kirby, "I completely understand and so will the public, but may I suggest that we add some photos and White House interviews with you and the first lady to get ahead of any rumors?"

"Rumors, what rumors?"

"Mr. President, during the first campaign your wife was a fixture by your side and the contrast will be noticeable, sir," added Spencer providing some air cover for Kirby who was beginning to struggle.

"Security is a greater concern today, and after what my wife and children went through on Nantucket I really don't give a damn what anyone thinks," snapped the president.

"Certainly, sir," said Kirby. "We can make this work, but Sterls is correct. We just need to ensure that we provide some interviews with you both. Maybe we do a remote from Camp David."

"Look, I understand the optics. It isn't lost on me, but it is secondary to my wife's health. Ron, we have the Bartlett wedding coming up. Work with your team and we can make that a good photo op, and then we can work something into our vacation plans," relented President Russell.

Sterling Spencer knew it was time to bring this topic to an end. He stood and said, "Thank you, Mr. President," which was the cue to Kirby to end the meeting.

Commander Bartlett was up early to meet with Admiral Fraser before he and Jim Hartel helo'd out to the USS *Florida*.

"Commander, keep me apprised on the Torchlight tests. Good luck."

"Aye, aye, Admiral," Bartlett said with a salute.

Bartlett met up with Hartel in the preflight room in the *Stennis's* tower. There the pilot of the MH-60S Seahawk helo, a lieutenant with HSC-14, the Chargers, went over the mission.

"We'll travel approximately 120 nautical miles north to rendezvous with the *Florida*, which is patrolling about one hundred miles off Gunsan, South Korea. Once we meet up with the *Florida*, we'll winch you down onto the deck."

The lieutenant could detect hesitancy in Hartel's face.

"Not to worry, sir. The Chargers will get you to the *Florida* as planned—and safely."

Hartel just nodded.

Commander Bartlett inserted earplugs in his ears and put on his cranial helmet with headphones and googles. A crew member of the MH-60S Seahawk then checked both Hartel and Bartlett to ensure that their equipment, which included a life vest with a strobe, dye marker, and shark repellant, was correctly attached to their flight suits. Where safety was concerned the US Navy didn't take any shortcuts.

Bartlett gave the crew member a thumbs-up, as did Hartel. They then were escorted, single file, out onto the *Stennis* flight deck by another crew member, wearing a white safety vest, where they boarded the MH-60S helo. The loudspeaker on the flight deck announced the helo's departure.

Three minutes later the MH-60S lifted off the flight deck of the mighty *Stennis*. Once they were twenty feet in the air, the nose of the helo tilted forward and to the left as the helo cleared the *Stennis*. They were on their way to the *Florida*.

The USS *Florida* was the sixth ship of the United States Navy to bear the name of that state. It began life as an Ohio-class missile submarine—or what the submarine community calls a "boomer." Later it was redesignated as SSGN-728, as it was converted to a cruise missile submarine.

As SSGN-728 it was selected for further modifications as the test platform for the Torchlight technology, which included the installation of six next-gen nuclear reactors, the Navy's brand-new SPY-6 3-D radar, which employed an active electronically scanned array for air and missile defense, and, of course, the Torchlight laser weapons system. Together they represented a giant step forward in terms of defensive missile standoff capabilities.

Torchlight, simply put, was intended to track and destroy any missile fired at the United States or its NATO allies.

The USS *Florida* with the Torchlight weapon system installed was dubbed the Death Star of the Fleet by its crew. Of course, that name was used only on board the submarine and by approved personnel. Any mention of Torchlight outside the skin of the submarine would be a serious violation of security.

In order to maximize time at sea, the *Florida*, like all US Navy ballistic submarines, had two crews assigned to it—designated Blue and Gold. The concept was that when one crew manned the submarine, say, *Florida*

Blue, the Gold crew would be on land training and enjoying family life.

On board the *Florida* this April morning was the *Florida* Gold crew, with Captain Ted "Dutch" Reagan in command. He turned to his officer of the deck. "OOD, surface the *Florida*. Once on top, bring us to a stop."

"Aye, aye, Captain," responded the lieutenant as he grabbed the 1MC microphone and ordered, "Surface, surface, surface. Ten degree up bubble. All stop."

A second later the chief of the boat, or COB, repeated the OOD's order: "Aye, aye, sir, surface, surface, surface, ten degrees up on the planes. All stop."

Dutch Reagan ordered, "Sonar, Con. Is everything clear?"

"Con, Sonar. The surface is clear, sir," responded the sonar operator.

After green lights appeared across the Christmas tree that monitored all the main valves on the submarine, a crew member climbed a few steps up the ladder to check the hatch's pressure valve and, once satisfied, said, "Sir, request permission to open the hatch."

After glancing at the relief valve, the XO barked, "Granted."

Next Reagan ordered, "Station the lookouts. I am going up top. XO, COB, you're with me."

As per procedure, the COB and the captain all waited until the lookouts had been stationed topside before climbing up the ladder and smelling the fresh sea air.

The lookouts were scanning 360 degrees around the *Florida* for any surface or air contacts. Their sonar and radar readings told them not to expect to see anything other than their visitor.

The starboard lookout was first to spot it.

"Captain, helo at four o'clock," he yelled.

Dutch Reagan, the XO, and the COB all turned to locate the inbound US Navy MH-60S Seahawk as it approached the now stopped *Florida*, which had surfaced with the express purpose of picking up Jim Hartel and Commander Bartlett.

The COB got on the microphone and called for the airborne arresting team to man the deck just aft of the sail in order to bring Hartel and Bartlett aboard as they were lowered from the Seahawk.

The deck crew flashed hand signals to the Seahawk crew as the first of their guests was lowered sixty feet by the helo's winch.

The deck crew used a retainer pole to capture the winch wire and haul Hartel on board. With Hartel now secured, the winch was retracted and Bartlett was lowered to the deck of the stationary submarine.

"COB, get them aboard quickly. I want this deck awash in three minutes," ordered Dutch Reagan, knowing full well that time spent on the surface risked exposing his ship to either detection or attack, or both.

"Aye, aye, skipper," responded the COB smartly. He was the highest-ranking noncommissioned officer on the *Florida* and as such was a cross between a deity and an NFL coach to the crew. He turned to his deck crew, barking a series of orders to ensure that the sailors under his command were focused on expeditiously and safely getting their visitors on board and belowdecks in the shortest amount of time possible.

Once on the deck, Hartel and Bartlett were escorted into the *Florida* through the aft hatch on the sail.

Two minutes and forty seconds after surfacing, Dutch Reagan turned to his XO and said, "XO, take her down."

"Aye, aye, Captain," replied the XO as he turned to the watch stander, ordering, "Clear the bridge, prepare to dive."

That command set off a series of actions and responses that have been in place in the submarine community for decades.

The watch stander, whose sole responsibility is to monitor all topside sailors and officers, went into action, calling, "Lookouts, clear the bridge."

As the lookouts flew down from their positions high up on the sail, they yelled, "One's down." "Two's down."

The watch stander then repeated to the XO, "Lookouts down, deck crew down."

The XO added, "Copy, clear the bridge, prepare to dive."

The captain descended as the watch stander reported, "CO's down." A moment later the XO slid down the ladder—"XO's down"—followed by the COB—"COB's down. Watch stander's down. Deck clear, sail's clear. Ready to seal the hatch."

The XO and COB were now in the control room and asked the OOD, "What's the sounding?"

The OOD ordered, "Navigator, report on the sounding."

"Ocean depth eight hundred feet, sir."

The XO next grabbed the 1MC: "This is the XO, dive, dive, dive," and in time-honored tradition, the diving klaxon was sounded as the XO turned to the OOD and ordered, "Five degree down bubble, make your depth four hundred feet, right standard rudder, ahead one-third."

Commands were repeated and the warship that was the USS *Florida* vanished from the surface and reentered the safety of the depths of the ocean.

While the *Florida* submerged, Dutch Reagan was welcoming his visitors in the officers' mess.

"Welcome aboard, gentlemen."

Commander Bartlett saluted the O-6 captain of the *Florida*, who was one grade above his O-5 commander rank.

Jim Hartel, a civilian, did not salute but responded, "Thank you, Captain. We're eager to get started."

"I understand," he replied. "This yeoman will see you to your cabins. Once settled, we will reconvene in the mess with the engineering officer, weapons officers, ops, and the XO to discuss the mission."

And with that Hartel and Bartlett turned to follow the petty officer to their cabins. Thirty minutes later everyone reconvened in the officers' mess as the culinary specialist brought in a tray of sandwiches and cookies and made sure the coffee was hot and the refrigerator was stocked with Red Bull, Monster Energy, and Mountain Dew, which had become staples on every ship in the Navy—especially submarines.

With the introductions out of the way, Dutch Reagan turned the briefing over to Jim Hartel.

"Thank you, Captain," began Hartel. "As you know, we're here to test the Torchlight weapon systems. We'll be conducting some real-life exercises of dummy missiles fired from Hawaii, South Korea, and other subs in the area. These tests will include Tomahawk cruise missiles and Minuteman III ICBM shots.

"In addition to testing the integration of the SPY-6 with the Torchlight laser weapon system, we're interested in all operational aspects of the system: tracking, targeting, power consumption, and Torchlight's ability to track multiple targets as well as operate with one or two offline reactors."

First up was a report from the operations officer.

"Up to this point Torchlight has checked out. We have successfully tracked, targeted, and shot down missiles fired from the Kauai Sandia Labs installation in Hawaii and Vandenberg Air Force Base in California." The ops officer handed a copy of the report to Hartel—a report Hartel had already seen.

Next to report was the weapons officer. "Torchlight employs a weapons-grade laser beam in the 1,550-nanometer wavelength. When the beam is correctly columnated, it can reach distances of approximately 250 miles."

Commander Bartlett asked, "Commander, what happens if a bird, for example, flies into the path of the beam?"

"Then we'll be having fried duck for dinner," Weps said, laughing.

Hartel interjected, "Yes, there is a risk if something travels into the path of the beam when it's at full strength."

"And what about an aircraft of some kind?" questioned Bartlett.

"It would be catastrophic, but we would know from SPY-6 if there are any aircraft in the beam's path so we wouldn't hit the aircraft. Unless we wanted to," added Hartel.

Next the engineering officer handed Hartel the latest updates on the performance of the new Bechtel reactors.

"There's a lot to like about these new Bechtel A1B nuclear reactors," said the chief engineer. "They're half the size of the old reactors and generate three times the output. They're deadly quiet and we haven't experienced a failure of any major components yet. They check out.

"There is one area of concern on which I would like your opinion, Mr. Hartel," said the chief engineer. "These new Bechtels run hot—and they need a lot of water to keep cool. Our water input is three times higher than a typical Ohio-class submarine. In and of itself it isn't a problem, but I was surprised by the amount of water we need to take in to keep these units cool."

Hartel jotted down some notes as the engineer spoke, then entered some commands into his laptop. After a few seconds he said, "Yes, I see the intake is higher than a normal boomer, but our consumption is within spec and we do have two separate intakes to collect the water."

The captain then asked, for the benefit of the room, "Does taking in all this water create any acoustic problems for us, Chief?"

The chief responded, "Negative, Captain. The intakes are similar to what we used as a boomer. They don't give off any acoustic signature. We are taking in more water than we used to but we're doing it quietly."

After concluding the operational review of Torchlight, Hartel began the briefing for the missile exercises they would be conducting over the next several days. As he spoke, there was no mention of North Korea, the DF-26, or the *John C. Stennis* Strike Group. That discussion was held for later, when Commander Bartlett, Captain Reagan, and Hartel were alone.

CHAPTER EIGHT

It was Saturday afternoon and Collins had called her staff in to brief them on the newly initiated project Badger.

"NetRiot just offered us the hack into the Chinese missile systems," Collins shared with everyone in the room.

"Do we think it's legit?" asked her DDI.

Collins smiled since that was the first question she'd asked La Rue. She liked the way her DDI thought and how he went about building his positions. Collins thought the DDI would be the right person to succeed her when the time came.

Lisa Collins, the first woman to lead the CIA, was a trailblazer. That said, she hadn't accomplished everything she wanted to yet. Her sights were next set on secretary of state and ultimately a run for president of the United States. But she would have to wait, as Andrew Russell, the president, and Jack McMasters, the vice president, who was one of her mentors, were in their first term and enjoyed enormous popularity and support.

Getting back to Badger, Collins answered her DDI. "Yes, we think the offer is legit and we expected it. The NSA has picked up some chatter about a possible Chinese missile hack. We need to move fast and, of course, we'll need to validate the hack."

As odd as this conversation seemed, it was increasingly becoming the norm. Leading cybergroups would regularly converse with national intelligence organizations around the world and offer their latest hacks.

And business was picking up. One group would perpetrate a cyberattack and in the next hours another group would offer their services to defeat it. It was an increasingly alarming situation and harkened back to the early 1900s, when organized crime in the US offered protection from its own violent offenders. But now it was all being achieved with software.

It mattered little that it was "just software" when attacks prevented people from withdrawing money from ATMs, purchasing gasoline, or encrypting the files on their PCs and when hackers demanded a ransom payment—it quickly became a national security issue.

"NetRiot wants a hundred million for the code," said Collins.

The CIA's cyber chief spoke up. "They must have found a back door into the operating system. They could exploit it to insert their own code. If that's true, and we could keep it a secret, it would be a very valuable asset for us to own.

"And at $100 million it would be a good value. Recall that the recent Tomahawk cruise missile attack of sites in Syria cost us approximately $60 million and produced only nominal damage," the cyber chief reminded the room.

The DDI spoke next. "Can you imagine paying $100 million for software? I worry as we continue to promote this behavior we'll get caught in a vicious circle."

Collins responded, "Simon, spying has been around for as long as countries have existed. This most recent variant just takes advantage of the latest technology. Spying and stealing technical secrets will never stop."

The DDI shook his head, with the CIA's cyberchief adding, "Yes, $100 million is a lot, but to put it in perspective, Facebook paid $19 billion for WhatsApp. Again, if the hack is valid, $100 million is a steal." With the NetRiot hack the US could penetrate the entire Chinese missile system with the potential to take control of their targeting system.

That was what Lisa Collins was waiting to hear. "Put a plan together to validate the hack. If it's bona fide, we are going to purchase it. I need the plan in the next six hours. La Rue tells us we only have twelve hours to get back to NetRiot before they shop it elsewhere. And that was four hours ago. So the clock is ticking, folks. Thank you."

As the meeting broke up, Collins reflected on their discussion. Her DDI was right; they were entering an unending cycle where cyber attacks were involved. But she also agreed with her cyberchief that the price was a good value for the asset. Going further, she was beginning to refine her own views about the nation's defense. While she knew President Andrew Russell, being an ex–naval aviator, was a strong advocate of the US Navy and actively campaigned on increasing the fleet size from its current 308 level to 355 ships, she knew it was too expensive and that money could be put to better use, especially if invested in cybertechnology.

Her vision for the country included a strong cybercapability, both defensive and offensive. She was also an advocate of drones over piloted aircraft. Lisa Collins represented the next generation of leadership for the country. She was readying herself to become a change agent and had little concern for injury to past ways of doing things. However, she was clever and knew in order to enact her vision she would need to gain the support of important allies—especially the tech community in Silicon Valley.

Lisa Collins was the future with a progressive vision for the United States.

In Croatia, Pavo Ludovic had just completed a Skype call with the leader of Guccifer 2.0 to obtain the source code for the Chinese missile operating system hack.

"I'll be back later. Make sure you get the files FTP'd from Guccifer," said Ludovic to his staff as he packed up to leave his office in order to meet up with his girlfriend, Katija.

At twenty-eight, with scraggly hair, a two-week beard, black jeans, and a T-shirt, Ludovic looked like any other Silicon Valley Java coder with his laptop bag slung over his shoulder.

As he left on the short walk into town, his thoughts turned to his life.

Pavo knew the time for an exit was nearing. In the past a hacker could live a life under the radar, make the occasional political statement, and earn more than a decent living. But because of the recent high-profile ransomware attacks as well as the interference in national elections, a bounty had been put on hackers. The best hackers were big targets, and Ludovic was considered one of the best.

Pavo entered the Dubrovnik version of a Starbucks and kissed his twenty-four-year-old girlfriend, a tall blonde with Madison Avenue good looks.

"You always brighten my day," said Pavo, evoking a smile from Katija Buric, who worked in a local travel agent office and did part-time modeling on a vlog with a local advertising group.

Katija opened her folder, saying, "I've found several villas in Marbella, just south of Málaga, that are available for the entire summer."

Pavo started to flip through the stack of Spanish properties with mild interest.

"Actually, I was thinking about America."

Katija lit up upon hearing Pavo's words. In addition to the general appeal that moving to the United States held for many Europeans, Katija had three cousins who had immigrated to the US during their teens, and she was eager to reunite with them.

"America? Where exactly in America are you thinking?" she asked, trying to hide her enthusiasm.

"I'm beginning to think maybe the time is right for us to move," he said, not revealing his full intentions.

Ludovic had several motivating factors to consider in making a move to the US. Like many of his hacker colleagues, he liked to spread his money around the globe to protect it, as a diversification strategy.

To that end, Ludovic had amassed a significant amount of real estate—especially for a twenty-eight-year-old.

"I was thinking of buying some real estate in the US. And if we owned property there, then why not consider moving there too?" said Pavo. "Manhattan and Southampton, or maybe Nantucket. Both are beach communities on the East Coast of the US. Southampton would be good because it's close to New York," said Pavo.

Having both grown up in Dubrovnik, they were used to being in close proximity to the water, so Pavo's thinking made sense.

"What about immigration? Can we get green cards to enter the US?" asked Katija.

"I think I can take care of that," said Pavo, knowing that Lauren La Rue would be more than cooperative about getting Ludovic to move to the US.

"You should go to the US first and look for some real estate for us," continued Pavo.

This was moving much faster than Katija had anticipated.

"You want me to go to the US to look for a house—for us—when?" a visibly excited Katija asked.

"How about next week? Once you are in New York, look for an apartment. When we have that, we can look for the beach house. I think we should spend no more than $6 million each for the apartment and for the beach house."

Pavo added, "Katija, let's keep these plans between us for now. I have a lot going on at work and I don't want this information beyond us for now."

Katija knew enough about Pavo's business to understand when Pavo said to keep something private, he meant it.

Pavo's thoughts turned to whether he could make this move to the US without incurring Moscow's wrath. Pavo knew it would be useless to try to hide his move from the Russian FSB, the Federal Security Service, better known as the modern-day version of the KGB. Pavo would need to convince the FSB that his move to the US would be in the Russians' best interest. Even someone with Pavo's intellect knew it would be dicey at best. But Pavo also could tell his time in Croatia was quickly coming to an end. Pavo knew his work for the North Koreans, this Chinese missile system hack, and now having Sheik Abdul Er Rahman's security force taking out Kordic would only make him an even higher-profile target. In the world of hacking, today's client could become tomorrow's assassin. There was no loyalty, and paranoia was beginning to spin out of control.

Moving money around was becoming even harder too.

Ever since the Chinese put a clamp on Macau, things had gotten much harder. It used to be that a wealthy gambler could fly on a private jet into Macau as a guest of one of the large casinos. Invariably he brought a suitcase—or sometimes three or more—full of US dollars, euros, or British sterling and passed it thru several LLCs owned by the casinos. The cost would only be losing $1 or $2 million at the tables.

The real win was a cashier's check that could then be deposited, without recourse, to either a Swiss or Bermudan bank account. The system worked well until the Chinese decided that it wasn't worth the headaches and shut it down.

India had also recently put in place much stronger restrictions on cash transactions. That left countries like Thailand and Indonesia as the remaining bastions of easy money laundering.

Of course, Pavo also had a few tricks of his own. He would say, "Antonija," referring to his banking expert, "we need to move some cash."

With a nod, Antonija would arrange for a nondescript motor launch to take packages of cash, usually of several million euros, across the Adriatic and be placed in a series of storage lockers in Italy.

From there, a small, highly trusted team of airline pilots, ship captains, and even a Catholic priest would take the euros, dollars, and pounds into specific targeted countries.

The end result was a series of storage facilities in Brooklyn, New York; Florence, Italy; and Bath, England, that all held a fortune of Ludovic's cash.

Back from dinner with Katija and discussing their potential move to America, Pavo was now reviewing with his team the Chinese missile operating system hack that had been earlier downloaded to their servers.

The code of the hack was displayed on a large flat-screen in a room that doubled as their conference room and dining room. Pavo's lieutenant Antonija spoke first. "Pavo, as you know, many of China's and

Russia's weapon systems relied on stolen operating system code from the US. In this case the Chinese used an old IBM operating system that was utilized years ago on mainframe computers."

Pavo nodded. "Yes, crude by today's standards but nevertheless very compact at only two hundred megabytes and reasonably feature-rich, as long as you weren't planning to play 3-D games on it."

"Correct," replied Antonija. "The area that we can exploit is the operating system code that handles interrupts. IBM never expected a one-way device, like a card reader, to actually write data, but the I/O subroutine that controls the card reader is authorized to both read and write data. That's the vulnerability. By hacking the I/O driver specifically for the card reader, we now have the ability write into the operating system. From there it is quite simple to insert some new code into the O/S and then have the operating system branch to our new code. And just like that we can take control of the operating system."

After a pause Ludovic said, "So you are saying all we need to do is emulate an IBM card reader from the 1980s?"

"Precisely," replied Antonija.

"I see. When the OS gets an interrupt from a card reader, we'll implant our hack via a payload module while remaining in supervisor state."

"We've identified the device type as an IBM 3505 card reader. And not only that; we've already acquired a copy of the original IBM device driver."

"Elegant," said Ludovic, using the term that was the highest compliment a coder could bestow on another system programmer. This hack was elegant.

"Antonija, when will you have the hack ready for testing?" asked Ludovic.

"It's rather simple. I would say in twelve hours if we push it."

"Perfect and well worth the price," Ludovic replied, referring to what he had paid Guccifer for the hack. They had given Guccifer a copy of their SWIFT banking system hack, which would bring the hackers tens, if not hundreds, of millions of dollars. That is, as long as the hack remained viable. Cybertechnology moved at such a blinding pace, hacks had a half-life of only a couple of months—and in some cases only a couple of days.

"Antonija, put all our resources on this," ordered Ludovic.

"On it," said Antonija.

Ludovic knew by gaining access to the missile OS he could insert more of his own code. But Ludovic also knew he would only be able to use the hack once. Once the hack was triggered, the Chinese would be able to easily and quickly detect it and shut it down.

As such, this hack was known as a "silver bullet," meaning it could be used only once before becoming obsolete. Still Ludovic thought that one use could be very valuable in the right circumstance.

It wasn't like China fired ballistic missiles every day. So in the advent of a planned missile launch, the owner of this hack could, theoretically, defeat the attack. That is, they could defeat it *before* the missiles were launched. Once the missiles were launched, the hack would have no value. But in the right hands, this hack would be worth a fortune—say, to the Americans, Russians, or Japanese. Not to mention what ISIS, Iran, or the Saudis would pay for this hack. Ludovic was already wealthy, but this hack could potentially get him a spot on the Fortune 100 list of wealthiest individuals in the world. Of course, he would need to stay alive to enjoy his wealth. He was anxious to hear the American response to his offer.

It was late in the day when Kristin McMahon asked for a few minutes of time with CIA director Lisa Collins. As she was the deputy director of the NSA, her request was not unusual, plus Lisa was something of a mentor to Kristin.

As dusk fell over the metro DC area, Kristin was shown into Lisa Collins's office at CIA headquarters in the McLean neighborhood of Virginia.

"Hi, Kristin. Nice to see you. You'll have to catch me up on the wedding plans," said the director of the CIA.

"Director, thank you for seeing me," replied Kristin, following the proper protocol of addressing Collins by her title first and then using her first name for the rest of the meeting.

"Sure. Do you want to talk business first?"

"Yes, if you don't mind. Lisa, the president sent Mike on a mission, something to do with North Korea and a new laser missile weapons system—something that will replace THAAD."

Lisa Collins, a practiced professional, kept a poker face and did not react to anything McMahon had said.

"I did some checking at the NSA, but there isn't much I could find out about it," said McMahon.

"I thought you said we were going to start with business first—this sounds pretty personal to me, Kristin," said the director of the CIA.

Given the director's reaction, Kristin wondered if she had made a mistake bringing up this topic.

"Well, it is, Lisa," said Kristin, regaining her momentarily lost confidence.

For a minute Collins just waited, another tactic she had refined over her career.

"Kristin, there is a new submarine-based weapons system the Navy is testing off North Korea," admitted the director.

"What puzzles me is that Mike's a fighter pilot. Yes, he just checked out the F-35 Lightning for fleet readiness, but he isn't a missile weapons specialist and certainly not on submarines."

"Kristin, I think you hit on your answer in your first statement. You said the president sent Mike on this mission. You know Mike gained the president's confidence on Operation Warlord after the Nantucket kidnapping," said Collins.

Very little was known about the exact details of Operation Warlord. But Washington being Washington, no one would let a dearth of facts stand in the way of creating their own story of what they believed went down on Warlord. Regardless of what version you heard, every scenario had President Andrew Russell piloting the F/A-18F that shot down the sheik's private jet over the Mediterranean. That's how President Russell earned the nickname Gunslinger. But what very few people knew was that the aviator in the back seat of the president's F/A-18F was Commander Mike Bartlett.

"I understand," said Kristin McMahon. "I'm just trying to piece together what I can so I can get some sleep. Plus, knowing how these missions go, I worry that he won't be back in time for our wedding on the twenty-eighth."

"Kristin, listen to yourself. You aren't even married yet and this is how you're reacting the first time Mike goes on a mission."

"Come on, Lisa, we both know a mission from the president isn't just *any* mission."

Collins couldn't disagree. Instead she picked up a notepad from her cocktail table.

"Let's talk about the wedding," said Lisa as she ripped a piece of paper from her notepad and handed it to McMahon with a single word written on it: "Torchlight."

Kristin McMahon glanced at the word and handed the paper back to Collins.

Collins got up. "So, what's it like preparing a wedding where the president is attending?" she asked as she walked over to the shredder behind her desk and fed the note into it.

"Well, it takes the normal wedding planning and increases the details by about a hundred or so." McMahon smiled. "The first lady wanted to make sure their attendance doesn't upstage the bride," said McMahon with a forced smile.

Now it was Lisa's turn to be encouraging. "Kristin, when you walk down that aisle, you'll have every eye riveted to you—you know that."

McMahon did know that.

They spent the next fifteen minutes talking about the wedding, until a knock on the director's door indicated that she had a call from Senator Stephen Krone of Texas and the chairman of the Senate's Intelligence Committee. With that Kristin thanked Collins for everything and left, having gotten what she wanted from the meeting.

As she left Langley for her home in Potomac, she reflected on Collins's words. They weren't even married yet and she was already asking for favors—and losing sleep over Mike's missions. She wondered how this was all going to work out.

Kennedy Russell's schedule indicated that it was time for her weekly session with her doctor, Dr. Frank Gleason. In the aftermath of last summer's kidnapping ordeal, she was seeing a psychologist once a week.

Not surprisingly, she and her doctor had formed a close relationship as they worked on the issues she was dealing with in the aftermath of the kidnapping.

The children also were seeing therapists, but only twice a month. Given their ages and general resiliency, they had recovered almost completely from the kidnapping and accompanying events.

Kennedy, on the other hand, was still struggling.

"Kennedy, last week you mentioned you and the president began discussing some ideas for your vacation this summer. How did that make you feel?" asked Dr. Gleason.

"Anxious and a little angry," replied Kennedy.

"I understand the anxiousness, but why angry?" asked the doctor.

"Andy has always had the ability to compartmentalize. Maybe it's a pilot thing. I'm different. I internalize and hold on to things until there is nowhere for them to go, and then it all comes spilling out."

The doctor nodded, having heard this statement from the first lady more than once.

"Different people react differently. We've discussed that."

"I sometimes get the feeling that Andy has already moved on from the kidnapping," said Kennedy, revealing an assessment that was very accurate, in the doctor's opinion.

"You say the president has moved on, but hasn't he added layers of new security for you and the family?"

"Yes, he has, and he's trying to be understanding, but I'm not ready to move on, let alone forget."

"You'll never forget—no one would," said the doctor, "that you and your children were exposed to extreme violence. The wonder of the young mind is that it moves on and continues to develop. But in adults the flexibility and cognitive development are more static and in some cases sclerotic. That's what you are dealing with. You find it hard to forget because of your cognitive development. We tend to remember important events in our lives more as adults than children do."

Kennedy sighed. "But I find myself cutting Andy off and not even considering some of his suggestions, like about traveling with the kids."

"The president no doubt understands, and I am sure he is trying to give you as much space as you need."

"And that's another issue—time. Soon we're going to have the discussion about running for a second term. And I know firsthand what that means in terms of travel and the pressure it brings. Yes, we can spare the kids from the campaign trail, but I'll need to be out there, which will mean being away from them."

"Time and patience are your best allies, Kennedy. When you start feeling yourself tense up, remember our exercises," added the doctor.

Kennedy shot him a look of displeasure.

"Look, Kennedy, after all you've been through—remember it's only been eight months since the ordeal. Give yourself time to recover. And try not to be so hard on yourself. I think you'll find if you lighten up on yourself, you'll also lighten up with others, including the president."

Kennedy nodded, but the grimace on her face told the doctor she still wasn't yet where she needed to be in terms of healing.

"Should we finish up with some breathing exercises?"

"Sure, but I think I'd do better hitting the gym and punching something," replied Kennedy.

Fifteen minutes later, Kennedy was feeling centered and calmer.

As the doctor left the White House, he was pleased with the progress the first lady was exhibiting, but he knew they still had a lot more work to do, especially as the campaign for the president's second term would begin next year.

General Goh entered the Eden Club at 7 p.m. for his scheduled massage and changed into a robe before the masseuse entered the room.

After lighting candles and putting on music that was especially created for its acoustic signature, which masked out listening devices, the masseuse began.

"General, how are the plans progressing for the April fifteenth missile launch?" asked the South Korean agent working on the general's back.

"Testing is proceeding as planned. The schedule is on track. We will select the launch sites and the exact time of the launch over the next few days," said the general. "What about my family? What is the plan to get them to safety?"

"General, coinciding with the Day of the Sun celebrations, your family will come to your office for a tour along with their classmates as a cover. After, just your family will be taken to the whale-watching boat out of Namp'o. That boat, the *Soft Wind*, will depart Namp'o and motor twenty miles, where it will rendezvous with a Chinese submarine, the *Deagal*. Once on board, your family will be taken to China, where they will remain in safety awaiting your orders to travel to America or to rejoin you in the newly unified Korea."

"Whether they ultimately go to America or return to Korea, I will need financial security. I want your superiors to deposit US$20 million into a bank account in Bermuda that only my wife will have access to. Do you understand?" demanded the general in a tone that brooked no argument.

The agent, who had been told not to let any issues jeopardize the plan, answered the general in the affirmative.

Getting back to the details of the plan and the missile launch, the agent handed the general a pen, saying, "General, on Friday night you will have food delivered to your home. Take the menu that comes with the food and run the menu under water, then use this pen to write the time and the coordinates for the launch on it. When the menu dries, the ink will disappear. Place the menu in your trash and we'll get it out of your garbage the next day."

"How are you going to deal with Paek and his circle of advisers?" asked the general.

"Turn over," said the agent, wanting to look the general in the eye for this next part of the conversation.

Before the agent could continue, Goh added, "Once threatened, Paek will either order the launch of more of our missiles, including the Hwasong-14s, or reach out to China and the US and say the launch of the DF-26 was unauthorized."

"Quite right," said the agent. "We will have a plan in place to deal with either eventuality."

The general said, "Keep in mind, even after the launch of the test DF-26, we will still have another DF-26 that will be ready to be fired."

"Yes, we understand, General, but the technology that will defeat your first DF-26 will defeat the second and your Hwasong-14s, should Paek decide to launch them as well," responded the South Korean.

Goh responded, "You seem very certain of your ability to take out our missiles."

Getting back to the general's original question about how they planned to deal with Paek, the agent said, "Chinese authorities will reach out to Paek with an ultimatum: Either he and his family will leave North Korea immediately for his compound in the Philippines, where they will be allowed to live in comfort and safety, or the facility he is in will be attacked and destroyed within minutes. As for the senior staff, they will be detained and their release will be predicated on their willingness to support the go-forward plan."

"What confidence do you have that you will be able to destroy Paek's bunker? It is highly fortified."

"You've heard of the MOAB?" asked the agent, referring to the US's Mother of All Bombs, the twenty-thousand-pound bomb.

Paek nodded.

"Well, the US has a new version of it, even more powerful," said the agent. "If Paek does not agree to leave North Korea, his bunker will be obliterated," said the agent dryly.

"And getting back to me, you said I will be put in communications with the South?" asked the general.

"You will be surrounded by our security force for protection as we work to establish control and communications. Once power is consolidated under your control, you will appear on Korean television claiming that Paek is no longer in the country and that you have assumed control and have opened discussions with the South about unification. You will say you have reached out to the UN, China, and the United States and have been given assurances that no hostile acts will be taken against the North and that they support the discussions around unification. You will state, 'The time for prosperity, peace, and unification is at hand.'"

It was time for the massage to end. *Yes,* thought Goh, *Everything should work—that is, if everything goes according to plan, and that rarely happens . . .*

The *Florida* was now stationed in the Yellow Sea just off Sinan, South Korea.

"Today's test-firing of Torchlight will be against a Minuteman III launched from South Korea," said Captain Reagan, the CO of the USS *Florida.*

With that intro, he turned the briefing over to Jim Hartel.

"Thank you, Captain. The operation calls for us to immediately surface once we detect the missile launch. We'll be conducting what we call a Snapshot maneuver," explained Hartel to Reagan's department heads, who were already familiar with the action.

"The SPY-6 radar will detect and track the inbound vampire," continued Hartel. "Once SPY picks up the vampire, we'll quickly surface, feed the tracking data into Torchlight, energize the weapon, and knock it down. We should be on the surface for only a matter of minutes, hence the name Snapshot."

"Gentlemen," Reagan added, "as you all know, the surface is a dangerous place for a submarine—especially a US submarine operating in the Yellow Sea. We're going to drill on Snapshot until we get the timing down to the absolute minimums. Brief your department heads. That is all." Captain Reagan then ended the briefing and headed to the control room.

Four hours later, the *Florida's* radar officer rang out with the following call: "Vampire, vampire, vampire. Sir, I have detected a launch of a Minuteman III from South Korea. Confidence is high, tracking 063 degrees and accelerating. She is inbound *Florida*, estimated time to target three minutes, sir."

"Navigator, what is the best course for intercept?" ordered the captain.

"Sir, SPY is telling us to come right to 180," called the navigator.

"OOD, come to 180 smartly," ordered the captain. Then he got on the 1MC and ordered: "Man special weapons stations; prepare for Torchlight test-firing. Prepare to execute Snapshot."

Commander Mike Bartlett and Torchlight project manager Jim Hartel were also in the control room as they prepared to test-fire the top secret Torchlight weapons system.

Less than a minute later, the alarm sounded as the officer of the deck commanded, "Surface, surface, surface. Quick stop."

Next the chief of the boat called, "Sir, the sail has just broken the surface. We're on the roof, sir. All stop."

The captain turned to Hartel, saying, "Mr. Hartel, we're ready. It's your show."

"Thank you, Captain. Weps, energize Torchlight, bring power up to one hundred percent. Radar, continue to feed data into Torchlight," directed Hartel.

The weapons officer responded, "Torchlight at one hundred percent power."

The chief engineer called into the control room, "All reactors are online and performing at one hundred percent output. We're ready to engage the laser, sir."

Hartel nodded as he focused on his laptop, which was connected to the *Florida*'s network and was monitoring all the Torchlight system outputs.

"There, we're locked on the Minuteman," Hartel said to the captain and Bartlett, pointing to his screen. Next Hartel toggled the tab on his screen to a graph showing the output of the six Bechtel reactors that powered the Torchlight laser weapon. The graph showed an increasing line, with the colors changing from yellow to green indicating Torchlight becoming energized.

"Sir," called the weapons officer, "we have a lock on the Minuteman, inbound 065 degrees, accelerating past Mach 2. We're ready, sir. Awaiting weapons commit."

Bartlett and Reagan were looking over Hartel's shoulder at the screen, which showed a white triangle surrounding the blip that represented the inbound Minuteman. It had just turned red, indicating the lock.

"Con, Engineering. Reactor 4 has just scrammed. Remaining five reactors are online producing eighty-five percent power needed for Torchlight," called the chief engineer.

Hartel looked up from his screen and nodded to the captain, saying, "We have enough power for Torchlight. We're okay to fire, Captain."

"Weps, commit. Snapshot. Take the Minuteman out," commanded the CO of the *Florida*.

"Aye, aye, sir," replied the weapons officer as he raised the plastic cover and depressed the red arming button. He then waited for his fire trigger to become active and called, "My weapons are committed. We're firing, sir. Snapshot."

It was deadly silent. No noise whatever. No swoosh typically associated with the launch of a missile. Just the silence of a highly concentrated columnated beam of photons targeting the inbound missile.

The radar officer called, "Sir, kill, kill, kill. That's a hit. The inbound vampire has been destroyed."

The captain responded, "Secure Torchlight. Officer of the Deck, dive the boat, take us down 350 feet, ten degree down bubble, come to course 055 degrees left standard rudder, ahead full."

"Aye, aye, Captain, chief of the watch on the 1MC," called the officer of the deck as he grabbed the overhead handset.

"Torchlight secure, sir. Ready to dive," called the OOD.

Reagan nodded, indicating his concurrence to the OOD's command.

"Dive, dive, dive. COB, make your depth three five zero, ten degree down bubble, course zero five five, left standard rudder, ahead full," ordered the OOD.

"Secure from action stations," commanded the captain, with the ODD echoing his command.

"Mr. Hartel, Commander Bartlett, we'll convene in the officer's mess at 14:45 for an operation debrief. XO, have Weps, Ops, and the chief engineer ready with readouts."

"Copy, sir," said the XO of the *Florida*.

Immediately after the captain left the control room for his stateroom, the ODD called, "Captain's off the bridge."

Commander Bartlett took note of how things were done on the *Florida*. Reagan ran a tight ship. This was Bartlett's first encounter with the US Navy's submarine force, and beyond being impressed with the crew, Bartlett had just witnessed the operational capability of Torchlight. In a matter of barely two minutes, Torchlight had tracked and destroyed an inbound missile traveling at high speed. As tests went, it was a success. Of course, the *Florida* was alerted and prepared for this test, and Bartlett's job was to determine if in a real battle situation Torchlight would perform as well. Then there was the issue of the scram of reactor 4. Why did that happen? That cut the margin for error down considerably. But for now, Bartlett would begin putting together his operations report for Admiral

Fraser and the president. He would then add to it any of the data that came out of the mission debrief the captain had scheduled for later that day.

All in all, though, Bartlett was impressed and felt like he had just witnessed the future of naval warfare.

CHAPTER NINE

On the sunny Rockaway Beach peninsula in Queens, New York, just a few miles outside of New York City, Lauren La Rue and Chris Dunbar were still holed up in their safe house. La Rue was immersed in the details of finalizing the payment to NetRiot for the Chinese missile hack.

"Thank you, Director Collins," said La Rue on her secure line. "I see the payments have been transferred to the staging account. I'll work to complete the transaction. Once I have the code from Ludovic, I'll send it to CyberOps for validation."

La Rue had done transactions like this many times for Sheik Abdul Er Rahman. She was expert in moving money and leaving little or no trace.

Chris Dunbar just watched as La Rue's fingers flew over the keyboard.

"Why don't we just deposit the money into a Swiss bank account and be done with it?" he asked.

La Rue, who had taken a liking to Dunbar, responded, "How you move the money today is critically important. Every major government in the world sifts through millions of SWIFT records to uncover payment patterns. The last thing we want are any footprints that show the US government, or worse, the CIA, has made a $100 million payment to a Croatian cyberhacking group. If discovered, not only would it become a political crisis, but adversarial intelligence agencies could dispatch teams to identify the recipients of the funds, which would put NetRiot at severe risk."

Dunbar looked over La Rue's shoulder as she logged on and off a maze of banking systems.

To be truthful, La Rue wanted to impress Dunbar. It was her turn to show off a little after Dunbar had saved their lives in Croatia a few days ago.

La Rue turned to Dunbar and said, "Pull up a chair and I'll take you through this."

Dunbar said, "I will, but first I want to do a check of the perimeter."

La Rue smiled as he went to check the video monitors. She was beginning to understand Dunbar.

A few minutes later Dunbar pulled up a chair. "Okay, how does all of this work?"

"So," began La Rue, "we want to transfer funds, in this case $100 million, but more importantly we want to obscure the source, right?"

Dunbar nodded.

"A year ago, we would have used a middleman like a casino and created a series of shell LLCs as the best way to move funds with little ability to trace them. But China clamped down on the Macau casinos, so that path is no longer viable. Also, that approach was too slow for sophisticated players like the United States. Today, more than anything else, we use Bitcoin."

La Rue explained, "The system allows for transactions to take place directly between users without an intermediary, but that's not the magic. The magic is these transactions use a digital currency. Since the system works without a central bank, no single currency is used. Without an actual currency, it is next to impossible for a bank to track. And that's how the term 'Bitcoin' came into being."

Dunbar replied, "Sort of like Venmo or PayPal?"

"Sort of."

La Rue brought up different bank accounts. "First, we create a series of bank accounts for a bunch of shell LLCs. Once that's done, we start depositing funds into each LLC. Now, here comes the magic. We then distribute, via dividend payments, the funds from one LLC to another, but instead of using a hard currency, we use Bitcoin. To make a long story short, we now have untraceable funds in Bitcoin. Now I can transfer those funds to Ludovic. Ludovic will basically duplicate the same steps and eventually convert his Bitcoin funds into the currency of his choosing. And voilà, your funds are now laundered and untraceable. Easy, peasy."

In fact, La Rue had not yet transferred the funds to Ludovic; she had just shown the process of how she would do it to Dunbar. Now she was ready to make the transfer, but first she needed to send a message to Ludovic.

Powering up one of the safe house's cell phones, one La Rue was certain was clean, with a brand-new number, she opened WhatsApp and sent Ludovic a message. The WhatsApp ID that Ludovic had created would be used just this one time. At least officially it would be used only once. Once Ludovic received La Rue's text, he would post the WhatsApp ID on a bunch of tech bulletin boards monitored by college computer labs, where it would no doubt be quickly picked up and used by a host of college students for whatever silliness they had in mind.

It was for these reasons governments around the world were building cyberorganizations and investing hundreds of millions of dollars with tech firms like Palantir, Teradata, and IBM's Watson to capture, store, and analyze petabytes of data in the hopes of uncovering covert operations. It was a daunting, expensive, and time-consuming endeavor.

La Rue typed into WhatsApp, "My vacation plans are confirmed."

A moment later came the response: "Great. Once you arrive, call me on 52 071 6876."

La Rue dialed the number and a few seconds later Ludovic answered.

"Hello," said Ludovic.

"Yes," La Rue replied.

Ludovic said, "8-6-5-4-5-6-1-1-0-2-5,"

La Rue repeated the number, waiting for Ludovic to confirm with a simple, "Correct."

Then they both hung up.

La Rue had been directed to substitute 1s with 3s and 5s with 7s from an earlier message from Ludovic which yielded 8-6-7-4-7-6-3-3-0-2-7 as the account number where she would deposit the Bitcoin payment. If anyone had picked up the communication it would be next to impossible to tie the WhatsApp data with the verbal account number Ludovic had given La Rue.

Now La Rue needed to move fast. In a Dropbox account, which had been set up specifically for this transaction, a file had just been uploaded by Ludovic. It was the Chinese missile hack. The file would remain in the Dropbox account for only five minutes; then it would be deleted and replaced by MP3 tracks by Metallica.

La Rue downloaded the hack from Dropbox and now would send it, via their secure network, to the cybersleuths at Langley. Once the code was received in Langley, she would be authorized to make the payment to Ludovic.

But that wasn't the end of it.

In the nefarious world of cyberterrorism, there was little trust—which was to say there was no trust at all.

La Rue typed, "Lisa, I have uploaded the files. I'm ready to make the payment, but first we need to obtain the encryption key."

La Rue was referring to the key needed to unlock the file that Ludovic had sent them. Without the encryption key, the files were basically worthless.

The plan to pick up the encryption key was also elegant.

Ludovic's girlfriend, Katija, was now in New York City looking at real estate.

Pavo instructed her to buy a MetroCard for the New York City subway system. Once she had the card, she gave the serial number on the MetroCard to Pavo during one of their calls. That number would eventually become the encryption key to unlock the Chinese missile hack.

And here was the clever part.

Katija had just entered Kava Cafe on Washington Street off Horatio in the West Village of Manhattan.

As she waited to meet her Realtor, who would be showing her a loft at 68 Jane Street that day, Katija ordered a latte.

Finding a table and sitting down, she placed her MetroCard under the napkin dispenser. A few minutes later, her Realtor joined her and they reviewed their plan for the day.

Taking their coffees with them, they left to go to their first viewing just a couple of blocks away.

As Katija and her Realtor left the café, a young man wearing a beanie and carrying the ubiquitous millennial backpack entered Kava. He ordered a mochaccino and sat at the table just vacated by Katija.

Moments later he slid the napkin dispenser aside, picked up the MetroCard, and put it in his pocket. With coffee in hand, the CIA agent left the café and walked several blocks toward the High Line park, where he stopped, sat on a bench, and took out his iPhone. He took a photo of the back of the MetroCard and sent the JPEG to an anonymous Gmail account. And that is how covert data transfer is accomplished in the age of the iPhone.

With the MetroCard key now in the hands of the CIA, their cyberteam de-encrypted the FTP'd file. Lisa Collins then authorized La Rue to transfer the funds to Ludovic.

A few minuts later, La Rue turned to Dunbar and said, "It's done," breathing a sigh of relief.

"And just like that, Ludovic is $100 million richer. Wow. I guess I should've been nicer to all the computer nerds in high school," remarked Dunbar.

"You don't look like the bullying type to me," responded La Rue.

"I wasn't. Actually, I was a pretty shy jock."

"I can understand the jock part, but I don't see you as shy. Maybe a little technically challenged, but not shy," said La Rue, smiling at him.

"Well, that's me, a shy, technically challenged ex-SEAL who knows how to cook a pretty good omelet."

"You left out the handsome part."

The president was finishing up a briefing with the budget director and his chief of staff, Sterling Spencer, when Alice Ahern came in and handed Spencer a note.

Turning to the president, Spencer said, "Mr. President, would you mind if I excused myself? There's a matter I need to address."

The president nodded as he continued to look at the budget figures with the director.

A few minutes later Spencer reentered the Oval Office just as the president was giving his final comments to his director of the budget.

With the budget meeting over, Sterling turned to the president. "Mr. President, I just received an operations report from Commander Bartlett on board the *Florida*. Today they successfully intercepted a Minuteman III missile fired from South Korea. The system worked flawlessly."

"Excellent," responded the president.

"The *Florida*'s SPY-6 tracked and locked on the Minuteman, they quickly surfaced, and the Torchlight laser took out the Minuteman. The *Florida* was on the surface for a matter of minutes. During the test, they took down the Minuteman with what they called a 'Snapshot.' Bartlett says he's very encouraged by what he's seen with Torchlight so far."

"Good. Do they have any other tests planned?" asked the president.

"Yes, Commander Bartlett says their next test will be more ambitious. It'll be a multimissile test—with Tomahawks fired from the *Connecticut* and *Washington* and a Minuteman fired from Hawaii. They're keen to do the Hawaii launch because it will result in the Minuteman on a downward trajectory and at maximum velocity, something the Torchlight PM is eager to test."

"Good, good," said the president. "When's it scheduled for?"

"Two days from now, sir," replied Spencer. "Bartlett was impressed that a laser beam made up of just photons could knock down a missile," he added. "Bartlett also pointed out the cost aspect of Torchlight. To fire a laser costs us virtually nothing, as opposed to the cost of a traditional missile like a Tomahawk or THAAD. Not only is Torchlight operationally superior to THAAD, but the economics of it are also remarkable."

"That's good news to finish the day with, Spence. And you can see that Bartlett was the right person for the assignment," commented the president as they left the Oval Office, with the president headed to the residence.

But not before President Russell issued some lighthearted kidding. "So the money we save with Bartlett's ray gun will allow us to increase the defense budget by more than three percent, Spence," said the president, purposely not using the top secret Torchlight code name, as they were now walking through the halls of the West Wing.

"Yes, sir, Bartlett's work is important, but the new Columbia-class submarines that will replace the old Ohio-class submarines are costing us $100 billion over the next twenty years, and we both know it will swell to well over $150 billion before it's complete. That's $15 billion per sub, sir, and the new Ford-class carriers are $14 billion each. Sir, your Navy is getting too expensive."

"For another day, Spence." The president smiled as he turned to take the stairs to the residence. Andrew Russell, the ex–naval aviator, rarely took the elevator.

"Yes, Mr. President. Good evening, sir," Spencer replied.

With dinner finished and the kids now doing homework, Andrew Russell and Kennedy had some time to catch up on their day.

"I was thinking, Andy," said Kennedy, "if you want, we can go to Colorado for our vacation."

"Is that what you want to do?" asked the president.

"It's the easiest," said Kennedy, "and the kids like it."

"Colorado's fine with me, and the staff will love the choice," said the president.

But then he added, "On the other hand, we could do Yosemite

and the Grand Canyon. I'll just close them while we're there so we can have the entire parks to ourselves," the president said, laughing.

"That would go over great, closing the national parks at the height of the summer season. As I recall, that didn't work out so well for Governor Christie," kidded Kennedy.

The president just smiled.

"By the way," asked Kennedy, "have you ever heard of the website called ImAFighterPilot.com?"

"No, what's that? A website that tracks pilots' traps?" asked the president.

Kennedy couldn't tell if he was playing her or not.

"It's not about carrier landings. It's a hookup website for pilots," said Kennedy, showing her disapproval. "I was talking to Kristin McMahon about the wedding and she mentioned that Mike Bartlett's best man, a lieutenant commander, created a website called ImAFighterPilot.com to help pilots hook up, especially when on liberty or assigned to a new base."

"Really," said the president. "I knew I retired too soon."

Kennedy just frowned.

"And what's wrong with the aviators today that they need a website to help them find a date? In my day . . . ," the president began, and then caught himself.

"In my day, what?" taunted Kennedy.

"I'm just saying, when I flew. . . we didn't need to rely on the Internet or mobile technology to find dates," said the president as he tried to cover his tracks.

"No, you didn't need a website. But as I recall you did use your uniforms quite a bit," replied Kennedy, remembering when they first met in the famous New York bar Tortilla Flats.

"Ken, it was Fleet Week and we were encouraged to wear our uniforms. As I recall, Harper and your friends were more than willing to show us around the city."

"Show you around the city—is that what you called it? Maybe you and that lieutenant commander have something in common." Now it was Kennedy's turn to goad the president.

"Well, I was just trying to be respectful of your sister and your friends," the president said with a smile.

Without a comeback, Kennedy took the pillow from the couch and hit the president with it.

"Hey, hey, all I have to do is yell and the Secret Service will be in here with guns drawn," kidded the president. But as soon as he spoke, he realized he had said the wrong thing. His comment was too close to their experience last summer on Nantucket.

"Ken, I'm sorry."

Kennedy knew he didn't mean anything—it was just banter—and she regrouped.

"You better have the CNO or JAG look into this lieutenant commander's website. All you need is to be asked at a press conference what your position is on ImAFighterPilot.com."

"Hmm," said the president, "I guess I better take my profile down from there, huh?"

Kennedy smiled, "Yes, I think that would be a very good idea."

A white van had been following his staff car for several blocks. That was enough for General Goh to convince himself he was being followed.

As the date for the missile test drew closer, now only six days away, Goh was becoming paranoid.

His sixth sense was telling him he was under surveillance from the North Korean State Security Department, the SSD. As a result, he suspected everyone—his driver, his flag lieutenant, Yong, the man cutting his lawn—everyone of spying on him.

His blood pressure was up, he wasn't sleeping, and he was chain-smoking.

Last night his wife had said, "Chul, what's bothering you?"

"Just work, nothing to be concerned with," was his short answer.

To calm himself, Goh tried to meditate, but he couldn't clear his mind. Details, timetables, and more would flash constantly across his mind.

In the meantime, North Korean agents had learned that there was a traitor on Paek's senior staff. That discovery, when shared with Paek, who himself was also paranoid, left the president wondering how to deal with the situation.

Paek's father would have simply executed his entire staff, and in fact, Paek considered that. But the fact that Paek was so young would make it very disruptive to remove his entire staff, not to mention it could put his own leadership at risk. No, Paek would first wait to see what the SSD uncovered.

And while neither Goh nor Paek's men knew it, the South Koreans were also surveilling Goh.

And it was the agents from the South who first detected the SSD tails on Goh.

But in discussions with the CIA, the South Koreans decided not to tell Goh about the SSD shadowing, as they worried about his refusing to go forward with their plan.

Today, Goh was on his way to Namp'o to inspect the progress on arming the DF-26 missile.

Once Goh arrived in Namp'o, he gathered his staff.

"What's the status of the eight decoy DFs and the two live shots?" Goh asked his assembled staff.

"General, we have successfully created the decoys. From a satellite photo they will look identical to the real missiles. In addition, we have successfully installed both live missiles onto their mobile launchers, and the warhead has been mated to the 'special' DF-26," reported Goh's head of missile operations.

Goh nodded and asked, "When will we be ready to fire a test shot?"

"Sir, we need to finish our system testing. It will take another two days, sir."

"Gentlemen, today is the tenth. The president wishes to fire a test shot in honor of the Day of the Sun celebrations on the fifteenth. Continue with your plans to make everything ready for the fifteenth. If anything deviates from our plan, inform me at once.

"Captain, which launchpad will we launch the test missile from?" asked Goh.

A map came up on the screen, showing the ten locations of the missile pads for the DF-26 mobile launchers.

"General, we have the capability to fire from either our Namp'o or Haeju location. The Namp'o staff is senior to the Haeju staff, so my recommendation would be to fire from Namp'o, sir," said the senior captain as he pointed to the location of each site.

"It is decided, then. We will plan to fire a test DF-26 from the site in Namp'o on the fifteenth at noon. Make everything ready. We will stage dry runs on the twelfth and thirteenth. There will be no failures, no errors, no mistakes," directed Goh as the meeting broke up.

Despite being fraught with worry, Goh knew how to conduct a staff meeting, and no one present could pick up anything different in Goh's demeanor.

Next Goh went to the underground facility where the mobile missile launchers were kept under strict security.

"General, here are the two live DF-26s," said his captain as they walked up to the mobile launchers.

Goh could see the two missiles with white noses and he detected two red stripes around the base of the nose cones.

"Captain, the stripes?" asked Goh.

"General, the red stripes designate the missile as a special."

The captain brought Goh to the other launchers, on which the decoy missiles were loaded. They, too, were housed in the same garage as the live DF-26s, but the decoys all had different-colored stripes.

"Captain, the colored lines on the decoys?" asked Goh.
"Yes, sir, we felt, once deployed, it would work to confuse any enemy intelligence organization that spied on us. They are there to distract them," said the captain.

Goh asked the missile operations commander, "Commander, if we had a mobile launcher failure, how fast could we move a missile from the inoperative launcher to a new one? And do we have additional launchers at the ready?"

"General, yes, we keep a spare launcher at both the Namp'o and Haeju locations. If a launcher failed it would take about three hours to swap it out," replied the commander.

"Captain, three hours? That's unacceptable. I want that time down to ninety minutes. Drill on it," commanded the general sternly.

Goh's captain in charge of missile operations replied immedi-ately, "Yes, General, we will commence at once."

Paek had agreed to allow the *United States* to visit North Korea for the April fifteenth Day of the Sun festival. The *United States* would put into Namp'o on the fourteenth and conduct tours for Paek's staff and a small list of well-vetted North Korean VIPs along with North Korean TV news teams. Paek was determined to make this a propaganda victory for his country. But more important, he saw the advantage of having an American liner with hundreds of American citizens on board in his harbor. It was a golden opportunity to hold the liner for ransom from the US government.

CHAPTER TEN

On board the *Florida*, Jim Hartel briefed CO Reagan and his staff on the next Torchlight test.

"Captain, sometime in the next thirty-six hours a multimissile attack will be fired at the *Florida*. Your mission is to defeat that attack." Hartel didn't share the information that during this exercise he would execute a program from his laptop that would scram two of the reactors for an added challenge.

Hartel added, "SPY-6 is more than capable of detecting and tracking multiple vampires. Once SPY-6 locks on the first inbound missile, Torchlight will fire, and then reacquire and destroy the other targets."

Turning to his staff, Reagan said, "For the test we've been ordered to clear the Korean Peninsula and run a speed course through the Japan-Okinawa gap. That'll put us in the Philippine Sea," he said, pointing to the chart in the officers' mess.

The ops officer spoke up. "Skipper, we'll be passing at close quarters to the *Stennis* Strike Group, according to this plot."

"That's affirmative, but we will be at a depth of six hundred feet and under the thermal, so they won't even notice us."

"Copy that, sir, but the *Washington* and the *Connecticut* are also in the area," answered the ops officer.

The ops officer was referring to the USS *Washington* (SSN-787), a Virginia-class US attack submarine attached to the *John C. Stennis* Strike Group, and the USS *Connecticut* (SSN-22), the Seawolf-class attack submarine that was also in the area, operating independently of the strike group.

"That's right, so we better be quiet," ordered the captain.

The COB responded, "We will be, sir."

The captain picked up the phone on the wall, pressing the button for the bridge. "Officer of the Deck, Reagan. On the sounding make your depth six hundred feet, come to course 120 degrees, right standard rudder, ahead full."

Regan addressed the group before him. "Gentlemen, if I were running this drill I would launch the land-based missile and then fire the Tomahawks just as the land-based missile penetrated our air space. So we need to keep our heads on a swivel. Luis, make sure your watch standers are alert and remind them that this drill will be multitargets. If an ASBM comes in, it will no doubt be a ballistic shot. But any Tomahawk fired at us will be wave hopping, so we need to be prepared to shoot high and then drop down to defeat the Tomahawks. That's exactly what I would do. Drill on that scenario."

Hartel was impressed. What Captain Reagan had just described comported almost one hundred percent with his test plan. He thought about changing it but knew it was too late to do so.

"Aye, aye, sir," responded Luis Lopresti, the *Florida's* sonar officer. He made a note to ensure that SPY-6 was in multi-mission mode and that the scale on the watch stander's screen was set to long range. Any advantage they could get by detecting the inbound vampire early would improve their chances of success.

"Mr. Hartel." The captain now turned his attention to him. "We haven't used your ray gun to defeat multi-targets yet. What can you tell us about that scenario?"

Hartel responded, "Captain, as you know, Torchlight is mounted on a gimbal pedestal. It's capable of firing at multiple targets regardless of their bearing. Given the range, Torchlight will need only a few seconds to fire on each inbound missile. Also, it is important we monitor the A1B reactors during the test."

Everyone in the room was taking notes as Hartel spoke. In these types of drills, the DoD representative was forbidden from given any advantage to the crew. That said, it wasn't unusual for the DoD rep to emphasize elements of the test that would be crucial. Therefore, the crew hung on every word Hartel said.

"All right, gentlemen, once we clear the Korean Peninsula we'll go to missile stations. We aren't going to let the *Connecticut* or the *Washington* get the drop on us. Copy," said Reagan, referring to the two attack subs known to be in the area, both commanded by academy classmates of Reagan's.

Reagan was well-known for his competitiveness. He would get the best out of his crew and made it a point of professional pride for them.

Everyone in the room responded with a loud, "Aye, aye, sir."

Bartlett was gaining tremendous respect for these submariners. Their competitiveness would be right at home in any squadron ready room in the fleet, thought Bartlett.

Lauren La Rue and Chris Dunbar were going a little stir-crazy at this point. It had been almost a week since they were transported from JFK to the safe house in Far Rockaway, Queens.

"Chris, how about we blow this joint and go for a walk on the boardwalk?" asked La Rue.

"No can do, amigo. We're stuck here until we get the green light from Langley," responded Dunbar. "Look, we have a briefing with the director in an hour. I can ask her about moving us to another safe house or bringing us back to Langley," he said.

"Well, I am going to tell her we need to get out of this place," said La Rue.

"I would warn against that approach with the director," replied Dunbar.

"Really," sassed La Rue. "I didn't know SEALs were such pussies," she admonished with a smile on her face.

"Okay, then." Dunbar chuckled. "Good luck with that. See how Collins reacts." And with that Dunbar started to open up the secure conference bridge as the time approached for their call.

A few seconds later the image of Director Lisa Collins along with some of her staff came up on the flat-screen.

"How are my Dubrovnik tourists holding up?" Collins asked.

La Rue was first to reply, "Well, Director, that's something we'd like to talk to you about. When can we get out of this place? The walls are beginning to close in on us, as you can imagine."

"I understand and we'll come back to that, but first we want to discuss project Badger with you," said Collins.

La Rue felt the unease of having misread the situation; she'd brought it up too early on the call.

Dunbar tilted his head at La Rue with an "I told you so," look.

"We're running into some trouble with the hack. It seems Ludovic omitted some critical sections of code," said the director of the CIA.

One of the director's staff members added, "Eventually we will be able to develop the missing modules, but it will take time and it will introduce risk."

"Forget all that," said Collins. "We paid Ludovic $100 million for a hack that doesn't work. Lauren, reestablish communications with NetRiot and tell them we want the entire hack. Remind him that we know his fiancée is in Manhattan."

Dunbar spoke: "Director, I would advise against that last point, knowing Ludovic now. When we tell Ludovic that he shorted us on the hack, I want to see his reaction. Let's see if he did that on purpose or by omission. I think threatening him at this point could spook him."

Director Collins, as was her style, turned to her staff for their reaction.

"Director, Agent Dunbar is right," said her DDI. "Ludovic is smart enough to know that with his fiancée in the US we have certain leverage over him."

After a short pause, Collins agreed.

"Agreed. Now, about moving you. We can relocate you to another safe house, but we can't take you out of the bubble yet." Collins added, "Lauren, we're picking up chatter that the sheik's son has made capturing you his top priority."

La Rue nodded. "Salman—he's twenty-two and has his father's temper."

"Just so you know, Lauren, while you may be a top priority of his, he is a top priority of ours," said Collins with a cold conviction that everyone on the call could read.

"We'll move you to another house in the next twenty-four hours. But we'll keep you nearby in case we need to pick up Ludovic's fiancée. Your role in that could be helpful. Stand by to get the details on the house move. And let us know once you reestablish contact with Ludovic and what his response is to the missing code," ordered Collins as she ended the call.

With the bridge terminated, Collins turned to her staff.

"We need to keep La Rue under wraps until we nail the sheik's son. Tell the Grey Wolfe team to get on with it," Collins directed, revealing that the CIA had tasked a Special Forces team code-named Grey Wolfe to assassinate the sheik's son ASAP.

"He's proving harder to find than a virgin on Bourbon Street during Mardi Gras," Collins's ops director replied flippantly.

Collins turned to her ops director with a cold look and fired her next directive at him: "Greg, keep your sexist bullshit comments out of my conference room. Do you understand?"

"Yes, ma'am. Sorry."

Nodding, Collins continued. "Keep the tail on Ludovic's girl-friend. If La Rue doesn't get the missing code quickly, we are going to grab her."

"Director," said the DDI, "we can move La Rue and Dunbar to the safe house on Staten Island. I can put the steps in motion to make that happen."

Collins, having grown up in New York City, just shook her head. "Great. If they didn't like Rockaway, wait until they hear we're moving them to Staten Island."

As the meeting broke, she was impressed with Dunbar and thought he could be moved up the chain and given more respon-sibility. But she was still upset over her ops director's Mardi Gras comment. Collins had fought the "good ole boy" network her entire career and worked hard to extinguish that sort of nonsense from the Agency, especially on her staff. As she went to her next meeting, her thoughts turned to whether or not she needed a new ops director.

It was a new Agency and a new world, and that sort of male chauvinism was something that Collins simply would not tolerate. As she would often say, "You lead by example. And change comes from the top."

He didn't know it yet, but the ops director was history.

Katija Buric was using Cyber Dust, the app funded by Mark Cuban that Pavo Ludovic had told her to utilize in communicating with him.

It was morning in New York and afternoon in Dubrovnik when Katija texted, "Pavo, I have narrowed our search down to two places that I love."

A moment later came Ludovic's reply: "Good, tell me about them."

"The first, 68 Jane Street, is a loft in the neighborhood called the West Village. It's beautiful and large with 4,300 sq. ft., and it's on the 6th floor so it has nice views. But it's expensive. It has an asking price of $10M, which I know is more than you wanted to spend."

"And the other?"

"39 Bank Street is a three-story carriage house. Right now, it is a duplex so there would be some work to convert it to a single-family home. But it has a perfect location, in the heart of Greenwich Village."

"How much?"

"The Realtor says we could get it for about $4.5M but we would need to put another $2.5M into it."

Feeling flush from the $100 million infusion from the Chinese missile hack, Pavo had an idea.

"Why don't we buy both. We can live in the loft while we reno the other place. Then pick the one we like best to live in and keep the other as an investment."

Katija was thrilled by Pavo's response.

"Offer $9m and $4m all cash."

"Okay, I will, Pavo. I'll let you know what they say. I love you," texted Katija as she signed off.

This plan fit Ludovic's goal to move more of his cash into real estate, and he considered Manhattan real estate, like London real estate, to be a rock-solid investment.

Plus, this would help pave the way if he decided to move to the US, which he thought was becoming an increasing likelihood for him.

Katija texted her real estate agent, "Krystal, I have news. I'll meet you at the Starbucks at Grove and West 4th at 10."

Katija was staying at the Mercer, the fashionable hotel located in the center of the equally fashionable Soho area of Lower Manhattan.

As she left the hotel she walked one block west, to the corner of Prince and Greene Streets, to the Apple store. There she purchased a new iPhone with a Verizon plan. As instructed by Pavo, she bought new iPhones every week, always paying cash.

After activating her new iPhone, Katija crossed Houston Street, headed to Washington Square Park.

As she walked through Washington Square Park, she placed her previous iPhone, now powered off, with the SIM card removed, in a folded newspaper and deposited it in a nearby trash can.

As she turned onto West Fourth Street to meet her Realtor at Starbucks, about half a block back, a twentysomething man in a black leather coat, jeans, and sunglasses followed her.

The disguise was perfect for the surroundings, as he could be any millennial on his way to work in downtown Manhattan.

But in this case, he wasn't. He was a CIA agent whom Director Lisa Collins had authorized the day before to follow Katija.

As Katija entered the Starbucks, Krystal could tell, having done hundreds of real estate deals, that her client had good news to share.

Not wanting to appear overeager, Krystal opened with, "Let's first order something."

Katija nodded and the two attractive, statuesque women moved to the counter to place their orders.

Moments later, with lattes in hand, they sat at a nearby table, both now eager to get down to business.

Neither noticed the hipster sitting at the next table.

To show just how easy it was to eavesdrop in the day and age of the mobile phone, the agent, wearing earbuds connected to his iPhone, activated a CIA-developed app that allowed him to listen clearly to the women's conversation.

Katija said, "Krystal, I spoke to my fiancé and you won't believe this, but he wants to put offers in on both properties."

Krystal's eyes widened. "Both, really," she shot back.

"Yes, we'll live in Jane while we reno Bank," said Katija, equally excited.

"You know, that's a very smart idea," said Krystal. "They are both located in such prime spots. Personally, I think you'll get the most appreciation from the Bank Street property, but either way both will be great investments."

As Katija and Krystal discussed their pricing strategy, the agent at the next table not only heard all of it but was also recording it.

Again, it was a powerful demonstration of how iPhone technology was used by intelligence agencies around the world. In this case, the app was quite simple—it boosted the iPhone's microphone acuity to a higher than normal level.

The agent then used the directional positioning feature to refine the microphone on the iPhone to capture the conversation of the intended subjects.

Later, using other software, the background noise would be washed out, leaving only the audio print of the targeted subject's conversation.

Few people, other than those in the intelligence community and real tech heads, understood just how powerful a device the iPhone was. Without a doubt, not only were the iPhone and Android smartphones boons to the typical cell phone subscriber wanting to use them to hail an Uber or pay for lunch with Venmo, but they also were indispensable to those in the espionage and covert communities.

As they finished their coffees, Katija said, "Krystal I'd like to visit both properties to take some videos and pictures to send to Pavo."

Krystal headed back to the office to communicate the offers to the owners and to arrange Katija's afternoon visits, while Katija headed back to the Mercer for a late morning Orangetheory class.

A minute after both women left the Starbucks, so did Katija's tail.

The *United States* had put into the Port of Busan, South Korea, as scheduled, on April 11. It would spend two days there and then make the voyage to Namp'o, North Korea, arriving on the fourteenth as the guest of President Paek. While in South

Korea, in addition to conducting workshops and tours for many of the VIPs, the *United States* would embark one hundred new passengers.

The cover for the team was as a group from IBM. The group kept to themselves and were seldom seen on deck. However, they seemed to make extensive use of the *United States* weight room.

Lauren La Rue had just finished packing her few clothes for their move to the Staten Island safe house. But before they left, La Rue had an important call scheduled with Pavo Ludovic.

La Rue turned to Dunbar, saying, "I finished reading the briefing doc that the director sent over about the missing code from the Chinese missile hack."

"What'd you think?" responded Dunbar.

"Well, there's definitely code missing. Ludovic must have known that there was no way we wouldn't have noticed it. So if Ludovic did it on purpose, he'll be expecting my call. On the other hand, it might have been an oversight, but let's see how he reacts."

La Rue sat down and typed a few commands into her laptop, opening up an instant message session with Ludovic that was only to be used for emergencies. A few seconds later, Ludovic responded. It was only a few minutes later that Pavo Ludovic's image came up on the monitor on a video Skype call.

"Pavo, my friend, we have a problem."

"What problem?"

"Your hack is missing the payload module."

La Rue could tell her comment had caught Ludovic off guard.

"So now you're a systems engineer," Ludovic said sarcastically, not able to help himself.

"Pavo, we paid you $100 million. No one's in the mood for jokes," shot back La Rue.

"Hold on for a minute," said Ludovic as he muted the line and called one of his team members into the conference room. The hands of both Pavo and his team member flew over the keyboards as they checked their build process.

Still typing furiously, Ludovic unmuted the line after a few minutes, "Miss La Rue, I apologize. When we packaged the code we inadvertently used a back-leveled link library, which caused the omission of several modules. Not only are you missing the payload module, but you are also missing the data definitions file and test data."

"Well, I'm glad to hear that you know what happened. When can we expect the missing files?" askedLa Rue.

"My team will get them to you by the end of the day. I will personally review the package before we FTP it to you," responded Ludovic.

Sensing an opening, La Rue pivoted. "Pavo, we want you to deliver the files in person."

Not only was Ludovic caught off guard, but so was Dunbar, who was sitting next to La Rue.

Ludovic thought for a moment before replying, "I don't make house calls. Aren't your IT people skilled enough to get the code working?"

"They were good enough to discover your team's errors," shot back La Rue. "Pavo, we're on a tight deadline and your 'we inadvertently omitted a step' faux pas has put us behind schedule," lectured La Rue.

After a minute or so, Ludovic replied, "Twelve million dollars. That's my price to come to the US to assist you."

"There's no way we are going to pay you another dollar. We paid you $100 million and you acted in bad faith," shot back La Rue.

"Miss La Rue, my team and I take pride in delivering a quality product," said Ludovic with a tinge of defensiveness.

"That might be—but how was your quality in this case?" La Rue demanded, pressing harder.

Chris Dunbar was impressed by how tough La Rue was and how she put Ludovic on the defensive.

"If I were to come, I would not go to Langley or any of your facilities. You'd need to set up a remote lab where I can work with your people. It needs to be a closed facility with no network connections to the outside—no Wi-Fi, no LANs, nothing, no cell phones," said Ludovic, regaining some of his swagger.

"Pavo, do you think this is our first rodeo? We know how to set up a lab. We'll set you up with what you need and you'll work alongside our SMEs at a secure, undisclosed location near New York," replied La Rue.

"And what about my fee?" queried Ludovic.

"There is no fee. I told you to forget it. We aren't going to pay anything more. No, wait, I take that back. We'll pay your airfare," La Rue said in a snarky tone.

Ludovic thought about it for a minute. He could use Katija's real estate purchases as a reason to tell his team that he needed to go to the US. That would help tamp down any suspicion from them. It would be good to see Katija, plus he could look at the properties she wanted to buy. Ludovic was warming to the idea.

"Give me a minute," said Ludovic.

"No problem; we'll keep the link open," said La Rue.

La Rue put her link on mute and turned to Dunbar to ask, "What do you think?"

"Getting Ludovic in the US would be huge for us. A lot better than just having his fiancée as leverage," said Dunbar.

Ludovic unmuted his conference line. "Okay, I'll be on Lufthansa Flight 402 from FRA to EWR landing at 3:45 p.m. tomorrow. I want to be met at the airport by you and your partner from Dubrovnik. No one else. And have your IT team ready to work once I arrive. We'll work nonstop until your superiors are satisfied that the code is working."

La Rue was writing down the details.

"What name are you flying under?" asked La Rue.

"Lauren, please. This isn't my first rodeo either. I'm agreeing to come to the US. Don't insult me with such questions."

"Fine. I'll put the wheels in motion to set up the lab and Chris and I will meet you at Newark tomorrow," said La Rue.

And with that the conference line was disconnected.

What Ludovic hadn't told La Rue was that he would be flying into Newark on United Flight 961, which landed an hour and forty-five minutes earlier than the Lufthansa flight.

La Rue next dialed Langley, saying she needed to talk to Director Collins at her earliest convenience.

An hour later the laptop in the Rockaway safe house flashed and Lisa Collin's image came up on the screen.

"What do you have?" asked CIA director Collins.

La Rue went on to recount the Ludovic call. As she did, Collins called in her DDI and her cyberchief. After a few minutes of discussion, their plan was agreed.

Collins recapped the plan. "The CIA will use the Staten Island safe house as a lab. It'll be perfect for the op. La Rue and Dunbar will still move to the Staten Island house today so they are closer to Newark to pick up Ludovic."

With the plan decided upon, Collins rang off. She kept her DDI and cyberchief back in her office for a few more minutes to discuss the matter further.

"What do you think about Ludovic agreeing to come to the US?" asked Collins.

The DDI spoke up first. "Well, we know his fiancée is in NYC, so that could be part of his motivation."

"Perhaps," responded Collins.

The cyberchief said, "Regardless of his motivation, I'm happy to have him on site to work with our coders on the CM hack."

Collins nodded in agreement and then said, "We're going to need to put a response team nearby to protect La Rue." She turned to her DDI and said, "Simon, work out the details to make that happen."

Collins then added, "I'm bringing the NSA in on this."

There was no pushback or surprise in reaction to her statement. Often the NSA would be brought in on cyberassignments.

Collins closed with, "Thank you, gentlemen," and then picked up the phone and said to her assistant, "Pascal, get me Kristin McMahon at NSA. Have her review the Operation Deadeye file first."

Deadeye was the Agency's code name for the plan to deploy the CM hack. Deadeye was a Navy term to describe an inoperative laser weapon. If the operation was successful, it would make the Chinese missiles inoperative too.

A few minutes later, having reviewed the Deadeye file, Kristin McMahon placed a call to Director Collins, opening with, "Good afternoon, Director."

"Kristin, you've reviewed Deadeye. What you didn't read is that Pavo Ludovic is flying into Newark tomorrow. We are putting him up in a safe house on Staten Island to work with our cyberpeople on the CM hack. I'd like you to be there," said the CIA director.

"You'll square it with George?" asked McMahon, referring to her boss, George Riordan, director of the NSA.

"Already done," said Collins. "Kristin, you know Mike's working on Torchlight," said Collins.

McMahon nodded.

"Torchlight, if successful, will replace THAAD and be a huge step forward for us. But President Russell has directed us to pursue additional steps as well. That's where Deadeye comes in. We want to have the ability to hack into any Chinese-made missile system and disable it. Ludovic is helping us on that. He sold us the initial hack, but some of the code is missing. He's agreed to come to the US to help us complete the hack."

"The leader of NetRiot has agreed to come to the US?" questioned McMahon.

"I'm not sure what Ludovic's real motivation is. His fiancée is in New York looking at properties, so some on my team think he agreed to come just to see her," summarized Collins.

"I'd hate to be the one to put a damper on the romantic explanation, but it doesn't sound quite right," opined McMahon.

"I agree," said Collins. "I think he agreed to come to the US for other reasons. He may be willing to defect. That's why I want you to be there—to find out why he's really here."

As Collins spoke, McMahon brought up Ludovic's bio from the NSA's database.

"Director, is it really defecting? It says here he's a Croatian national," said McMahon.

"Yes, he's a Croat, but trust me, Moscow owns him. The KGB won't let him go willingly. So be careful. We'll have a senior agent on site plus a response team close by. Also, Lauren La Rue will be there. Keep in mind she is still being sought by the Saudis over her role in the Nantucket attack and the Sheik Rahman matter," said Collins. "Kristin, you'll leave tomorrow morning. Keep me apprised and be careful," Collins said as she concluded the call.

CHAPTER ELEVEN

"Con, Sonar. We have a missile launch from Pearl. Tracking Vampire 1," called Luis Lopresti from the USS *Florida*'s sonar station.

"Copy, Sonar," replied Captain Reagan. "Officer of the Deck, sound action stations, missile."

"Aye, aye, Captain," replied the OOD. "Bosun mate on the 1MC, action stations, missile. I repeat, action stations, missile."

"Weps, ready Torchlight for energizing, sync with SPY-6," commanded Captain Reagan as Commander Bartlett and Jim Hartel both entered the control room.

As the Torchlight laser began the process of energizing, the chief engineer dialed up the power from his six Bechtel nuclear reactors.

"Sonar, Con. What's the track and speed of the inbound vampire?" asked Reagan.

"Con, Sonar. We are tracking Vampire 1, bearing 080 degrees, range four thousand miles, speed approximately fifteen thousand knots, or Mach 23, sir. She's coming on fast. Expected intercept of *Florida* is thirteen minutes."

"Weps, status of Torchlight," called the captain.

"Sir, we are eighty percent power. Expect to reach one hundred percent momentarily," replied the weapons officer.

Back in the engineering spaces, the chief engineer was over-seeing his vast array of screens and dials. His six A1B reactor plants' total power output was classified, but the power generation could be estimated by the fact that the new Gerald R. Ford class aircraft carrier needed only two A1B reactors to produce six hundred megawatts of power. With six A1B reactors, the *Florida* could produce 1.8 million megawatts of power. All from a new generation of reactors that were smaller and weighed less than the Nimitz-class carriers' A4W reactors.

But that was just part of the story. Torchlight also employed devices known as EDFAs, or erbium-doped fiber amplifiers, which increased the A1B power output another tenfold.

Torchlight took the electricity generated by the A1B generators and converted the electrons to photons; then the EDFAs took over, amplifying the strength of the photon beam another ten times. Next an array of top secret chips columnated the beam, and fast-steering mirrors and tracking computers targeted the laser beam on the inbound threat.

"Maneuvering, five degree up bubble, surface, surface, surface, standard rudder, quick stop, prepare for Snapshot," ordered Reagan.

The OOD and chief of the boat carried out the captain's order immediately as the *Florida* rose from its six-hundred-foot depth to the surface in order to fire the Torchlight laser weapon at the inbound missile.

"Sonar, when we surface, put SPY in surface mode. Keep an eye out for inbound Tomahawks. Gentlemen, fight's on." Everyone on the bridge knew this was the test they had expected.

"Engineering, status," called the captain.

"Sir, reactors at one hundred percent throughput. All readings are nominal. We're ready to fire, sir," came back the chief engineer.

The captain picked up the 1MC mike. "Prepare to Snapshot Torchlight. Radar, give me a three-sixty sweep," ordered the captain as the surface alarm was sounded.

As the 560-foot, eighteen-thousand-ton *Florida* broke the surface, the captain called, "Sonar, Radar, status."

"Con, Radar. All clear. No surface contacts."

"Con, Sonar. SPY just picked up two new inbound Tomahawks, starting tracks Vampire 2 and 3."

"Weps, prepare to fire Torchlight on Vampire 1," said Reagan.

The weapons officer flipped the cover to the commit button for Torchlight and depressed it, signaling Torchlight to fully power up and to accept guidance in real-time mode from SPY-6.

"Aye, aye, sir. Torchlight commit, ready to fire on your command," replied the weapons officer.

Just then Hartel triggered the program on his laptop that would initiate a scram on two of Torchlight's reactors.

A few seconds later, in Engineering, reactors 1 and 5 started to spit out alerts.

"Bridge, Engineering. Reactors 1 and 5 are scramming," reported the chief engineer.

Jim Hartel looked up on hearing the engineer's report to see how Reagan would deal with the scrammed reactors.

Without missing a beat, Captain Reagan responded, "Can we fire Torchlight with four reactors online?"

"That's affirmative, sir," replied the chief.

"Weps, are you ready to fire?" was the captain's next question.

"We're ready, sir, on your command," replied Weps.

"Sonar, range of inbound vampires," asked the captain.

"Con, Sonar. Vampire 1 is one thousand miles out, bearing 082 degrees, closing fast, intercept Alpha Bravo 3 minutes 42 seconds; Vampire 2, bearing 170, range ninety miles, intercept Alpha Bravo 8 minutes; Vampire 3, bearing 172, range 150 miles, intercept Alpha Bravo 12 minutes," responded the sonar operator, using "Alpha Bravo" as the *Florida*'s designated call sign.

"Weps, Snapshot, Vampire 1, Snapshot, Snapshot," ordered Reagan.

The weps officer depressed the trigger button on his handset. Immediately the Torchlight laser fired a concentrated beam of high energy at the inbound Minuteman missile approaching the *Florida* in excess of fifteen thousand knots. One hundred forty miles from the *Florida*, the inbound Minuteman III missile disintegrated as the Torchlight beam accurately hit it, vaporizing its electronics in an instant.

"Con, Sonar. Kill, kill, kill, Vampire 1 is down," called the sonar operator.

The captain asked, "Range and bearing of Vampires 2 and 3?"

"Con, Sonar. Vampire 2, bearing 165, range 60 miles, intercept Alpha Bravo 7 minutes; Vampire 3, bearing 175, range 120 miles, intercept Alpha Bravo 11 minutes," replied the sonar operator.

Next the Torchlight gimbal spun the Torchlight laser gun eighty-eight degrees to starboard, locked on to the slower and much lower altitude of Vampire 2.

"Weps, Con. Vampire 2, Snapshot, Snapshot, Snapshot," ordered Reagan.

The weapons officer again depressed his trigger three times, firing Torchlight.

"Con, Sonar. Kill, kill, kill, Vampire 2," called the sonar operator.

"Copy," said the captain. "Distance and bearing on Vampire 3?"

"Con, Sonar. Vampire 3, bearing 174, range 90 miles, intercept Alpha Bravo 10 minutes. Sir, Vampire 3 is very low—she's wave hopping," called the sonar operator.

"Weps, Con. Is Torchlight locked on Vampire 3?" called the captain.

"Con, Weps. Sir, SPY keeps losing Vampire 3 as it dips toward the surface, sir. I don't have a lock."

Reagan knew he had little time to sort the issue.

Just then the chief engineer called the control room. "Sir, Torchlight is operating at sixty percent with reactors 1 and 5 down. We're okay as long as we don't lose any more reactors."

"Copy, Chief," said the captain.

Reagan took a moment to summarize his tactical situation. He had the power, he had about nine minutes before Vampire 3 would intercept *Florida*, and the target was echoing in and out of target lock. That was all the time Reagan needed.

"Weps, Con. Vampire 3, Snapshot, Snapshot, Snapshot," ordered Reagan.

Again, the weapons officer fired Torchlight.

Then there was silence. There was no report of a kill from sonar.

A moment later came the report. "Con, Sonar. Vampire 3 still inbound, bearing 172, range ninety-eight miles, intercept Alpha Bravo 8 minutes."

"Con, SPY now has a lock, sir," came the call from the radar officer.

Without waiting, the captain yelled, "Snapshot, Snapshot, Vampire 3—take it out, Weps."

The Torchlight laser beam fired multiple times at a very low angle as SPY-6 took into account the curvature of the Earth and the distance to the inbound Tomahawk.

With Vampire 3 approximately 93.2 miles south of the *Florida* and at an altitude of fifty to seventy-five feet, SPY-6 corrected for a 7.98-inch-per-mile curvature and fired a deflection shot.

"Con, Sonar. Kill, kill, kill, Vampire 3. All inbound vampires have been defeated, sir."

Cheers and yells broke out in the control room and through the ship as they heard the sonar operations report. The Death Star of the Fleet had just defeated three inbound threats.

The captain barked, "Dive, dive, dive, come to course 000, depth four hundred, right standard rudder, ahead two-thirds."

Immediately the diving alarm was sounded as the OOD and COB carried out the captain's orders.

"Operations, how long were we on the surface?" asked the captain.

"Four minutes, thirty-six seconds," came the reply.

"Chief Engineer, power down Torchlight. XO, schedule the department heads to meet in the officers' mess for a post-op debrief at 15:00," ordered the captain, giving his department heads two hours to collect the operational data from the missile shoot downs.

Captain Reagan looked at Jim Hartel and Commander Mike Bartlett for the first time since the operation started and just nodded. He was proud of his crew and equally impressed with the way Torchlight had performed.

As the excitement and stress of the exercise subsided, Reagan thought to himself, *Damn, this Torchlight is a game-changer.*

Reagan ordered the *Florida* to head back to the operating area off Namp'o at best possible speed. The Torchlight tests, as far as he was concerned, were over for now.

Two hours later, with the captain's staff assembled in the mess, Hartel began, not able to hide his exuberance, "Captain your boat and crew performed flawlessly. What we just saw was the most impressive test of Torchlight to date. The system handled the three inbound vampires effortlessly."

"Thank you, Mr. Hartel," began Reagan. "Department heads, let's hear your reports."

First up was Engineering.

"Captain, Torchlight performed very well. We were able to successfully execute the mission despite losing reactors 1 and 5 due to a scram."

Hartel, who had been looking over the readouts from the test, questioned, "Chief, the scrams, do you know what caused it?"

"We're looking into what caused the scrams, but it looks like we have a bad pump bearing on 1. We don't know what caused the scram on 5 but we're running diagnostics as we speak, sir. We think 5 shut down over a software issue. We'll ship all the sensor trace data back to Bechtel so they can analyze it, and in the meantime we'll swap out the pump bearing."

"That won't be necessary, Chief," said Hartel. "I programmed reactors 1 and 5 to scram as a test to see how Torchlight and the crew would respond," added Hartel.

That caught Reagan's attention. "Well, Mr. Hartel, how did we do?"

"Captain, the scrams were a good test for Torchlight and your crew, and both handled it without a problem."

Next up was the weapons officer.

"Sir, I forwarded our results to Mr. Hartel, but there really isn't much to add. We defeated three inbound vampires with ease. And note that one of the vampires was traveling more than Mach 20 on its downward trajectory. That's the most difficult shot, sir. Torchlight is amazing. Truly amazing.

"However, sir, there is some concern about SPY-6's ability to lock on a wave-hopping Tomahawk. Things were getting a little dicey around the Vampire 3 shoot down," added the weapons officer.

Jim Hartel nodded and took more notes, as he acknowledged the weapons expert's assessment. He thought enhancements were needed to SPY-6 to address the ghosting issue.

Then the XO chimed in. "Sir, the one area worth pointing out is with all the space in engineering taken up with reactors and Torchlight technology, the *Florida* does not have much room left for torpedoes. Are we going to require a fast attack with us just like the boomers?"

The XO was right. The *Florida* did not possess the torpedo firepower of a traditional SSBN. And just as boomers never deployed without a fast-attack submarine riding shotgun, so, too, should be the case for the *Florida*, thought Reagan.

"XO, put that note in our operations report we send to Pearl and the *Stennis*," Reagan said.

An hour later, with the briefing concluded, Commander Bartlett spoke with Captain Reagan. "Sir, I think my assignment here is done. I'd like to get back to the *Stennis* as soon as possible. I committed to keep Admiral Fraser and the president briefed on Torchlight and right now I'm just taking up space on your sub," added Bartlett.

Reagan had come to like Bartlett and he couldn't argue with his assessment. As a warrior, Bartlett liked to be able to contribute, and right now on the *Florida* his observer status was wearing on him.

"I understand, Commander," replied Reagan. "I'll have the XO coordinate with the *Stennis* to chop you back as soon as practical. But before you go, I would appreciate hearing your assessment of Torchlight."

"Thank you, Captain," replied Bartlett. "I'm not sure I have much to add to your staff's readout on Torchlight. I will say my assignment in Pax

River with the Navy's Test and Evaluation squadron has taught me that all new weapons systems have surprises and flaws. Often, they come from areas that are totally overlooked. I, too, am impressed with Torchlight, but the first two years of deployment are going to uncover some design issues that we haven't seen yet. Torchlight is off to an impressive start, but in my opinion the system needs more testing before it can be certified for use in the fleet."

Reagan nodded and noted Bartlett's comments in his operations reports, knowing they were well-founded and came from firsthand experience of testing and certifying the F-35C Lightning II for fleet readiness.

General Goh said to his wife, "Are you almost ready?"

They were preparing to leave to attend their son's school science fair.

"Yes," said Goh's wife, and she picked up her pocketbook and checked her makeup in the hall mirror.

General Goh's driver was already waiting in front of his black government sedan.

Goh looked at his wife. "You're a nervous wreck."

"I know, I know. Hwan's worked so hard on his project," she said.

"He'll do fine. He prepared well and knows his facts," said the general with the confidence that came from a career of knowing that when an officer or a soldier had prepared thoroughly, it almost always led to a successful outcome. But truth be told, Goh felt the same excitement and nervousness as his wife.

And while it was not an official event, Goh had decided to wear his uniform to the science fair to honor his son.

Out of respect, the principal and assistant principal along with Hwan's science teacher were outside waiting to greet General Goh when he arrived. After pleasantries were exchanged, General Goh and his wife were escorted into the gymnasium, where all the students had set up their science projects.

As Goh and his wife walked the aisles reviewing the students' projects, occasionally Goh's wife would lean in and whisper in the general's ear to remind him of the name of a particular student who was either a friend of Hwan's or whose parents were friends of the Gohs.

General Goh was skilled in the art of making an individual feel special.

"Hello there," the general would say with a warm smile. "Your project looks very interesting. Can you tell me about it?"

The excited student would launch into his explanation, with his beaming parents taking pictures with their smartphones. While not a politician, Goh had a charisma and gravitas that lit up any room he entered.

Eventually the Gohs came to their son's stand. Not able to hide their pride, both smiled as the general said, "Now, this project looks very interesting to me. What can you tell me about it?"

Hwan couldn't help blushing as he smiled and began his talk on photosynthesis.

The general listened to his son's explanation of his project and then asked a few questions. His son beamed as his father complimented him on his preparedness and knowledge of the subject matter.

After reviewing the remaining projects, the Gohs attended a reception in the school's library, where the general worked the room, pausing to take photos with staff and parents.

It was during the reception that the general was approached by the South Korean agent he had previously met with in his dentist's office.

The general greeted the agent with, "I was impressed by your daughter's project."

The agent played the role of a proud parent. "Thank you, General, that is very kind of you."

The general concluded the discussion with the agent with a handshake. It was during the handshake that the general secretly passed an Apple iPod Shuffle on which the general had recorded his comments about new details regarding the launch of the DF-26 missile, which was scheduled to occur in three days. He also put in a note regarding the bank account he wanted set up for his wife with the $20 million deposited in it.

The iPod Shuffle wave file included a file with identification numbers for each mobile launcher as well as their GPS locations. And finally, the general added detailed comments about his family's plan to escape on the whale-watching boat.

If the iPod Shuffle fell into the wrong hands it would spell doom for the general as well as his family. But the general's tradecraft was exceptional, and no one, not even the agents whom Paek had tailing the general, detected the sleight of hand that facilitated the iPod transfer.

Even though this event was taking place in North Korea, some behaviors persisted and transcended politics, and celebrating a student's accomplishment was, of course, universal. And so, once the reception was concluded, the children and parents departed to the local ice cream shop, where a less formal celebration would take place.

Typically, Goh would never attend such an event, but tonight he had a reason to do so.

In the hour that elapsed from the reception to the time at the ice cream shop, the South Korean agent had time to listen to Goh's recording and respond.

At the ice cream shop the agent mixed into the crowd and made his way to the general again to say good night. As he did, he passed a memory stick back to the general with his responses recorded on it as well as a software back door that would allow the CIA to gain access to any secure network. With the back door in place, the CIA would be able to upload the Chinese missile hack into the North Korean networks, which was the next critical step for Deadeye.

Every four to six weeks, the president and his wife would host a small informal dinner party with some of the most innovative and interesting people in the world. It was always an eclectic group, one that would provide thought-provoking conversation.

Tonight's guest list was Elon Musk, founder of the Tesla and SpaceX, Lin-Manuel Miranda, the writer and star of the hit musical *Hamilton*, Casey Neistat, the YouTube vlogger extraordinaire, Dr. Patricia Moore, the CEO of Sloan Kettering, John Sexton, the recently retired president of NYU, and Lisa Collins, the director of the CIA.

Once everyone was seated, Kennedy Russell remarked, "Casey, my children were thrilled when I told them you would be coming to dinner."

Neistat, who had become something of a sensation with the younger generation, replied rather awkwardly, "Thank you, Mrs. Russell. I mean Mrs. First Lady," which drew a laugh from the table.

"Please, everyone, let's keep it informal tonight. Please call me Kennedy."

The president smiled, knowing that no one would be calling him Andrew tonight other than Kennedy.

The president began, "John, NYU just opened a remote campus

in Abu Dhabi. How is that going?" "Yes, Mr. President, we opened it in 2010, and after some initial start-up issues it has become a very popular campus for us. Sixty-three percent of our undergraduate students spend at least one semester in the UAE."

"Extraordinary," said the president. "Whatever we can do to promote multiculturalism."

This opened the door for a comment from Lin-Manuel. "We recently brought *Hamilton* to Abu Dhabi, sir."

"And is it popular?" asked the first lady.

"Ma'am, just as popular there as here. Sold out every night."

Lisa Collins didn't know it, but this dinner was an opportunity for the president and first lady to size her up as a possible running mate. Other than Kennedy Russell, no one in the president's inner circle knew about Vice President McMaster's leukemia diagnosis.

Kennedy supported the idea of Lisa Collins as a running mate, but there were other viable candidates on the list as well, and, of course, she and the president were rooting and praying for Jack McMasters's recovery.

The idea of mixing business with social occasions comported with the president's style. He liked to see how people reacted when their guard was down. Even so, he knew no one ever really lowered their guard when having dinner in the White House.

"Lisa, what is your reaction to *Hamilton* being as popular in the UAE as it is here?" asked the president.

"Well, Mr. President, I don't doubt that Hamilton's popular over there. But I suspect it's only the well-heeled Emirati that are going to see it. And more because of its reputation as a musical sensation than any interest in American history or democracy."

Elon Musk then interjected, "I was recently in the UAE and Saudi Arabia and I was struck by their rapid adoption of solar—especially given the region's economic dependency on petroleum. I think the region is changing. That said, I still observed many human rights issues. Especially on how they treat women."

"Some of our best surgeons are now coming from the Middle East as well as India. And some are women," added Patricia Moore. "If I had made such a comment ten years ago I would have been laughed at."

"India may not be a military power, but they are definitely an economic power and their IT skills are beginning to rival Silicon Valley's," remarked Collins.

"I agree with that point," said Elon Musk. "India is the next China."

The president then asked, "Casey, what is your opinion of India?"

"Mr. President, I agree that India is coming on, but currently they lack the innovative spark that exists in the US. I do think the amount of Indian engineers working in Silicon Valley as well as attending our universities will aide them immensely to catch up, but it's still a generation off in my opinion, sir."

"Elon," asked the president, "what are you looking at as the next *big* thing?"

"Mr. President, we're studying the impact of global warming and how the Northwest Passage will soon become navigable twelve months a year. We're buying vast amounts of Canadian real estate betting on the fact that an open Northwest Passage will cut days off oceanic shipping and commerce. We believe there will be a race to develop the area. And I should add we're seeing large investments from Canada and Russia in the area, sir."

"Interesting," was the president's only response, but he took note of the point. This was another example of how these dinners helped provide the president with information on issues without the spin added by his staff.

And so the evening continued. It was one of the perks that came with the White House—the ability to host such an interesting and influential group of individuals.

Before the guests left, the president asked Dr. Moore for a few minutes in private, during which he inquired about Vice President Jack McMasters's condition. The report wasn't encouraging.

As Ludovic headed to the Dubrovnik airport for the first leg of his flight to the US, he received a message on the Telegram Messenger app. Telegram, developed by a pair of Russian brothers, was another technology coveted by the dark web because its messages were encrypted and untraceable.

"We have a client who is very interested in the whereabouts of La Rue." It was sent from the account used by Imperial Imports LLC, the front used by North Korean president Paek.

"I don't know where she is but I suspect she's in the US," replied Ludovic, knowing not responding would raise alarms with his powerful and vengeful client.

"Whatever additional info you can tell us will be generously rewarded," was the final message from Imperial.

"Understood," was Ludovic's response.

But Paek had already achieved his goal. He wanted to alert Ludovic that he was interested in Lauren La Rue.

Paek next passed the information on to the late Sheik Abdul Er Rahman's son, Salman.

What interested Salman more was that his intelligence team had learned that Ludovic was booked to travel today on a United Airlines flight from Frankfurt to Newark, New Jersey. It took some doing and cash but the sheik's son was able to arrange for his security team of three to get seats on the same United flight from Frankfurt. Ludovic now had a tail on him.

"So, this is Staten Island," said La Rue as she and Dunbar crossed over the Verrazano-Narrows Bridge from Brooklyn into Staten Island.

"My first time here too," added Dunbar.

"It doesn't look that bad," commented La Rue.

Dunbar was amazed as he slowed to pay the toll for the Verrazano Bridge. "Seventeen dollars for a toll," remarked Dunbar. "That has to be a record."

After exiting the toll plaza, Dunbar took the Hylan Boulevard exit, which led them a few minutes later to a small, well-kept house on Sparkill Avenue in the center of the island.

One of the attractive features of this particular safe house was the garage, which provided direct access to the house through the basement without having to go outside.

La Rue said, "I'll wait while you check the house." La Rue was now quite familiar with Dunbar's behavior.

When Dunbar said the place was secure, La Rue selected two bedrooms on the upper floor for them, leaving the other two bedrooms in the basement for their guests.

A little over an hour later, a light blue Honda CR-V pulled into the driveway. Behind the wheel was the deputy director of the NSA, Kristin McMahon. She grabbed her bag and approached the front door, setting off the Nest cameras. McMahon was driving what was know as a "white car." The CIA had purchased a fleet of used, non-descript cars for field operations. Gone were the days of driving around in black Suburbans.

"Welcome to Staten Island," said La Rue as she opened the door. McMahon was one of La Rue's main contacts at the NSA, and it was clear she was happy to see the deputy director. McMahon was the first person other than Dunbar La Rue had seen in almost two weeks.

"Lauren, it's good to see you. Looking no worse for the wear, I see," returned McMahon as she entered the house. La Rue closed the steel-reinforced door behind her.

"I heard your trip to Dubrovnik was a little more exciting than planned," said McMahon.

"You could say that. Kristin, do you know Chris Dunbar?" she said, introducing the CIA agent to the DDI of the NSA.

"No, I don't think we've met," said McMahon, nodding to acknowledge Dunbar.

Dunbar shook her hand and then made sure the front door was properly locked.

"We only have about two hours before Chris and I have to leave to pick up Ludovic," said La Rue.

"No problem. I have a call I need to take, plus the IT folks should be here any minute now," replied McMahon.

Dunbar went to check the windows again and review the video streams from the Nest cameras installed at every corner of the house. The CIA had cleverly placed the Nest cameras in the eaves, and while someone trained in tradecraft would be able to pick them out, it would take that level of expertise to do so.

Half an hour later a van pulled up to the house and three of the CIA's best cyberengineers got out and quickly entered the house, after which the van pulled away.

The engineers showed their IDs to Dunbar and quickly got to setting up their equipment in the basement for the soon-to-arrive Ludovic.

Meanwhile at Newark Airport Ludovic had already arrived on the earlier United flight. As he exited US Customs, he made his way to the AirTrain that would take him to the rental car and parking areas. Ludovic surveyed the crowd on the platform and entered the front section of the first car of the AirTrain.

Once on the AirTrain, Ludovic opened up his laptop and started to type furiously. As the train came into the P3 Station, the doors for his compartment opened while all the other doors of the train remained closed.

Ludovic exited the train, crossed the platform, and boarded another AirTrain that would take him back to terminals A, B, and C and then continue on to the Liberty Airport Station, where one could change to trains for Manhattan and other areas of New Jersey.

His plan worked perfectly. If he had been followed, his pursuers were now stuck in the AirTrain, thanks to his successful hack of the AirTrain door system.

With his tail dropped, Ludovic made his way back to Terminal B and waited for La Rue and Dunbar.

Over the last few weeks, Ludovic had become fond of La Rue and considered her an asset. So, while Ludovic had shared information that was clearly being used by the Saudis to find La Rue, at the same time he wasn't going to make it easy for them.

It was going on 3 p.m. when Dunbar said, "Lauren, time to go. We'll take the Honda."

McMahon nodded and handed Dunbar the keys. Forty minutes later, after stopping for gas, La Rue and Dunbar were at Terminal B looking for Ludovic.

"Ludovic's flight has landed," said Dunbar, looking up at the screen, which indicated that Lufthansa Flight 402 had arrived.

"He'll be coming out one of those doors." Dunbar pointed to the US Customs area.

A moment later La Rue heard a quiet, "Hello, Amy," at her ear. She turned to see Ludovic's six-foot-two frame right behind her. He sported his typical two-week beard but was now wearing a New York Yankees baseball cap and Ray-Bans that he had purchased as he waited.

La Rue said, "Welcome to America, Pavo."

Dunbar asked, "Were you followed?"

"No, and if I were, I've lost them," replied Ludovic.

Not wanting to spend any more time than necessary at EWR, Dunbar said, "This way," pointing to the down escalator.

While Dunbar didn't identify himself to the US Customs agents, he had shown his ID to the Port Authority police as he parked the light blue Honda at the departures drop-off area.

Ten minutes later they were crossing the Goethals Bridge back into Staten Island. They would be in the safe house in a matter of minutes.

All in all, Dunbar considered it a successful pickup, but Ludovic's comment about having dropped any tails left Dunbar on heightened alert.

Once in the safe house, Ludovic got to work with the CIA's cyberengineers.

The engineers and Ludovic spoke in half sentences as they worked to link the missing files into the CM hack code.

Dunbar interrupted, "Do any of you have cell phones? I want to take to make sure we aren't emitting any signals."

The engineers and Ludovic looked at Dunbar and then turned back to their screens without providing the hint of an answer.

McMahon chuckled at their reaction, saying, "Chris, I don't think you need to worry about that with this group."

McMahon then went upstairs to call Director Collins about their progress.

With the secure line established La Rue said, "Director, I wanted to give you an update."

"Good to hear from you, how is it going?" asked Collins.

"Fine, the IT guys are working with our guest as we speak," said La Rue. "Chris thinks our guest came in on an earlier flight than planned. You may want to look into that," continued La Rue.

"We will. Just so you know, we have a response team just minutes from your location if required. All you need to do is yell and they'll be there. Chris knows how to reach them," said Collins.

Alpha Team was five blocks away at the FDNY Engine 160 and Rescue Company 5 firehouse. On operations that took place in New York City, where the CIA wanted to keep a low profile, they preferred working with the FDNY rather than the NYPD.

There was no insult implied in that decision. The CIA worked closely with the NYPD when needed, but where possible it was preferred to keep local law enforcement out of the loop to limit the chance of leaks.

Director Collins was due at the White House to brief the president on Deadeye.

When she arrived, Director Collins, wearing her A-code security pass, was escorted not to the Oval Office but to the underground Situation Room. There the directors of the FBI and NSA, along with the chairman of the Joint Chiefs as well as the vice chairman of the Joint Chiefs, Admiral Johnson, were already seated.

"Good afternoon, gentlemen," said Collins as she entered the room.

A moment later the door opened and President Andrew Russell, followed by his chief of staff, Spencer Sterling, entered. Everyone stood as the president made his way to his seat at the head of the table.

"Afternoon, everyone. We'll start with Torchlight, then cover Deadeye, and end with a status report on the North Korean operation," said the president.

Admiral Johnson began, "Mr. President, I spoke with Commander Bartlett this morning and read the report from PM Hartel. Yesterday Torchlight successfully defeated a three-missile attack. The *Florida* surfaced and in less than five minutes destroyed an inbound Minuteman III fired from Hawaii traveling at high Mach speeds and two incoming Tomahawks launched from the *Connecticut* and *Washington*, operating in the area. It was a complete success."

"Any surprises?" asked the president.

"The Torchlight PM on the *Florida* scrammed two of the reactors during the test to see how the crew and Torchlight would react. He said both the crew and Torchlight handled the situation perfectly," replied Johnson.

The president nodded. "Anything else from Bartlett's report?"

"Mr. President, as you know, Commander Bartlett comes from the Test and Evaluation squadron at Pax. That community tends to obsess on testing," said Johnson.

"Rightly so," replied the president.

"While the Torchlight test was a success, he stresses that more testing is needed before Torchlight can be counted on for an operational mission," ended Johnson.

"He's correct," said the president, "but as long as Torchlight continues to check out, we're moving ahead with the North Korean operation. I see no reason to delay it. Director Collins, status on Deadeye," the president said.

Bringing up her first slide, the director of the CIA began, "Mr. President, we have our team in Staten Island working with the high-value asset from Dubrovnik who sourced the Chinese missile hack. We believe we'll have a viable hack available by sunup tomorrow."

"What's the security plan for this team in Staten Island?" asked the president.

"Security is a concern, Mr. President," replied Collins. "We know the Saudis are still looking for La Rue, who is on-site. And the asset there is also considered high value to the Russians. To that end, we have a response team stationed nearby should they be required. We also have an evacuation plan in place in case our team needs to get out of there in a hurry," said Collins.

The president nodded but then added, "Do we need La Rue there?"

Collins smiled as she recognized Russell's tactical expertise. "Mr. President, you are correct. La Rue's presence complicates the mission, but her relationship with Ludovic is key. He specifically requested that she be there—he trusts her. If La Rue were removed I think it could spook Ludovic. We can't risk that until the hack is finished and tested."

"Twenty-four hours," said the president. "That's all you have. After that I want you to bring the entire team in."

"Understood, Mr. President," was Collins's reply.

Next to speak was the president's chief of staff. "As you know, we are planning to use the advantages of Torchlight and Deadeye to force a regime change in North Korea. The Chinese are on board with the plan, as are the Brits and Japanese. Going further, we expect the North Koreans to fire a test missile as part of their Day of the Sun celebration on Sunday, April fifteenth. After defeating that missile shot with Torchlight and disabling their remaining missiles with Deadeye, we'll use these events to issue an ultimatum to Paek and his cabinet to cede control and leave the country or face attack. If Paek doesn't agree to leave, we'll be prepared to handle that situation with our Special Forces, which will be on-site, delivered by the *United States*. Once Paek sees we have neutralized his missiles, especially his Hwasong-14 long-range ICBMs, we believe he'll have no choice and must leave the country. We know Paek has a retreat on a private island in the northern Philippines. En route to the Philipines the Chinese will take down Paek's plane."

Everyone in the room had already been briefed on the plan—it was bold, it was big, and it was risky.

President Russell picked up the hesitancy of his team and addressed it. "Nec metu, nec spe. Without fear, without hope," translated the president.

"Gentlemen, ma'am," said the president, "the two biggest threats that exist to our way of life are North Korea and Al Qaeda. Like a cancer, the longer we leave either to fester, the larger the threat grows. The fact that Paek now has nukes makes him our number one threat. We are going to eliminate this threat. Yes, it carries risk, but the risk is much greater if we do nothing. We tried that for the last fifteen years, and look where it has gotten us. Over that time, we've seen Paek develop longer- and longer-range missiles with larger warheads. The time is now for us to act. With Torchlight and Deadeye, we have the advantage. As everyone in this room knows, military technological advantages are fleeting. We're going to seize the initiative and remove this threat once and for all. Today is the twelfth. We have three days until the mission goes active. Make sure everything on our side is ready. I will give the order once they fire their missiles at the *Stennis* on the fifteenth. That is all."

CHAPTER TWELVE

Commander Mike Bartlett had landed back on the *Stennis* and was in the admiral's conference room along with the admiral's chief of staff, the CO of the Stennis, Captain Craig Ryan, and CVW-9's CAG (Commander of Air Group), Sara "Clutch" Cunningham.

As COMCARGRU-3 entered the room, all participants stood at attention.

"At ease," said Fraser as he entered. "Commander Bartlett is just back from the *Florida* and is going to brief us on the latest with Torchlight."

"Admiral, the *Florida* surfaced and in four minutes and thirty-six seconds was able to successfully defeat three inbound vampires. The first was an LGM-30 Minuteman III fired from Hawaii traveling inbound *Florida* in excess of Mach 20. Then Torchlight and SPY-6 detected and defeated Tomahawks fired from *Connecticut* and *Washington*."

Fraser asked, "Commander, at what altitude was the LGM-30 shot down?"

"Admiral, the Minuteman was destroyed at altitude of two miles above the earth and 143 miles from the *Florida*. The missile was on its downward or terminal trajectory and was just reentering the thermosphere," replied Bartlett.

The CAG, who had the distinction of being the first female CAG in the Navy, spoke out. "Whoa, Commander, at Mach 20 that only leaves two minutes before the Minuteman would've been on us."

"That's correct, CAG, but Torchlight had been tracking the vampire since its launch was detected. Torchlight with SPY-6 had a lock on the vampire and calculated that the two-mile altitude was its optimal range and best angle of attack," replied Bartlett, bringing up a supporting slide.

The admiral's chief of staff noted, "The DF-26 is reported to have a top speed of Mach 5 to 10, much slower than the LGM-30. That would double the time we have. So instead of two minutes we'll have four minutes to react. Great."

"Captain," replied Bartlett, "there's good news and bad news in the Dong-Feng speed. True, the DF-26 is slower than a Minuteman III, but its operational ceiling and range is shorter too. To account for that, Jim Hartel and I think the best scenario is once the DF-26 is launched that Torchlight take it out while it's still on its upward trajectory. That's something THAAD can't do."

Rear Admiral Fraser asked, "To accomplish that, Commander, just how close does the *Florida* need to be to the launch site?"

"The closer, the better, Admiral," replied Bartlett. "We'll want the *Florida* to be no more than thirty miles off the North Korean coast."

"Knowing Dutch Reagan, I'll bet he'll be closer than that," opined Rear Admiral Fraser.

"Admiral, the XO of the *Florida* had a good idea. He suggested we dispatch the *Connecticut* to ride shotgun for the *Florida*, just like we do with boomers. It will allow Captain Reagan to focus on Torchlight and not worry about any enemy sub threats," added Bartlett.

"Bring up the plot, will you, Captain?" asked Fraser of the USS *John C. Stennis*'s CO, Craig Ryan.

On the screen in the staff room came the tactical plot. It showed the location of the *Stennis* Strike Group as well as all other US Navy assets in the East China Sea.

It showed the *Stennis* Strike Group approximately eight hundred miles south of Seoul but well within the DF-26's fifteen-hun-dred-nautical-mile range.

The *Connecticut* was five hundred miles away from *Florida* in the Philippine Sea.

Fraser turned to Ryan. "Captain, issue immediate orders for the *Connecticut* to make best possible speed and rendezvous with the *Florida*. I want the *Connecticut* on station within twenty-four hours. Let *Florida* know they'll have company. We'll keep the *Washington* with us."

"Aye, aye," replied Ryan, who picked up the handset on the desk and relayed the admiral's orders for the *Connecticut*.

"Admiral," said the CAG, "getting back to the DF-26, at Mach 8 it can be on us in fifteen minutes."

"CAG, once we detect the launch of the Dong-Feng, we'll have the strike group start SP-JASHOing," answered the admiral, referring to the defense condition specifically designed to defend the strike group against an inbound missile attack.

Commander Bartlett added, "CAG, as soon as the *Florida* detects the DF-26 launch, they'll surface and Snapshot the Dong-Feng. They should be able to hit it no more than two minutes into its flight path."

"What about THAAD? Should we look to fire them at the DF-26 from South Korea?" asked Fraser.

"Sir, Hartel is dubious about THAAD's ability to catch up to the DF-26. I don't see any reason not to fire them, if they have a lock, but Hartel said we shouldn't count on THAAD. And, of course, they only have a sixty percent kill rate," said Bartlett.

With that, the briefing ended, and Commander Bartlett asked to meet with Admiral Fraser one-on-one.

Admiral Fraser was contemplating what the impact of a fifty-kiloton DF-26 warhead would do to his carrier group. A fifty-kiloton warhead would produce a fireball the size of three football fields, or roughly the length of the *Stennis*. There would zero survivors in the blast area.

Beyond the fireball would be the radiation zone of over a square mile, where there would be a seventy-five percent mortality rate due to acute radiation poisoning. Those affected would die in a span of several hours to several weeks.

The outer edge of the blast zone would cover sixteen square miles, where third-degree burns would occur, destroying nerves and causing severe scarring, which could require amputation.

"Sir," said Bartlett, "I'm as impressed with Torchlight as anyone, but as CO of VX-23 I know that Torchlight is just too new of a weapons system for us to rely one hundred percent on it. And Jim Hartel's assessment of THAAD is less than glowing."

"I don't disagree, Commander. Do you have another plan?" asked Fraser.

"Yes, sir, I do. We launch a flight of F/A-18s and tank them so we get them as far from the *Stennis* as our fuel will allow. If Torchlight fails we can fire our Sidewinders at the inbound DF-26. We'll be able to pick up the heat source either from the missile's exhaust or from its skin heat. Admiral, keep in mind, if the

DF-26 is traveling at Mach 7, it will be radiating a lot of heat. "Go on, Commander. I'm listening." ""The AIM-9X Sidewinders travel at Mach 2.7, so while they're not fast enough to catch the DF-26, the Sidewinders have extreme maneuverability with thrust vectoring, something we tested thoroughly at Pax River. Sir, if we approach from a head-on aspect and stack our Hornets at various altitudes, we should be able to launch our Sidewinders at the DF-26 and hopefully blanket it. It's a tough shot, no doubt, but if we launch twenty to thirty Sidewinders, we stand a chance of scoring a kill," said an enthusiastic Bartlett.

"You're suggesting we take down the DF-26 with a Sidewinder shot.

Is that what you're saying, Commander?" clarified the admiral. "It's possible, sir. Only if Torchlight doesn't succeed in its mission. The F/A-18s will be a lot more useful in the air than on the deck. We need to work out the details, but that's the idea, sir."

The admiral thought for a minute, then said, "Commander, you've intrigued me." He picked up the handset and called the bridge. "Have CAG, the CO, and my chief of staff report to my conference room at once."

Once they were assembled the admiral began. "Bartlett here has an idea. I don't know if it will work, but I want you to talk it through. Vet it and if it holds water put together an operational plan. Call me once you have the plan ready for review."

Pavo Ludovic opened another can of Red Bull as he banged away at his keyboard, saying, "That's it. I have the data description files ready to be linked."

The senior cyber engineer nodded and replied, "Send them to me. I'm almost ready to begin the compile." With the data descriptions finished, assuming they were correct, they would have the final build ready in less than an hour. While the compile ran, it would give them time to take a short break, which was good, since they had been going at it all night.

All Ludovic did was nod. He was in his zone and his level of concentration was such that he had little bandwidth for conversation.

McMahon wanted a more thorough explanation and so she descended the stairs to talk with the cyberteam.

"Where are we?" she asked.

"Almost done," said the lead engineer. "We've completed our tests. Everything looks good. Once we finish this build, we should have a working hack. I'll double-check that the compile has no errors, and then we'll be ready to FTP the file to Langley. We should be done shortly."

"Good," was all McMahon said, but her mind was racing ahead. While not a field agent, she knew every hour she and the team spent out of the protective bubble of Langley was another hour at risk.

Upstairs, Ludovic turned to Dunbar and said, "I'd like to get some air. Okay if I go out in the yard?"

"One second," said Dunbar as he scanned the screens from the Nest security cameras again.

"Okay, let's go," said Dunbar, opening the rear door.

"Wait up," said La Rue, "I'll join you."

Dunbar stopped on the threshold to wait for her.

The three made their way into the backyard. It was a crisp April morning and the air felt good, revitalizing them after having been cooped up inside for so long.

La Rue began, "So, Pavo, what would you think about moving to America?"

Ludovic wasn't surprised. He knew sooner or later La Rue would bring up the topic.

"Family is important to me, Lauren. My people are in Dubrovnik," he replied.

"I understand," said La Rue, "but not all of your people are in Dubrovnik, right?"

"I don't follow you," said Ludovic, trying to play dumb.

"Katija," said La Rue.

"Ah, your secret police."

"Pavo, let's get to the point," said La Rue. "Our government would be supportive of your moving to the US," said La Rue.

"What makes you think I'm interested?"

"Please, Pavo. We know Katija's been here for two weeks. We know what places she's looked at. We know the real estate agent she's using," La Rue fired back.

Ludovic paused, more for dramatic effect than to contemplate his response. He knew already what he would say.

"Katija and I would need new identities. I would want your government to help transfer my funds to untraceable tax-free accounts. And I would need your government to get Moscow's assurances that they would not come after me. I would need these things to move to the Land of the Free and the Home of the Brave. And that's just for openers."

Anticipating those points and having already discussed various options with Director Collins, La Rue was about to respond when Dunbar heard a noise from the front of the house.

Dunbar slowly looked around the corner of the house, when a burst of automatic fire rang out.

"In the house, now," shouted Dunbar to an alarmed La Rue.

As he followed Ludovic and La Rue inside, Dunbar pressed the talk button on his headset. "Paper Dragon is taking fire. Repeat, Paper Dragon is taking fire."

That call was immediately picked up by the CIA's response team. They grabbed their gear and headed to their van.

Dunbar returned fire as he made a dash to the back door. He lunged at his chair to survey the images from the security cameras. He saw three men dressed in black tactical gear approaching the house carrying FAMAS G-1 assault rifles. A moment later he saw one of them throw several small canisters that released smoke intended to obscure the view from the cameras.

Dunbar got up, yelling to those in the house, "Everyone into the basement now."

McMahon grabbed La Rue's arm as they headed to the basement.

Ludovic yelled at Dunbar, "Give me a weapon."

Dunbar was at the closet grabbing a SCAR 17S, the US Special Operations newest assault rifle. He handed Ludovic a SCAR, saying, "This is the safety." He also handed him four magazines of extra ammo.

And then it began.

A burst of automatic weapon fire raked the front of the house, running a line of bullets across the windows and front door.

Dunbar took a position near the corner of the blown-out picture window and let off a burst from his SCAR.

As he fired he called, "Paper Dragon under fire from three assailants with automatic weapons."

The CIA response team responded, "Copy, Paper Dragon, Alpha Team en route, ETA four minutes."

NYPD sergeant Tom Walsh lived in a nearby Cape Cod at the corner of Holly and Sparkill.

As Walsh turned onto Sparkill Avenue with his dog, Winston, he saw a sight he never expected to see in his Staten Island neighborhood. Yes, a terrorist attack in Manhattan was plausible where he was assigned, to the Fifth Precinct, which served Chinatown, Little Italy, and the Bowery. But here in Staten Island? He was shocked—but only for a second.

"Home, boy, go," he said to his dog, dropping the leash as he unholstered his Glock 17 Gen4. Because he was just walking his dog he had only the single magazine in the Glock, but that would give him seventeen rounds.

Walsh saw three men in black with automatic weapons firing on the Sparkill Avenue house. He ran to a parked car and crouched, sliding his thumb to take the safety off, then glanced over the car's rear fender to gain situational awareness.

It was a mess. Smoke covered the front of the house as three men sprayed it with automatic fire. There wasn't a window on the house that wasn't shot out at this point, and the CIA's safe-house-reinforced front door looked like the surface of the moon it had taken so many rounds.

Walsh sighted his Glock and fired five shots before claiming his first target.

The second assailant, upon seeing his partner hit, immediately spun around and let loose with a full auto burst from his G-1. Glass showered down on Walsh as the windows of the car he was using for cover exploded.

Walsh needed to move. He decided to run to the car parked in the driveway of the house directly across from the safe house.

As he ran, Walsh fired another five rounds for cover.

Suddenly he felt a burning sensation in his right leg, causing him to lose his balance and fall. Walsh had been hit in his right calf.

As he crumpled to the ground, he pulled himself toward the car in the driveway for cover. He looked down at his leg and knew it wasn't good, but at least it hadn't hit the bone.

Turning their attention back to the Sparkill house, the assailants continued to shower the front of the house with automatic fire. That's when they drew their first victim.

Chris Dunbar was returning fire when he was hit. The first shot grazed the top of his head, but a second shot hit his right shoulder. Dunbar was down and losing a lot of blood.

As he fell he called, "I'm hit. I'm hit." That call not only alerted Ludovic but also went out over the CIA radio.

Seeing Dunbar down and not being a trained agent, Ludovic retreated to the basement door. He opened it and backed down the stairs. In the basement he found McMahon, La Rue, and the CIA cyberengineers huddled in the corner with the lights out and terrified expressions on their faces.

The engineers asked Ludovic, "Where are the guns?"

"They're upstairs. We can't get to them. Dunbar is down." Ludovic aimed his rifle toward the top of the stairs.

Alpha Team was still 120 seconds out, but as Marines say, "they were cocked, locked, and ready to rock."

The two assailants approached the front door of the house and kicked it in after firing on its hinges and lock. As they entered the house, they passed by Dunbar, who had passed out from loss of blood. One kicked the SCAR away from his body. The second assailant was pointing his weapon at Dunbar, ready to shoot him again to ensure he was dead, but was distracted by a call from his partner: "Leave him, they're in the basement. Remember, we want the woman alive."

They found the basement door and took up positions on either side of the entrance. The leader signaled to his partner, who grabbed a small-round grenade-like device from his vest.

He flung the door open, pulled the pin on the grenade, held it for a second, and then threw it down the basement stairs. It was a flashbang, intended to stun the occupants in the basement.

The lead assailant raised his G-1 to let loose a clip worth of bullets down the stairs.

As the assailant raised his weapon to fire, someone yelled, "Hey."

Sergeant Tom Walsh, leaning on the frame of the front door, held his Glock in both hands and was already sighted on the head of the G-1-wielding assailant.

The assailant turned to respond to Walsh's cry. It was the last move he would ever make.

Walsh fired two shots—both head shots that found their mark.

As the remaining assailant also spun to fire, Walsh was abruptly grabbed from behind and pulled out of the doorway by two members of Alpha Team. At the same time a red dot appeared on the forehead of the third assailant. An Alpha Team sniper set up across the street fired a 7.62mm round, causing the head of the third assailant to explode.

In a cool voice the sniper called, "Target neutralized."

Walsh looked at the two Alpha Team members who had grabbed him and said, "I'm on the job, NYPD, I'm on the job."

The Alpha Team swept into the house. Two started to work on Dunbar, who was down and unconscious.

"In the basement," said Walsh, pointing the way. "In the basement."

The people in the basement were still incapacitated, unable to hear or respond to the calls from the CIA response team. They all lay motionless, deaf and blinded, awaiting their demise.

One of the Alpha Team was attending to Dunbar and radioed for an ambulance. Ironically, help would come from their host, FDNY Engine 160 and Rescue Company 5.

Another Alpha Team member started to work on Walsh's leg, asking him who he was.

"Sergeant Tom Walsh, NYPD badge number 2077."

Alpha Team was yelling, "CIA, the house is secure. CIA, the house is secure." It was a dangerous time, as the people in the basement couldn't hear and Ludovic was still holding his SCAR automatic weapon. The last thing anyone wanted was for Ludovic to shoot a CIA agent securing the house.

It took a good five minutes before the CIA ventured down the basement stairs. What helped was the sirens and horns of Ladder 160—the sounds were loud enough that La Rue, McMahon, and the techs could actually hear them.

Still yelling, the agents slowly descended the stairs, yelling, "CIA, don't shoot, CIA."

The attack was over—it had failed. The Saudi security team pursuing La Rue was defeated and the NYPD had proven once again that they were, in fact, New York's Finest.

Kristin McMahon had just finished briefing Lisa Collins on the Staten Island attack, which was timely because Collins in turn was called to brief the president's chief of staff.

On a secure line from the White House, Chief of Staff Spencer asked, "Is everyone safe?"

"Our agent is in critical but stable condition. The NYPD sergeant might be released as early as tonight," answered Collins.

"That's good. The president will want briefs on both to make calls to their families," Spencer added.

"Already in the works," Collins answered. "La Rue was the target," she added.

"You're sure about that?"

"One hundred percent. The shooters were Saudis with ties to Sheik Rahman's son. We're airlifting La Rue, McMahon, and the cyberteam out of McGuire AFB within the hour. They'll land at Andrews and we will bring them to Langley."

"How are they?"

"I just got off the phone with both. They're okay, considering. But it hasn't all sunk in yet. We'll need to monitor them over the next couple of weeks," said Collins.

"And Ludovic? What's his status?"

"Well, he's also pretty shook up, as you can imagine. They all are. Not to mention our cyberengineers. Regarding Ludovic, we're putting him under an assumed name with a protection detail at the Waldorf and we'll bring his girlfriend to him. That should help. La Rue said she had Ludovic leaning on immigrating to the US, but that was before the attack. We'll have to see how he processes all of this," Collins said.

"Now, what about Deadeye?" asked Spencer.

"It's ready. Fortunately, the team had finished their testing before the attack began. Our folks in Langley have confirmed that it works," replied Collins.

"No issues?"

"None that we know. We just need Goh to insert our back door into the North Korean networks, once he does that we'll be able to load and execute the hack on the president's order," said Collins.

"Thank you, Director. I'll brief the president," said Spencer, which was Collins's cue to end the call.

"By the way, the other day I told Ron and Sterling that you would be taking a much lower profile in the campaign," said the president.

They had just finished dinner and the children were either working on their homework or chatting online with their friends, so the first couple had some time in the den to themselves.

"And what was their reaction? I'm sure they weren't happy with that news."

"No, they weren't, but they knew well enough not to show it. I told them you would only be making five campaign appearances. Three at the convention, the Al Smith dinner, and then on election night."

"Andy, only five? I said I didn't want to hit the campaign trail with you, but I can do more than that," replied Kennedy, almost alarmed.

"I know, but I wanted to set a low bar with them so when we decide on your involvement it will be more than they expected. Managing expectations," said the president.

"Andy, I think I can do a campaign event every month. I don't think that would be too much. But I don't want to involve the kids other than at the convention and election night. We are agreed on that, correct?"

"Totally," said the president.

"You know what I fantasize about?" said Kennedy next.

"Me?" said the president with a big smile.

"That's not what I'm talking about," she said with a laugh.

"No, what I fantasize about is our place on Eighty-Second Street in Brooklyn. Going back to living a normal life. Anonymously. Being able to attend a teachers' night at the kids' school without having a Secret Service detail. I dream of not having to worry that the outfit I wore today, I wore last week. I think about being able to take the kids out to dinner or shopping without planning it three weeks in advance," said the first lady.

"Hon, we're doing some very important work," chided the president.

"I know, Andy, but I yearn to go back to the days before the White House. 'So was I once myself a swinger of birches. And so I dream of going back to be,'" said Kennedy with a smile.

The president, who also loved Robert Frost, didn't hesitate and smiled, saying, "But we have promises to keep, and miles to go before we sleep."

CHAPTER THIRTEEN

The sun was shining brightly, which was apropos for the Day of the Sun celebration on this Sunday, April 15, in North Korea.

As planned, General Goh was hosting his son along with his classmates for a tour of the Namp'o naval headquarters.

"Hwan, introduce me to your classmates," said the general as the group of thirteen-year-olds were escorted into the general's large office.

After a welcome and a short speech, the general said, "Flag Lieutenant Yong will now show you our Operations Center. Then I will join you to answer questions and sample some refreshments before I must leave for P'yŏngyang," said the general.

The Day of the Sun celebration was always a busy time, and this one, with the test missile, would be even more so.

After taking some questions from the group, the general bade them farewell. Next, he spent a few minutes with his wife. Goh didn't know when or where he would next see his wife or sons. It was an emotional good-bye.

The drive to P'yŏngyang was forty miles long, but Goh made it in less than thirty minutes, as his driver used the car's lights to clear their way through traffic.

Before Goh left, he went into the Missile Command Center and inserted the memory stick the South Korean agent had given him earlier.

As the memory stick went active, alarms went off in Langley, indicating that a back door had just been established into the North Korean network.

Arriving in the North Korean capital just before noon and the start of the official ceremonies, Goh was ushered into President Paek's office to review the plan for the missile test.

"General, is everything in order?" Paek asked.

"Yes Mr. President, we are ready to launch on your command," replied Goh.

"And we're targeting the US aircraft carrier in the East China Sea?"

"That is correct, Mr. President. The US carrier is approximately twelve hundred miles south of P'yŏngyang, within the fifteen-hundred-nautical-mile range of the DF-26."

"Once launched, how long will it take for the missile to reach the Americans?" Paek asked.

"Mr. President, given the distance, plus calculating time for the missile to attain its peak velocity of Mach 7, the missile will reach the Americans approximately twenty minutes after launch," said Goh.

"Goh, show me the location of our launchers," ordered Paek.

Goh booted up his laptop. "Mr. President, here are the locations. We plan to fire missile 174, a test missile with a dummy warhead, from Namp'o," explained Goh.

"And the missile equipped with the warhead? That's 188, correct?" questioned Paek.

"That is correct, sir; 188 is the special. It is located just south of Namp'o," said Goh, highlighting its location on the screen.

Just then an aide to President Paek entered his opulent office to remind the president that he needed to start making his way to the official reviewing stand.

Paek nodded and then turned to the general. "It's 12:05. At 12:20 I order you to launch missile 174 at the Americans. Understood?"

General Goh saluted and repeated the order: "Mr. President, you have directed me to fire test missile 174 at 12:20, targeting the American aircraft carrier operating in the East China Sea. I will execute your command as ordered, sir."

The 560-foot *Florida* was twenty miles off the coast of North Korea near Namp'o, where the crew's mission plan called for them to loiter just under the surface awaiting the detection of the launch of the North Korean DF-26 missile.

Captain Dutch Reagan issued the commands. "Right standard rudder, ahead slow, bring us up to one hundred feet, quietly, OOD."

Based on intelligence they had received from Washington, the *Florida* expected to detect the DF-26 launch at any moment, and Reagan wanted to be near the surface when the launch was detected.

At a shallow depth, the *Florida* was above the thermal layer of the ocean, creeping along the warmer surface water.

More than a thousand miles to the south, Admiral Fraser on the *John C. Stennis* had given the order an hour and a half earlier to launch sixteen F/A-18E/Fs of CVW-9 in support of Commander Bartlett's plan, now called Operation Shogun.

First to catapult off the mighty *Stennis* was CAG Sara "Clutch" Cunningham, flying VFA-41's aircraft number 100, which was known as the CAG bird. Jets whose numbers ended in a double zero were the aircraft that either the CO of the squadron or the commander of the air wing (CAG) flew. Each of the sixteen Super Hornets had large *NG*s on their vertical stabilizers, indicating that they were part of Carrier Air Wing 9 attached to the *Stennis.*

Following in rapid succession were three more F/A-18Fs of the Black Aces, call sign Fast Eagle, after which four F/A-18Fs of VFA-14, the Tophatters, call sign Camelot, launched, followed by four of the single-seat F/A-18Es of VFA-151, the Vigilantes, call sign Switch.

The mission called for the fighters of Operation Shogun to take up station five hundred miles from the *Stennis* to provide a protective barrier combat air patrol, or BARCAP, ready to fire their Sidewinders at the inbound DF-26 should Torchlight fail or miss.

In support of the mission, Fraser had also ordered the launch of an E-2C from VAW-117, the Wallbangers, to provide airspace battle management command and control.

In addition, four F/A-18E tankers of VFA-97, the Warhawks (which used Warhawk as their call sign), carrying added fuel stores, were airborne to provide fuel to the twelve fighters of the strike force as needed. With a range of two thousand nautical miles, the Super Hornets might not need to tank, depending on how much fuel they consumed during their BARCAP. But CAG Cunningham, like all CAGs, didn't want her fliers worrying about their fuel states in the heat of a combat mission. Should the need arise, Cunningham's pilots would hit the 20 button on their radios and call one of the Warhawks to tank their thirsty fighter.

Earlier that morning Admiral Fraser had issued the order for the ships of the *Stennis* Strike Group to take up positions at ranges varying from fifty to eighty miles from the flagship to provide maximum protection from any anti-ship ballistic missile attack. Meanwhile the *Connecticut,* one of the Navy's most capable fast-attack submarines, had taken up station behind the *Florida,* trailing her by approximately three miles, riding shotgun. If a North Korean submarine so much as entered the area, the *Connecticut* was under orders to take it out—without warning.

On that late Saturday evening in Washington, twelve and a half hours earlier than P'yŏngyang, President Andrew Russell and his assembled staff were in the White House Situation Room. In attendance were the president's Joint Chiefs and the directors of the CIA, NSA, and FBI, along with the president's chief of staff, as well as the secretaries of defense and state.

On board the *United States,* a message was received to prepare to get under way at a moment's notice.

Captain Clifford had anticipated the notice and had his chief engineer ready all of the new gas turbine engines on the *United States.* In addition, Clifford had his deckhands single up the bow and stern lines that kept the *United States* tied to the pier. He also had his crew members standing by, ready to retract the two gangways on his command.

Clifford and his Chinese counterpart, who knew the waters of Namp'o harbor, were both on the bridge waiting for the signal to depart.

General Goh's wife and two sons had been on the *Soft Wind* for a little over an hour and had traveled approximately twenty miles northwest of Namp'o.

The time was just a little before noon when the captain of the *Soft Wind* cut his engines. The captain and his crew of three were all South

Korean agents participating in the plan to extricate Goh's family from North Korea.

"Con, Sonar. Hull-popping sounds coming from Sierra One," called out the sonar operator on the *Connecticut*, which was operating eighteen miles to the south of the *Soft Wind*.

The CO of the *Connecticut* conferenced with his XO, saying, "We're sure Sierra One is the Chinese sub picking up the package?"

The XO called out, "Sonar, Con. Confirm Sierra One."

"Con, Sonar. The BSY-2 has classed Sierra One as a Type 041 Chinese attack sub," responded the sonar officer.

Hearing that, the CO went to the radio station and said to COMPACFLT, "Papa Juliet has detected the laundry being picked up."

On board the Chinese attack submarine *Deagal*, the captain ordered the sub to surface, rising within one hundred feet of the *Soft Wind*. Once on the surface the *Deagal* sent over an inflatable raft to pick up General Goh's family. The transfer took fifteen minutes, after which the *Deagal* disappeared under the blue-green waters of the Yellow Sea.

The time was now 12:18 P'yŏngyang time.

General Goh was in the North Korean version of the Situation Room along with the head of the SSD as well as the general of the army and the minister of defense.

Goh was on a videoconference with his missile command post in Namp'o. "By order of our president I order you to fire missile 174."

As a fail-safe mechanism, General Goh's launch order needed to be confirmed and repeated by another member of the president's staff.

General of the Army Sun echoed Goh's command: "This is General Sun. I order you to launch missile 174."

At the center in Namp'o, the North Korean version of a colonel, the most senior officer on duty, barked orders to his staff to initiate the missile launch. Because the missile would launch from a mobile platform, there were two modes of launch initiation. The first was an automated launch initiated from Namp'o, the second a manual process implemented by the missile crew on-site. This test shot involved the former option—an automated launch.

The missile operator lifted the plastic lockout guard and positioned his thumb on the red launch button. Before depressing it, the operator looked at the colonel one more time for confirmation.

Seeing the indecision in his operator's action, the colonel barked, "Launch the missile."

In response, the missile operator immediately depressed the red commit button and then pushed the launch button. There wasn't any more to it than that. Other than the size of its warheads and its missile technology, the rest of North Korea's command and communication structure was very rudimentary. If not for the brutal and unforgiving level of discipline they were forced to maintain for President Paek, their command and control systems resembled the organizational sophistication of a 1980s McDonald's restaurant.

A video image of missile launcher 174 came up on the main screen. Billows of smoke could be seen coming from the exhaust ports of the DF-26 missile as the ignition sequence began.

In the next ten seconds, the thirty-five-foot missile started to lift off its launch.

Nineteen seconds later the sonar officer on the *Florida* called the bridge, "Sir, SPY-6 has detected a missile launch. Starting track on Vampire 1, BRAA 101, 160, rock, 1,000, 120." The sonar officer, who was also responsible for the radar, was employing the Navy's nomenclature for tracking using the BRAA method, which stood for bearing, range, altitude, and aspect.

Dutch Reagan acknowledged the sonar officer's call. "Copy, Sonar. OOD, all stop, surface, surface, surface. Chief Engineer, prepare for maximum power on Torchlight. Weps, sync Torchlight with SPY-6."

The OOD repeated the captain's order. The chief of the boat, standing behind the navigation and diving petty officers, was repeating the order, "Surface, surface, surface," as he hit the alarm that would let the entire crew know they were surfacing.

As the *Florida* started its ascent, the chief engineer calmly instructed his team of engineers, "Come up on the power. Let me know when we reach max power."

Because the *Florida* was at a depth of only one hundred feet, it took less than thirty seconds for the sail to break the surface.

"Sir, all reactors are online. We're producing eighty-five percent output and we will be at one hundred percent within a minute. You have the power to fire Torchlight now," relayed the chief engineer to the bridge.

As that was happening, almost a thousand miles away, on board the USS *Mobile Bay* (CG-53), the Ticonderoga-class cruiser responsible for monitoring the airspace around the strike group, its BMD (ballistic missile defense) screens also started to light up.

"This is Red Crown on guard. Vampire, vampire, vampire. Red Crown is tracking an inbound ASBM BRAA, 017, 1,215, splat, 2,000." The *Mobile Bay's* BRAA call indicated that the DF-26 was 1,215 miles away from the *Stennis*. The splat call indicated that the missile had not yet reached Mach speed, and its altitude was two thousand feet.

Rear Admiral Fraser immediately headed to the *Stennis*'s Combat Direction Center, or CDC, the nerve center of the ship when it was either under attack or getting ready to attack.

Seconds after RADM Fraser entered the CDC, he was joined by Captain Ryan, his XO, the admiral's chief of staff, and the commodore of the DESRON, a captain who commanded the destroyer squadron that made up the bulk of the *Stennis* Strike Group's surface ships.

In the dark of the CDC, the group of officers focused on the large screens above its team of operators.

The CDC officer, or combat control officer, relayed information as it came in from Red Crown or from any of the other assets in the strike group.

"Sir, Red Crown has confirmed the launch. We have an inbound missile launched from Namp'o accelerating and increasing altitude. SPY-1D says it's tracking the *Stennis*. Confidence is high. I repeat, confidence is high."

RADM Fraser turned to Ryan and his staff captain. "Captain, sound general quarters, missile, and order the strike group to do the same."

"Aye, aye, admiral," Captain Ryan acknowledged, then turned to his XO. "Sound general quarters, missile."

The XO relayed the order to the bridge of the *Stennis*, where the bosun's mate sounded the alarm. Seconds later the entire crew of the *John C. Stennis* jumped to life as they ran to their action stations.

The captain of the *Stennis* next spoke with the carrier's air traffic control center, or CATCC, to instruct them to inform the E-2C to vector the BARCAP toward the inbound Vampire 1 track.

On the bridge of the *United States* the radio operator handed Captain Clifford a note with the message "Execute Vanguard."

Clifford, displaying the typical British coolness, simply picked up his handset and ordered, "Retract the gangways. Deck crew, slip the lines."

Clifford called to his chief engineer: "Chief, prepare for revolutions."

Clifford and his Chinese counterpart went to the starboard piloting bridge. Checking that the mooring lines were now free, Clifford grabbed the joystick and engaged the bow thrusters while at the same time ringing up "slow astern" on his four propellers. With that, the enormous mass that was the *United States* started to back away from the Namp'o pier, to the amazement and consternation of the North Korean security force that was stationed there.

Simultaneous to all this, in Washington the president and his staff in the Sit Room were notified by Colorado Springs as they detected the launch of the DF-26.

Also on the screen in the Sit Room were icons indicating the locations of all the US Navy assets in the area.

"Mr. President," said Admiral Johnson, "the mission brief calls for *Florida* to fire Torchlight at the DF-26 any moment now, sir."

The president simply nodded and rubbed his right index and ring fingers across his lips as everyone in the room kept their focus on the screen.

The E-2C orbiting in the East China Sea issued, "Shogun, Closeout, inbound Vampire 1, 015, 1025, rock, 5,000, 2200."

CAG Clutch Cunningham responded for the Shogun flight: "Closeout, Shogun 1, copies."

"Shogun 1 to Shogun flight, come right 015, climb to angels 38, copy."

On board the *Connecticut* the sonar officer called out, "Sir, Papa Kilo is on the surface. She's stopped, sir," said the sonar officer, using the *Florida* call sign.

"Sonar, Con. Is the sonar and radar clear?" asked the CO.

"That's affirm, sir, no submerged or surface contacts within twenty miles of Papa Kilo. Other than Sierra 1."

Sierra 1 referred to the Chinese submarine *Deagal*, which had picked up General Goh's family.

On board the *Florida*, Jim Hartel was in the control room observing the action with his laptop plugged into the *Florida's* LAN so he could monitor in real time the readings coming from SPY-6, the Bechtel reactors, and, of course, Torchlight.

"Con, Weps. Torchlight is ready for Snapshot. SPY-6 has painted Vampire 1, sir."

"Chief Engineer, what is our power output?" asked Reagan.

"Sir, we're ranging from ninety-eight to one hundred percent. We're got the power to fire, sir," replied the chief engineer.

"Mr. Hartel, is everything checking out on your screens?" asked Reagan.

"Good to go, sir," said Hartel, never looking up.

Captain Dutch Reagan spoke into his handset. "Weps, Con. Commit Torchlight, Vampire 1, Snapshot, Snapshot, Snapshot."

The weapons officer, hearing the CO's command, flipped the cover to his master arm button and depressed it. Two seconds later he got green lights on the Torchlight control panel and the system was enabled to fire. Next, he depressed the trigger on his firing mechanism and called, "Con, Weps. Snapshot." He paused for a second and then added, "Snapshot, Snapshot," as the *Florida* fired two more bursts from Torchlight.

In the engineering spaces on the *Florida*, the control circuitry of Torchlight began to route the output from the A1B reactors, amplified by the EDFAs, to the Torchlight laser gun, which had the targeting coordinates supplied by SPY-6.

A blinding light of powerful photons emitted from the laser gun in a tightly columnated beam skyward. The e nergy p ulse lasted only two seconds for each depression of the weapons officer's trigger. Three powerful pulses were now headed skyward toward the DF-26.

Torchlight tracked and targeted the DF-26 so quickly that the South Korean THAAD batteries had no time to fire. Not to mention that the DF-26 was at the outer limits of THAAD's 120-mile range.

General Goh, along with General Sun, the chief of the SSD, and the minister of defense, were all watching the track of the missile when a flash of light appeared on their screen where the DF-26 had been.

"What was that?" demanded General Sun.

The missile operators in Namp'o, who were online, began to issue control commands to the missile at sea. Moments later the missile commander called out, "We have lost contact with missile 174." "Sir," responded the missile commander, "missile 174 is no longer proceeding on course. It has either self-destructed or it has been destroyed by the enemy."

Half a world away, in the Sit Room, the mood was vastly different as the group saw the flash of light on their screen.

"Mr. President," said Admiral Johnson, listening to a headset he was wearing, "we have a good kill. Vampire 1 is down. I repeat, Vampire 1 is down."

There were no cheers or applause in the Sit Room—after all, the mission was still not complete.

The same information was witnessed in the CDC on the *Stennis* and on screens of the E-2C Hawkeye, as well as on the screens of the USS *Mobile Bay*, the Red Crown cruiser responsible for the protecting the strike group's air space, and, of course, the *Florida*.

CO Reagan turned to Jim Hartel. "Congratulations, Mr. Hartel. Torchlight has its first confirmed enemy kill."

Hartel just nodded, then let out a sigh of relief. After years of work and hundreds of man-hours of effort put in by his team, Torchlight had finally delivered in combat.

Hartel felt the intense pride and satisfaction that comes only from a job well done. As he began to smile, applause and yelling broke out throughout the *Florida* as the CO informed his sailors that they had just defeated the North Korean missile. The Death Star of the Fleet had scored a combat kill. Every officer present on the con of the *Florida*, including the chief of the boat, slapped Hartel on the back. It was a special moment, one Hartel and the crew of the *Florida* would remember for the rest of their careers.

The *United States* had just completed its pirouette corkscrew maneuver approximately three ship lengths from where she had been docked.

Captain Clifford, now back on the main bridge with his Chinese captain, ordered, "All ahead full, set your course 345 degrees smartly."

The Chinese master nodded as Clifford called out his order.

Immediately the four five-bladed screws of the Atlantic Blue Riband holder for the fastest crossing started to churn up a massive amount of water.

It took only about forty-five seconds for a rooster tail to develop out the back of the stern of the mighty liner as its speed increased quickly.

Clifford next called, "Come left to 281 degrees."

The Chinese captain was now running back and forth to each bridge wing to check his position. He cried, "Captain, five degrees to starboard, now."

Clifford nodded to the crew member manning the wheel.

The *United States* was at eighteen knots and accelerating quickly.

"Captain, port eleven degrees now," yelled the Chinese captain.

Clifford's number two reported, "Captain, a North Korean Coast Guard boat is readying to leave its mooring."

Clifford called, "All ahead emergency full."

"Aye, aye, Captain, all ahead emergency full, indicate 135 revolutions," called his helmsman.

"Now," yelled the Chinese captain, "hard over to port."

The helmsman immediately started to turn his wheel rapidly to the left.

The *United States* was at twenty-eight knots and still accelerating, creating a huge wake of brown water caused by the mud being stirred by the mighty liner's props as they spun at an amazing speed only a few feet from the bottom of the harbor.

The Chinese captain said to Clifford, "One more turn and we'll be out of the harbor and clear to the sea. Now come right ninety degrees," yelled the Chinese captain, who for all intents and purposes was now in command due to his knowledge of the waters.

In the Sit Room the director of the CIA said, "Mr. President, we're ready to execute Deadeye on your command."

The president surveyed the room, looking at his Joint Chiefs, his directors of intelligence, and his chief of staff. Spencer Sterling gave a small nod, which was the only movement in the room. The president paused for a second to absorb the enormity of his next order, then turned to Director Collins. "Director, you have a go on Deadeye. Execute."

Director Collins, who had the CIA Cyber Attack Unit on her handset, spoke clearly and loudly enough for everyone in the room to hear, "You have a go on Deadeye. Repeat, you are go on Deadeye. Execute."

At the Langley Cyber Operations Center, only twelve miles from the White House, operators input the commands that would deliver the Deadeye payload.

Within seconds the Deadeye code was penetrating North Korean networks and infiltrating their silo-based Hwansong-14 ICBMs, which were known in the west as the Mars-14s.

As condition codes were received by the Deadeye code, the operators in Langley could monitor each North Korean missile as it was neutralized. Deadeye was doing its job.

In the span of only a few minutes, every offensive missile in North Korea was rendered impotent. That is, all but the mobile DF-26 launchers, which were connected to a brand-new network, one not detected by or accessible to Deadeye. The mobile DF-26 launchers were connected by a wireless network that employed a military version of a commercial VPN, or virtual packet network.

"Do you see what I am seeing?" an operator in Langley said to the room full of colleagues. "There's another network. A wireless network. That wasn't on our list. I'm starting to hack it but it's probably going to take thirty minutes to jailbreak it."

Getting briefed via her headset, Director Collins asked, "What does this mean to us?"

"Ma'am, it means that Deadeye isn't able to infect the missiles on that network. They remain active and under North Korean control," said the lead analyst.

"Which missiles?" asked Collins.

"One moment, ma'am," said the operator. After a minute he said, "Director Collins, it is the network that controls their DF-26s."

"How long until we can infect them?"

"Thirty minutes, ma'am."

Collins turned to the president. "Mr. President, we have a problem."

CHAPTER FOURTEEN

In P'yŏngyang, General Sun yelled, "General Goh, you must inform President Paek of your failure and incompetence. He must be told immediately." Goh knew that Sun was no fan of his and had expected such an outburst.

But in truth, this was in keeping with the North Korean military code, which called for taking responsibility and sharing both good and bad news with their leader as soon as it occurred.

General Goh nodded. "Yes, it is my responsibility and mine alone. I will tell our president immediately." He left the control room to find Paek on the reviewing stand. Goh knew Paek's temper well and expected an immediate and emotional reaction to the news.

On board the *Florida* one of the assistant engineers called to the chief engineer, "Chief, take a look at the filter readings."

The chief engineer walked over to the assistant engineer's station and saw that the seawater intake filters were registering only fourteen percent throughput, meaning eighty-six percent of their filtering capacity was no longer available.

"Ben, show me the intake filter readings from an hour ago," the chief requested.

The petty officer picked up the clipboard next to the dials and replied, "Sir, an hour ago we were at seventy-eight percent."

The chief engineer looked alarmed as he took the clipboard from the petty officer to verify the data. It was correct. The filters were rapidly becoming clogged. At this rate they would be completely clogged within minutes.

The CE went over to his master control panel, where he checked the salinity and seawater temperature readings and noted they were both way above average.

The chief engineer muttered out loud, "We must have surfaced into a sea of seaweed or algae. Jesus Christ."

The chief engineer then checked the power readings on his six Bechtel reactors. They were all still performing to spec.

The chief engineer called the bridge. "Con, Engineering. Sir, our seawater filters are rapidly becoming clogged."

"What do you mean, Chief?" replied the captain.

"Sir, our salinity and water temps are way above normal. As a result, our filters are sucking in a ton of algae and it is clogging the Torchlight filters. We won't be able to take in enough water to cool Torchlight," said the chief.

Hearing that, Hartel toggled to the screen that monitored the reactor readings.

The captain replied, "Chief, we're above the thermal and we surfaced. Of course the salinity and water temps will be higher than normal."

"Not like this, sir. This sea we are in must have an above-average amount of plankton and biologics. Sir, it's clogging our filters as we speak."

The captain continued, "Chief, what's the impact?"

"Sir, we won't be able to cool the A1B reactors. Without the reactors, Torchlight will be offline. We need to get out of this area right away and then replace the filters. We need to find some blue water fast, sir."

"Chief, how long to change the filters?"

"About an hour, sir."

Reagan turned to his OOD. "I need a speed course to get us out of this area. We're staying on the surface."

The OOD spoke with the navigator for a few seconds and came back. "Sir, we recommend come left full to three hundred." Out of habit the navigator added, "The sounding is twelve hundred feet."

Reagan, not hesitating, commanded, "Left full rudder, ahead flank."

It didn't take more than a second for the control room crew to start repeating and yelling commands.

The *Florida* was going to get out of this East China Sea's version of the Sargasso Sea right now. The sub kicked up a big wake as it accelerated to its top surface speed of twenty-eight knots.

"OOD, call out water salinity and temperature readings every two minutes. Let me know when we hit blue water," ordered Reagan.

Hartel said, "Captain, I'd like permission to go to Engineering to work with the CE."

"Granted."

As the *Florida* started to get out of the area, so did the submerged *Connecticut*, staying close to its charge as ordered.

Captain Reagan next radioed RADM Fraser that Torchlight was offline due to the filter issue. The estimate was that it would be back online in a little over an hour.

RADM Fraser noted it and ordered Reagan to get Torchlight back online ASAP.

With Torchlight offline, Fraser turned to the CO of the *Stennis*. "Captain, Torchlight's offline. Alert the BARCAP and let them know we need to keep them on station longer. Have them hit the tankers as needed."

General Goh made his way to the reviewing stand and informed the president's aide he needed a few minutes with the president.

The aide relayed the message to President Paek, who nodded and left the reviewing stand, telling his vice president to take over the official duties.

On his way to meet with Goh, Paek was informed that the *United States* was sailing out of the harbor as they spoke.

Goh began, "Mr. President, I have no excuse. The test firing of missile 174 was a failure. It self-destructed shortly after takeoff. I do not yet have an explanation for what happened."

"I have an explanation," said Paek. "Goh, you're incompetent. Not only did you fail in this mission, but you have let the people of North Korea down. On this great national holiday. Goh, I want an investigation to begin immediately into the cause of this failure."

Just then the president's aide came in with an urgent message for the president.

There was a priority call coming from the Chinese president, Wei Zhang.

Paek left immediately, cutting short the number of insults he could shower on Goh over the failed missile test.

President Paek entered the North Korean version of the Sit Room, ordering General Sun and his ministers out as he got on the phone with President Zhang.

The Chinese president began speaking through his interpreter, "President Paek, thank you for taking my call. I have a serious matter to inform you about. All of your missiles have been compromised. Your Hwasong-14s are no longer under your control. You and your family have one hour to leave the country or face a combined military response from China and the United States."

Paek did not respond as the weight of Zhang's words set in. Then Paek said, "Who are you to tell me what to do?" Paek's volume and blood pressure were rising as he continued. "I will launch all my missiles and you will pay for your lack of loyalty."

"President Paek, perhaps you did not understand me. Your missiles are no longer under your control. They are useless to you. You must leave the country immediately. We know you have a compound in the Philippines. You must go there now. China will guarantee your and your family's safe passage, but you must leave now."

Paek just responded with a curse word and hung up.

He called his staff back into the room and started to shout orders.

General Goh immediately connected with the missile control center. "What is the status of our Hwasong-14s?"

The missile commander replied, "Sir, I cannot explain it, but none of our Hwasong-14 missiles are responding to our commands. I cannot tell you why, sir."

Out of control, Paek now yelled, "What missiles do we still have control over?"

"Mr. President, we still have control over our mobile-based missiles. Sir, the DF-26 missile network is still responding."

Paek knew he had only one "special" DF-26 remaining. He took a minute and then gave the command to his generals: "Ready missile 188 for launch. Target the American carrier group."

Paek then turned to his aide and quietly ordered him to get his family, who were on the reviewing stand, and move them immediately to his helicopter. Paek also ordered his aide to ready his jet.

Paek paused and entered a text message into his phone. He then turned his attention back to Goh, lashing out for the loss of control of the missiles and for the earlier failed missile launch. Paek threatened to relieve Goh of his command as he left the Sit Room.

Paek then joined his family as he executed his emergency evacuation plan. They would leave North Korea via a private jet and go to an island that had been purchased through a shell company years ago just for this sort of eventuality. The island was located in the northern part of the Philippines.

Before getting on his jet, Paek screamed at his generals, including Goh, "I order you to launch missile 188 now at the American carrier group. No one is authorized to countermand this order. Is that understood? Fire 188 now."

In the US Sit Room, the president was being updated by Director Collins. "Mr. President, we have confirmation that President Zhang has delivered our ultimatum to Paek. An update on Deadeye indicates we have successfully neutralized all silo-based missiles. The only missiles not neutralized at this point are the remaining Dong-Fengs."

"Good, good," said the president. "We can deal with any remaining DFs with Torchlight if we need to." Word had not yet reached the Sit Room that Torchlight was down.

With blue water ahead, Captain Clifford of the *United States* accelerated to the liner's top speed of thirty-five knots. The *United States*, the blue-ribbon record holder for the fastest Atlantic passage, still was a fast ship, given its sleek hull design and the fact that the retrofit had increased the output of its engines to more than three hundred thousand ship horsepower.

As the *United States* entered the Yellow Sea, unbeknownst to them they had picked up a shadow: a North Korean Sang-O diesel-electric submarine.

Before it sailed, the captain of the Sang-O had been given a direct order from President Paek himself. The order was if he received a text message with the Korean word *jae*, he was to immediately attack and sink the *United States* once in international waters.

The captain of the Sang-O, in command in his control room, had just been handed a piece of paper with the word *jae* on it.

The Sang-O was stationed eleven miles outside the harbor of Namp'o, bordering the twelve-mile line that demarked international waters. The captain of the Sang-O knew he couldn't keep up with the speedy liner, so instead he waited until the *United States* came into range.

In P'yŏngyang, the jet carrying President Paek and his family had already departed to take them to their secret compound.

Goh left the Sit Room for a moment to issue a text message with the code 1122334. That message would alert the team of Special Forces commandos that their mission was to commence. These commandos had arrived in P'yŏngyang on the *United States*. The eighty-member team of US Special Forces was joined by a team of twenty South Korean undercover agents, who were also in P'yŏngyang attending the Day of the Sun celebration.

The combined Special Ops teams started to move toward the Generally Assembly building, where the North Korean Sit Room was located. With everyone focused on the Day of the Sun parade, the

Special Ops team met with minimal resistance as they pressed their surgical attack on the General Assembly. Their goal was to quietly and quickly gain access to the Sit Room and to detain the head of the SSD, General Sun, and the rest of the senior members attending the Day of the Sun celebration.

After the Special Ops team secured the Sit Room, General Goh reentered the Sit Room and got on the radio with his Namp'o missile commander, saying, "President Paek canceled the order for the launch of missile 188. You are ordered to stand down."

The SSD had an asset embedded in the Missile Command Center. Hearing Goh's new order, the SSD agent drew his semiautomatic pistol and yelled, "I am an SSD agent and I am assuming command of this center. General Goh is a traitor as is anyone who cooperates with him."

The missile commander jumped from his seat to confront the SSD agent and was shot point-blank in the chest.

Wielding his pistol, the SSD agent yelled, "Who's next?"

No one remaining in the center had any appetite to challenge the SSD agent as he added, "Launch missile 188 as ordered by President Paek."

The remaining operators quickly turned their attention to performing the tasks necessary to launch the missile.

The Special Ops team administered a strong sedative to the members of Paek's cabinet to better manage the situation. Now Goh was the only member of Paek's staff still conscious and capable of issuing orders. But Goh knew he did not have control of the Missile Command Center.

General Goh tried to communicate to the Missile Command Center again, but the link had been broken from the Namp'o end.

Two minutes later, missile 188, the DF-26 "special," leapt into the North Korean air.

"This is Red Crown on Guard. We have detected the launch of a vampire. Vampire 2," called out the BMD operator on the USS *Mobile Bay*.

Similar calls were being made on the *Florida* and the *Connecticut*.

Brass Hat in Colorado Springs had also detected the launch and was now streaming data into the Sit Room.

"Mr. President, there's been another launch from Namp'o," said the chairman of the Joint Chiefs.

"Another DF-26?" asked the president.

"It appears so, Mr. President."

"Is *Florida* tracking it and ready to shoot it down with Torchlight?" asked the president.

Admiral Johnson was on his headset and was talking in an increasingly animated manner, which got the attention of everyone in the room.

"Admiral, what's going on?" demanded the president.

"Sir, Torchlight is down. They have clogged filters and can't take in enough water to cool the reactors that power Torchlight. It will take an hour to get Torchlight back online," added Johnson.

"What about THAAD? We can fire them, correct?" asked the president.

"Absolutely, sir, our stations in South Korea are tracking the DF-26 right now and are preparing to fire," replied Johnson.

"What's the flight time and target of the Dong-Feng?" the president asked.

"Sir, the DF-26 is tracking the *Stennis*. Estimated flight time twenty-two minutes."

"What about Deadeye? Can it help?"

"Sir, the missile is already in the air—Deadeye can't help," replied Collins.

"Gentlemen, options? What are our options?"

"Sir," began Admiral Johnson, "the *Stennis* has detected the launch, as has *Florida* and *Connecticut*. They'll be spoofing and jamming to the full extent possible. We need our THADD installations to knock down the DF-26, sir."

On board the *Stennis*, the CDC had detected the launch and knew that *Torchlight* was down.

Admiral Fraser said, "Tell the strike group to commence SP-JASHO."

"Have the E-2C direct our Shogun flight to intercept Vampire 2."

"Execute Battle Order Zulu," commanded Fraser.

In a matter of seconds, the USS *John C. Stennis* started to increase speed to accelerate beyond its official top speed of thirty-five knots.

Similarly, the other ships of the *Stennis* Strike Group increased speed and radically altered their course away from the *Stennis* at top speed, as set forth in the battle order. The Arleigh Burke destroyers of the group all were now nearing their top speeds of thirty-eight knots as every ship in the group ran for its life from the incoming North Korean missile.

The *Stennis* Strike Group had picked up the inbound Vampire 2 and was employing all their countermeasures, which included spoofing and jamming.

An urgent message was relayed to the Special Ops team in P'yŏngyang: "Can General Goh disarm or destroy the DF-26 missile?"

The commandos accompanying Goh asked him, and he replied, "I already tried once, but I will try again."

The conference link to the Missile Command Center had been disabled by the SSD agent who had taken over the center.

Goh didn't know the cell numbers of any of the operators, nor did he think they would answer their phones because the SSD agent would surely shoot them.

He could use their network and basically open an instant message chat with the operators. It wasn't brilliant, but it was the best he could come up with in that moment.

Goh sent an IM to the missile command group address. "This is General Goh. I order you to destroy missile 188. Initiate the self-destruct sequence."

There was no response.

Goh typed another message, "For the safety of your families and the future of our country, I order you to destroy missile 188."

A second later came back a message. "You're a traitor, Goh. The SSD will hunt you down and make you pay for your actions."

Goh turned to the South Korean agents, saying, "There is nothing that can be done on our end to defeat missile 188."

The agents relayed that response back through their channels. No one was surprised by the answer.

At the mouth of Namp'o harbor, the Sang-O loaded its firing solutions into torpedoes 1 and 2, opened their torpedo doors, and without hesitating fired at the *United States* as she came into range. The angle and range were all textbook—in a matter of two and a half minutes the captain of the Sang-O expected to hear an explosion.

"Con, Sonar. Sierra 1 is opening his torpedo doors," called the sonar operator of the SSN-777 USS *North Carolina*, a Virginia-class fast-attack submarine that President Russell had secretly ordered to escort the *United States* on its journey to Korea. The *North Carolina* had been shadowing the *United States* ever since it left Pearl Harbor and was also stationed at the mouth of Namp'o harbor waiting to join up on the escaping *United States*.

"Con, Sonar. Torpedo in the water. Sierra 1 just fired. Sir, a second torpedo has just been fired. Both torpedoes are tracking Alpha Panda, sir," called the sonar operator.

The skipper of the *North Carolina*, Frank Malfi, ordered, "Sonar, Con. Let me know when BSY-2 has a lock on Sierra 1."

"Con, Sonar. BSY-2 is locked, sir."

"Weps, Con. Load firing-point solutions into tubes 1 and 2 for Sierra 1."

Impatiently waiting to hear the reply, Malfi finally got the call. "Con, Weps, firing-point solutions loaded targeting Sierra 1, ready to fire on your command, sir."

Malfi ordered, "Open outer doors on 1 and 2. Fire 1. Fire 2."

The Sang-O was five miles from the *North Carolina* and well within the MK 48 torpedo's twenty-one-nautical-mile range. Traveling at fifty-five knots, the MK 48s would lock on and destroy the Sang-O, Sierra 1, in a little under five minutes.

The bigger challenge for the *North Carolina* was the need for it to intercept the two torpedoes that the Sang-O had just fired at the *United States*. The torpedoes would reach the *United States* in two minutes.

"Shogun flight, Closeout. Inbound Vampire 2, 010, 1000, rock, 2.5, Mach 3 and increasing. Your vector for intercept is 010," came the call from the orbiting E-2C Hawkeye that managed the airspace envelope for the strike group.

CAG Cunningham replied, "Copy, Closeout. Shoguns come right to 010, A Section take it upstairs to angels 44, B Section angels 46, and C Section angels 48. Master on Vampire 2."

The fl ight of tw elve F/ A-18E/Fs cl imbed to th eir va rious assigned altitudes as ordered by CAG. C Section, climbing to forty-eight thousand feet, would be near their maximum rated ceiling on a heading that would give them the best angle of attack to intercept the inbound Vampire 2.

In the fighter community, the preferred angle of attack was always to come in behind the target and fire a running-away shot. The issue now was that the F/A-18s were armed with AIM-9X Sidewinder missiles with a top speed of Mach 2.7, so the Shoguns couldn't make a running-away attack. The Sidewinders would never be able to catch the DF-26. Instead their only hope of shooting down the inbound Dong-Feng was a head-on attack—at the speed the DF-26 was traveling, Mach 7, it was going to be an extremely difficult shot.

The mission brief called for A Section of four F/A-18s, led by CAG Cunningham, to fire their AIM-9X Sidewinders from the head-on angle at the Dong-Feng. Then they would clear and the next four F/A-18Fs of VFA-14, the Camelots, making up the B Section, would roll in at a slightly higher altitude and fire again from a head-on approach.

Last would be the four single-seat F/A-18Es of VFA-151, call sign Switch, led by Commander Bartlett, in C Section, which would take their shot from the altitude of forty-eight thousand feet.

The key to Bartlett's plan—and this was crucial—would be to fire while the DF-26 was still ahead of the F/A-18s. If it passed them, the F/A-18s would never be able to shoot the DF-26 down. The trick was that the Shoguns must accurately lead the DF-26 as it approached.

"Shogun, Closeout, group, rock, 020, 425, 188,000, track south-east, Vampire 2."

The Shogun flight had picked up inbound Vampire 2 on their radars, causing them to signal a "commit" for the mission. With the commit issued, Shogun flight switched from broadcast to tactical control.

"Closeout, Shogun 1, commit," called CAG Cunningham.

B and C Sections pulled back and left on their sticks and broke from A Section so they could set up for their shots.

The E-2C provided another update: "Shoguns, Closeout, Vampire 2, BRAA 017, 8, rock, Mach 7, 22." The call meant the inbound DF-26 was eight miles away from the Shoguns at an altitude of twenty-two miles and flying at a speed of Mach 7, or approximately forty-five hundred knots.

The DF-26 would be on them in less than two minutes.

"Closeout copies, commit," came back the call; then: "Vampire 2, BRAA 027, 6, rock, Mach 7, 22."

"Shogun 1, target, single," came the immediate reply from the Shogun flight leader.

Shogun Section A flight moved into a spread formation, as the inbound Vampire 2 would be on them in a minute.

"Fox" is the code US pilots use to signal the release of an air-to-air missile. "Fox Two" is the call used for the firing of a heat-seeking AIM-9X Sidewinder.

It was critical that the pilots waited for the preceding section to clear—no one wanted to fire a heat-seeking missile with an F/A-18 out in front of them.

With an operational range of only twenty-two miles for the Sidewinder, it was going to be very difficult to judge the range of a missile traveling toward them at forty-five hundred knots, or more than five thousand miles an hour.

The A Section pilots pushed the selector switch on their control sticks to select the AIM-9X Sidewinder missiles. Three seconds later a solid tone was heard in CAG Cunningham's headset, as it was for the other pilots of A Section, indicating that the Sidewinder had locked on the heat signature of its target.

"Shogun 1, Fox Two," called CAG Cunningham.

She released the trigger, then pressed the selector switch a second time and heard the tone sound again in her headset. She depressed the trigger a second time and called, "Shogun 1, additional Fox Two."

As did all the pilots of A Section.

A second later CAG Cunningham called, "Shogun 1 to A Section, break, break, break. B Section, roll in."

The B Section followed the A Section and performed similar procedures, firing their combined eight Sidewinder heat-seeking missiles at the approaching DF-26.

Now there were sixteen Sidewinders in the air—all had some sort of lock onto the DF-26, but the DF-26 was traveling at Mach 7, and none hit.

It was now up to C Section, led by Commander Bartlett.

The DF-26 would pass by them in mere seconds. Bartlett could see the flash of light ahead and above him. He called to his section, "Steady, just one more second," and then Bartlett pulled back abruptly on his stick to get a higher angle of attack and called, "Switch 15, Fox Two."

Not waiting, he fired his second Sidewinder right away, "Switch 15, additional Fox Two."

Then Bartlett called, "C Section, break, break, break."

Meanwhile the US Army in South Korea were preparing to fire their complement of forty-eight THAAD missiles from their mobile launchers. The major concern was range and speed. The THAAD missiles had a range of 120 miles and the DF-26 had a range of more than twelve hundred miles. They had only seconds to fire in order for the THAADs to catch the blazing DF-26, which was on a southerly course headed toward the *Stennis.*

The Army colonel in-charge of the THAAD batteries was receiving reports from his missile crews.

"Colonel, we don't have a lock but we need to fire now or the DF-26 will be out of our range," said his most senior missileman.

Without hesitating, the colonel ordered, "All THAAD batter-ies, fire. I repeat, all batteries, fire."

Within seconds of the colonel's order, forty-eight THAAD missiles leapt from their mobile launchers. Now it would be up to the electronics on each THAAD missile to acquire and destroy the Dong-Feng threatening the USS *John C. Stennis.*

On board the *Stennis* the admiral commanded, "Order the group to set condition Yoke."

Condition Yoke meant that a ship would take steps to prepare for an imminent inbound missile strike. The ship would basically go into lockdown. All watertight doors were shut, any window that could be covered with a metal cover was secured. All deckhands were ordered into the inner skin of the ship. On the *Stennis*, the flight deck and hangar deck crews were all ordered into interior spaces.

The *Florida*, having found clear, cold water, was now getting on with the process of changing its filters in order to get

Torchlight back online. Captain Reagan ordered, "All stop. COB, prepare to deploy divers."

"Aye, aye, Captain."

With the lookouts posted, the hatch behind the sail was opened. There, wet-suit-equipped divers checked their gear. Also topside now was the chief engineer, going over with the divers the procedure for changing out the filters.

Captain Reagan and the XO were topside on the sail and were joined by Jim Hartel.

"Captain, we need to change six filters, three on each side of the hull. The filters are just aft of midships and about twelve feet below the surface. They are an ultrafine mesh stainless steel filter about six inches wide by eighteen inches long."

The XO added, "Sir, our divers have been drilling on the filter replacement procedure. We'll put two divers on each side. Diver 1 will open the retaining cap and remove the clogged filter. Diver 2's job is to hold the underwater light and ready the new filter so Diver 1 can insert it, lock the retaining cap, and move on to the next filter. The sea is calm. We should be able to get this done within fifteen minutes."

Reagan checked his watch. He knew there was an inbound missile headed for the *Stennis* a thousand miles south of them that was quite possibly armed with a fifty-kiloton warhead.

Just then Reagan had a thought. "Jim, what if we just remove the filters and not put new ones in?"

"Sir, you need to ask the chief engineer. I'm not up on the A1B reactor design," answered Hartel.

Reagan turned to his chief engineer, who was now on the sail with them, and said, "Bill, what do you think?"

"Captain, without filters the pumps will clog in a matter of minutes, even in this better water. If the pumps get clogged, the only way to fix them is to overhaul them," replied the CE.

"I know, I know, Chief, but without the filters can you get enough cooling to power up Torchlight for one shot?"

"I don't know, sir," said the CE as he called to check the water temp and salinity meters. They were steadily getting lower. "Sir, it might work, but no guarantees," said the CE.

That was enough for Reagan. He yelled to the COB, who was on the deck, "COB, tell them to just remove two of the clogged filters on each side. We don't have time to do all three. Pull the old filters. Don't put in the new filters. Do it now, on the double," yelled Reagan.

The divers were already in the water, so the COB went over and told them as Reagan slid down the ladder back into the control room, barking orders the entire time.

On the *North Carolina*, Captain Malfi had his hands full. "Are the Vectors locked on the enemy torpedoes?" Vectors were the US Navy's new solid rocket-propelled torpedoes. They had a top speed in excess of 150 knots, with a warhead as large as the MK 48. Because of their speed, Vectors were not wire-guided, meaning once they were fired, it was up to the homing technology on the Vector to track, lock, and destroy its target.

"Con, Weps. The Vectors are hot," answered the *North Carolina*'s weapons officer.

"Stand by," said the captain, looking at the digital stopwatch that hung from the cord around his neck. "Weps, Con. Fire Vectors 1 and 2," came the order.

The entire submarine could feel and hear the hiss when the Vectors shot out of their tubes, which was one of the drawbacks of the weapon. Yes, you could kill anything with Vectors, but they always gave away your position, as they made a hell of a lot of noise as they were launched and created an enormous wake as they ran. As a result, Vectors could be used only for specific tactical situations. And this was one of those situations.

Captain Malfi, with his two MK 48s already in the water and on their way to the Sang-O, wasn't worried about giving away his position. His concern and priority were intercepting the Sang-O's torpedoes before they put the *United States* on the bottom of the ocean.

"Con, Weps. Vectors are away and tracking the inbound fish to Alpha Panda," called the sonar officer, using the call sign the Navy had given the *United States*.

Captain Clifford of the *United States* never even knew he was under attack or that a North Korean and American submarine were off his port quarters.

As the *United States* entered the blue water of the Yellow Sea, Clifford ordered, "All ahead emergency. I want to put as much distance between us and North Korea as possible. Where's that North Korean Coast Guard boat?" asked Clifford.

"Sir, it's about three miles behind us in pursuit. At this speed, I doubt it will catch us," said Clifford's second-in-command, who was monitoring the cutter, as the *United States* started to accelerate past its certified top speed of thirty-five knots.

Just then, a thousand yards off the port side, two massive explosions boiled the ocean as the Vectors caught up with the Sang-O's torpedoes.

A minute later another great explosion occurred, this one farther from the *United States*. Again, the explosion set the sea to boil. That was the death of the Sang-O, as two MK 48 torpedoes from the *North Carolina* found their mark.

The North Korean Coast Guard cutter pursuing the *United States*, witnessing the explosions, put hard over and headed back to harbor, having no appetite to take on whatever had just caused those explosions.

Back on board the *Florida*, Reagan called, "Sonar, Con. Is SPY painting Vampire 2?" yelled Reagan.

"Con, Sonar. That's affirm, Captain. We have Vampire 2 locked."

"Weps, Con, prepare to Snapshot."

"COB, get those divers below decks as soon as they're done. XO, clear the bridge," ordered Reagan.

Reagan knew he couldn't fire Torchlight with crew members on the deck.

The divers on the port side were done and climbing back onto the deck of the *Florida*.

The COB yelled, "Go, go, go," pushing them to the hatch. The COB then went over to the starboard side and could see activity below but still no divers. "Come on," he yelled to no one.

The CE started to power up the portside A1B reactors. He knew he only needed four at full power to fire Torchlight.

If Vampire 2 struck, the burden and impact would fall on the *Stennis* alone. Admiral Fraser's order had scrambled the rest of the strike group far enough from the *Stennis* that even a direct hit on her would cause little to no damage—at least physical damage—to the rest of the ships in the strike group. That would be little consolation to the men and women of the *Stennis*, especially those in the CDC, who were tracking the inbound DF-26 with an estimated time of impact of five minutes. Three hundred seconds is not a long time to live. One of the operators in the CDC, a young petty officer, started to quietly cry.

Rear Admiral Fraser thought about relieving the sailor but thought, "Who could blame him." Everyone in the CDC was exhibiting signs of stress be it elevated respiration, perspiration or even praying.

On the *Florida*, the call came, "Con, Engineering. We are at sixty-five percent power. Torchlight is *not* yet online," added the chief engineer.

Just then the chief engineer saw A1B reactor 5 go offline. He'd expected it, as it was one of the reactors whose filter had not been removed. He also expected reactor 6 to scram any minute too.

A red light on the control panel started flashing as the chief yelled, "No, no, no." Reactor 2 was scramming due to a pump failure, as it quickly became clogged without any filter to protect it.

Twenty seconds later reactor 6 followed 5, also scrammed.

As the power on Torchlight dropped to forty-three percent, the chief engineer grabbed the handset and called to the bridge.

"Sir, Torchlight's done for. We just lost reactors 5, 6, and 2. We're offline until we can put into port, sir," reported the chief engineer.

"Copy that, Chief," replied Reagan.

Reagan knew he had just taken a big risk and that his decision could be challenged, maybe even by a general court. Nevertheless, he was sure he did the right thing and he would do it again if given a chance.

Admiral Johnson provided the Sit Room with a dour update. "All forty-eight THAAD missiles exhausted their fuel stores and fell into the Yellow Sea in pursuit of the longer-range DF-26. And Torchlight is still down, sir."

Both missile technologies had failed at the most crucial time.

"Can the *Stennis* evade the DF-26?" asked the president, already knowing the answer.

"Sir, they'll continue to SP-JASHO and they do have their Hornets up in a CAP," said Johnson.

The tension in the room was enormous. It appeared that President Russell's Torchlight gambit was going to fail at the potential cost of the USS *John C. Stennis* and its crew.

No one spoke. They just watched the screens and listened for updates, hoping for a miracle.

Bartlett and his section had just fired their Sidewinders, Bartlett's from a closer range and higher angle of attack. With their missiles released Bartlett called, "Switch flight, break, break, break."

As he made the call, a blinding light appeared directly above him. A moment later he felt his F/A-18E shudder as warning lights started to go off in his cockpit.

He wasn't sure if he had hit the DF-26 or if he was just experiencing its shock wave as it passed overhead, but either way he needed to stabilize his jet and dive to a lower altitude in case he needed to eject.

As the light subsided, Bartlett surveyed his aircraft. His right wing had three chunks missing and was streaming fuel. In addition, Bartlett's stick was getting heavy, so he suspected he had a hydraulic leak. Warning lights were going off faster than Bartlett could read them. Bartlett didn't know how much longer he would have flight controls.

Two issues were critical for Bartlett now—speed and altitude.

From his work at Pax he knew that any speed in excess of 600 knots would greatly increase the likelihood of significant injury or death even though the F/A-18's Martin Baker Mk-14 NACES ejection seat would fire at any speed. Compounding everything was his helmet.

The Joint Helmet Mounted Cueing System (JHMCS) was only rated to stay on at up to 250 knots. Anything above that speed risked severe neck injuries, as the helmet would be ripped off in the slipstream of the ejection.

Bartlett didn't have much time. First, his airspeed which indicated 700 knots. He needed to lose speed before he ejected – and lose it fast.

The challenge: In order to shed speed meant he would lose maneuverability which was already difficult given the damage his bird had sustained.

"Fuck it," he said as he he pulled back on the throttles.

As his altitude crossed forty thousand feet, Bartlett's F/A-18E started to buck, as warning lights were now coming from both engines. He knew he did not have much time left.

He retarded his throttles to idle, and his Super Hornet dropped to just under 600 KCAS (Knots Calibrated Airspeed).

"Switch 15. I'm punching out."

As he made that call, he lost the leading edge of his right wing, which caused his jet to pitch violently to the right.

It was time to get out of Dodge.

Bartlett reached down between his legs and grabbed the black and yellow ejection handle with both hands. A split second later rocket motors on the bottom of his canopy fired as the ejection sequence initiated. With the canopy flying off in the slipstream, Bartlett's Martin Baker Mk-14 ejection seat fired along its launch rails, sending him into the sky high above the Yellow Sea.

A flash of light appeared on the screen of the CDC of the *Stennis*. There was silence as the entire room tried to absorb what had just happened.

The silence was broken by the call, "This is Red Crown on Guard. Kill, kill, kill, Vampire 2. Repeat, Vampire 2, kill, kill, kill."

The CDC officer turned to Admiral Fraser. "Copy that, sir. Vampire 2 is no longer tracking Home Plate." A cheer went up in the CDC with the report of the news.

In the Sit Room, they, too, saw the flash on the screen.

A moment later Admiral Johnson updated the group. "Mr. President, it appears the F/A-18s off the *Stennis* were able to shoot down the DF-26 with a Sidewinder. It was a one-in-a-hundred shot, sir."

"More like a one in a thousand," commented a relieved Russell.

Then Admiral Johnson said, "Mr. President, there is something else, sir."

"Home Plate, Shogun 1. We have a down bird. Repeat, we have a down Hornet," was the sobering call from CAG Cunningham.

Everyone was now silent in the CDC.

Next the E-2C called, "Switch 15 is down. Repeat, Switch 15 is down. Posit 32.779, 124.045."

The CDC operator entered the longitude and latitude figures provided by Closeout. The location was approximately 425 miles north of the *Stennis* and too far to send a helo. The closest ship in the strike group was the USS *Kidd*, an Arleigh Burke destroyer of DESRON-21. The *Kidd* was just one hundred miles south of that posit. They could be on station in three hours, but they could launch their Seahawk helicopter in minutes.

Fraser then ordered the CDC operations officer, "Contact the *Kidd* and let them know we have a down bird and to launch a SAR at once."

"Little Bear, this is Home Plate. Scramble SAR, scramble SAR, posit 32.779, 124.045."

"Copy, Home Plate. Little Bear launching SAR," came the call from the USS *Kidd*.

Next CAG Cunningham radioed, "Shogun flight, commence tanking as needed. All others form on me. We're beginning a SARCAP at two hundred feet, 180 knots, in a racetrack pattern. Keep your distance so we don't lose another bird."

Fraser knew that Switch 15 was Commander Bartlett's jet. He also knew that while the Shoguns and the E-2C would conduct a SARCAP, he needed to get either a surface ship or helo on location fast. He didn't know the condition of Bartlett but was fully aware that any ejection always put the crew at great risk, especially at the altitude and speed Bartlett had been. If he survived, it was very likely he was injured.

"What commercial traffic is in the area?" yelled Fraser to the CDC commander.

The CDC commander had his operator move the cursor to the area of the downed Super Hornet, and then with a click of the mouse expanded his screen to show all radar contacts.

A dot showed up close to the position of the jet. "There"— Fraser pointed—"who's that?"

"Sir, it's the *Anna Maersk*. She's approximately twelve miles from the downed Rhino," said the CDC operator.

"Contact that ship immediately," ordered Fraser; then he turned to Captain Ryan. "Chaser," said the admiral, "let's get another E-2C up to manage the SAR. And we'll probably need more tankers too."

"Already working on it, Admiral," replied Ryan.

"This is the US Navy calling *Anna Maersk* on channel 16. Repeat, this is the US Navy calling *Anna Maersk* on channel 16. Priority traffic. Come in, Anna Maersk."

A minute later came the reply, "Roger, US Navy, this is the *Anna Maersk*."

The admiral grabbed the handset from the radioman. "*Anna Maersk*, this is Admiral Fraser in command of the *John C. Stennis* Strike Group. We have a down aircraft in your vicinity. We request you lend immediate assistance."

"Admiral, this is Captain George Pierce of the *Anna Maersk*. We're ready to lend assistance. What is the location of your down aircraft?"

"I am giving you over to our CDC commander, who will coordinate all the necessary information. Thank you, Captain." With that Admiral Fraser handed the handset to the *Stennis's* safety officer, Commander Ricardo Nuñez, who would be in charge of the SAR effort.

Back in the Sit Room, the president responded to Admiral Johnson's last comment. "What is it?" said the president.

"Sir, we have a down F/A-18."

The momentary elation was now clouded by Admiral Johnson's report.

"Is there a SAR under way?" asked the president.

"Yes, sir, they have a helo beginning the search. Also, we have diverted a cargo ship in the area to assist with the search. There's more, sir."

The president looked at the Johnson.

"Sir, the downed F/A-18 was Commander Bartlett's jet," added Admiral Johnson.

President Russell winced as he heard the news.

"Sir, CAG said it was Commander Bartlett's missile that knocked down the DF-26. Apparently he veered into the DF-26's flight-path in order to get his shot off. When the DF-26 exploded, CAG thinks debris damaged Bartlett's Super Hornet, forcing him to eject."

After a pause, the president slowly stood, as did everyone in the room, and he spoke in a low, reverent tone, "Shield our brethren from rock and foe, protect them wherever they go; Hear us when we cry to Thee, for those in peril on the sea."

Captain Malfi on the *North Carolina* decided to break radio silence to help explain what had just happened and to ease the nerves of the officers, crew, and passengers of the *United States*, who had just witnessed two tremendous explosions at close quarters and were probably concerned that the next one would find their liner.

"US Navy submarine hailing *United States* on channel 16, come in *United States*," called the radioman from the *North Carolina*.

Right away the radio officer on the *United States* responded. "*United States* acknowledges calls from US Navy submarine. I have alerted Captain Clifford, please stand by."

Once Captain Clifford was in the radio room of the great liner, Captain Malfi grabbed the transmitter and said, "Captain, this is the captain of the US Navy fast-attack submarine off your port quarter. You were just fired on by a North Korean submarine. That submarine is no longer a threat to you."

Captain Clifford absorbed the information he had just been given.

Captain Malfi added, "Captain, we have been shadowing you since you left Pearl. We have orders to escort you to San Francisco." For a little added drama, which Captain Malfi was known for, he added, "You have a guardian angel at your side, Captain."

The master of the *United States*, a well-read Brit, replied in a typical Cunard fashion. "Captain, many thanks. As the Benedictine nuns who taught me used to say, 'The music of your guiding voice is ever in my ear,' over."

CHAPTER FIFTEEN

In P'yŏngyang, General Goh was convening a meeting with the seconds-in-command of the army, air force, and navy as well as the deputies of the SSD and the Ministry of Foreign Affairs.

The senior leaders of the army, air force, and SSD were all under house arrest and being kept by South Korean agents in a secret location.

Goh began, "President Paek and his family have left the country. The entire General Command is under arrest. We're now the leaders of the country." Goh paused to let that sink in.

Goh continued, "For too long our people have suffered under the leadership of President Paek and his family. We have lived as separate people on this peninsula for too long. We have witnessed prosperity and growth in the South while we in the North have continued to struggle. I have been in touch with President Young-woo of South Korea and raised the topic of reunification with the South."

Again, Goh paused to let his audience absorb his words but also to measure their reaction. Of most concern to him was the deputy director of the SSD. If he could get the SSD on his side with the plan, things would proceed much more easily.

But he couldn't get a read from the deputy.

Goh continued, "I will now take your questions."

This was an abrupt departure from what the group was used to. They were typically given a plan dictated by President Paek or his staff. Never were they asked their opinions or allowed to put forth questions around policy.

After a moment the minister of foreign affairs spoke. "What is the position of the Americans and Chinese on this situation?"

Goh knew he had to answer carefully to make sure he didn't come off appearing as a puppet of either country.

"Both countries support the plan to unify with the South or for us to establish our own new government. The choice is ours. The US and China say they will abide by the decision we make today. Gentlemen, if we no longer need to spend a large percentage of our national budget on military spending, think of how we could help our people. And I say that as someone who has a life spent in the military."

"If we did consider reunification, would we just be absorbed into the South?" asked the army general.

"That all needs to be worked out and negotiated. For now, we must establish rule over our country. Again, the people in this room will make up a temporary ruling body until we can establish the rules for an election. Once we have elected leaders in place it will be their responsibility to decide if and how to negotiate with the South. We will elect a General Committee made up of seven members. The members will cover domestic and foreign affairs, the military, the national bank, health services, technology and communications, and a person to establish a system of courts. That committee would rule over our country and lead negotiations with the South around reunification. The negotiations with the South would be made up of an equal number of representatives from the North and South."

"Where is Paek and what will happen to him? As long as he is alive he would never agree to this plan."

Goh responded, "Paek voluntarily left the country. He will be kept in exile with no chance of returning or influencing any of the country's future direction."

Goh then said, "I am scheduled to conference in President Young-woo now. You are all invited to stay and monitor the session."

The image of President Young-woo of South Korea next appeared on the large screen in their room.

"Good afternoon, General Goh and the leaders of the North. Today, we have the opportunity to make history and to take action that will improve the lives of our citizens for the next one hundred years. Let us pause and pray together," said Young-woo, who then led the group in a short prayer.

It was the start of a new beginning for the people of Korea.

Meanwhile President Paek's jet was on its way to an island in the north of the Philippines. The original plan was for China to shoot down the jet carrying Paek and his family. But at the last moment president Wei Zhang of China rejected the plan and called President Russell to propose an alternative. Wei said, "The people of China do not agree with the plan to kill Paek or his family."

President Wei instead proffered, "Our special forces will keep Paek under surveillance but we will leave him and his family unharmed. He will basically be kept under house arrest on his island by Chinese security forces."

President Russell knew this proposed plan involved significant risk, but he had formed a relationship of trust with Wei, much of it based on China's role in the rescue of his family when they were kidnapped the year before by Al Qaeda on Nantucket.

After a moment of deliberation, Russell answered, "President Wei, we agree."

Wei then changed the subject. "Mr. President, we are concerned about your Deadeye project."

President Russell was expecting this and said, "President Wei, Deadeye was an operation strictly targeted at North Korea. As you know, it was imperative that the US neutralize all North Korean missiles. As you are also aware, our plan calls for all North Korean missiles to be disarmed over the coming weeks. To the extent Deadeye has any application to China, you have my assurance that we will not use it against you. Going further, I suspect Deadeye has a half-life of days if not hours, as we fully expect your technical teams to be working right now to upgrade your missile operating systems, making Deadeye obsolete."

Wei smiled on the video link and added, "Mr. President you are very astute. The imperfection in the Chinese software is being corrected at this moment, but I needed to hear your assurances not to use Deadeye against us."

"President Wei, by working together today we have impacted the world. The United States looks to continue to advance our relationship with China as we work to make our planet a safer place for all of its people."

President Wei nodded. "Yes, we have done a great thing today. Something that five years ago was unimaginable. By working together there is really nothing we cannot accomplish."

"President Wei, I agree. When we next meet I would like to discuss another challenge, as well as an opportunity for us. Without getting into the specific details, high levels of biologics in the ocean almost turned this operation into a disaster. The next great enemy we must confront is not a regime or a madman with a nuclear weapon— it is our carbon emissions and consumption of fossil fuels—we must work together to reverse the effect of global warming. And if we take the lead I am sure all the world's countries will follow our example," closed President Russell.

"We look forward to those discussions, Mr. President," responded Wei.

Those present knew they had just witnessed history in the making.

This was what real leadership looked like.

By now the USS *Kidd*'s helicopter had reached the location where Switch 15 had gone down.

Close by was the *Anna Maersk*, conducting a grid search.

It would still be two hours before the USS *Kidd* arrived on scene.

It was the trained observer on the MH-60 of HSC-14, the Chargers, who first spotted him.

Bobbing up and down in a churned-up sea was Commander Bartlett, his green dye marker long since faded into the depths of the ocean.

"Little Bear, Lightning 14. We've spotted the package," called the MH-60 copilot.

"Roger, Lightning 14," came back the radio operator on the USS *Kidd*.

"Little Bear, we're putting our rescue swimmer in the water, copy."

After the rescue swimmer reached Bartlett, the MH-60 lowered its basket and winched the downed pilot to the helicopter.

Once Bartlett was on board the helo, the crew updated the *Kidd*. "Little Bear, Lightning 14. We have the package on board. He's alive.

Returning to Little Bear." The pilot of the MH-60 couldn't resist adding, "Day and night, lightning strikes," the motto of the HSC-14.

It was not quite 5 a.m. in Washington when the president's phone rang.

"Yes," was all the president said, knowing that calls at this time of the morning were never good news.

"Mr. President," said his chief of staff. "Sorry to disturb you, Mr. President, but I thought you would want to know immediately. Sir, the MH-60 off the *Kidd* just picked up Commander Bartlett. He's banged up but will live, sir. Bartlett has a broken arm and a punctured lung, a lot of bruises, and a couple contusions, but otherwise he's in pretty good condition."

The president offered a silent prayer of thanks. He then thanked his chief of staff for sharing the news and hung up.

The president then connected to the White House operator. "Yes, Mr. President?"

"Get me Kristin McMahon."

Captain Clifford of the *United States* provided Tim Cook with an update from sea. Tim Cook called President Russell to express his gratitude. "Mr. President, I wanted to thank you for keeping our employees and crew safe during the operation. Captain Clifford just informed me about the submarine that you had dispatched to keep watch over them."

"Tim," said the president, "we weren't going to let a US-flagged ship with a thousand of our citizens on board venture into North Korean waters without providing them with a phalanx of protection. And, Tim, I want to thank you. I know it wasn't easy, but now you see what was at stake. You can take enormous pride and satisfaction in the role that Apple played in making this operation a success and thereby the world a safer place."

Cook later learned from Sterling Spencer that it was the USS *North Carolina* that provided the protection for the *United States*.

Cook put plans in motion that, once in port, every sailor and officer of the *North Carolina* was given a new iPhone, iPad, and MacBook courtesy of Apple. Cook was sure these gifts violated a long list of Navy regulations, but he didn't care, nor, he thought, would the secretary of the Navy, the CNO, or President Russell, for that matter. And he was right.

CHAPTER SIXTEEN

Pavo was settling into his new life in Manhattan with Katija.

Katija's excitement was palpable as she looked up from a text she'd just gotten. "Krystal says the closings are set for Monday." She was referring to the Bank Street house and the loft on Jane.

Pavo leaned over to kiss Katija. "That's great news," he said.

Pavo and Katija had just finished shopping at the tony shops of Manhattan's Upper East Side. Katija, who had the looks of a model, also had a model's fashion sense, and now, with Pavo, she had the budget to match. They had shopped at Chanel and Kate Spade and just finished at Tory Burch.

Pavo was finished, though. "Katija, don't you think we've done enough shopping for one day?"

"Do you want to go to the Apple store?"

Pavo didn't need anything, but he could use a technology fix after so much Chanel, so they headed a few blocks north to the corner of Madison Avenue at Seventy-Fourth street, which had once housed the United States Mortgage and Trust Company bank but now was an Apple store.

After a few minutes of browsing and taking in the state-of-the-art displays, they decided to look for a place to get some coffee.

After a short walk, Pavo saw Cafe Boulud and said, "Let's stop there."

As they entered and sat down, Pavo added, "This city is made of money, isn't it?"

"It is," she said, "but I love the energy of the city. There's always something going on and so many people."

They were young and in love and in Manhattan.

As they finished their coffees, Pavo picked up the bags containing Katija's purchases. They got up to leave, and another patron followed them as they exited through the door. Without Pavo's notice, the stranger slipped a device the size of an iPhone into the Chanel bag Katija was carrying.

Once on the street, the stranger turned and walked toward Central Park as Pavo and Katija headed in the opposite direction.

"Let's head back to the Waldorf," said Pavo, referring to the hotel where the CIA had put them up in since the Staten Island operation the week earlier.

Katija agreed, saying, "Let's walk. The air feels good. Pavo, let me carry some of the bags." They walked south on Madison and then crossed over Fiftieth to Park Avenue, where the Waldorf was located.

Pavo and Katija didn't know it, but they would not live to enjoy their newly purchased Manhattan property. The small device slipped into the shopping bag that Katija was now carrying was emitting a high level of a radioactive isotope. The dosage they both were exposed to during their twenty-minute walk back to the hotel was enough to inflict on them a deadly amount of radiation.

Katija showed the device to Pavo once they were back in the Waldorf. At first, he thought it was some sort of security device left inadvertently in the bag by one of the store personnel.

But after examining it, Pavo could tell it wasn't a simple security device but rather something very sophisticated. What it was he wasn't sure, but it immediately raised his suspicions. He called his contact at the CIA, and some agents came by and picked it up. The CIA lab determined it was what was known in the trade as a "kill box." It was a small and compact device that emitted a high dosage of radiation for only ten to twenty minutes, but during that time, anyone within a five-meter range and exposed continually to it would be fatally exposed. Furthermore, the CIA discovered that the "kill box" contained Soviet technology.

It was a couple of weeks later when Lauren La Rue visited Pavo Ludovic at Memorial Sloan Kettering Cancer Center on Sixty-Seventh Street and York Avenue in Manhattan.

"Hello, Pavo," said La Rue.

"Lauren, thank you for coming," said a weakened Ludovic, who was sitting up in bed with several tubes connected to him.

"Pavo, I'm so sorry," said La Rue, who was genuinely moved.

"You know my Katija is gone," said Ludovic with a faraway look.

"Yes, I know, Pavo. Are there any arrangements you would like to make for her?"

"That is why I asked to see you. There are several things I would like you to look after for me. First, I would like Katija and me to be buried at our family plot in Mlini. Second, I want you to take my funds and give $20 million each to my parents, brother, and sister, and then take the remaining funds, which I estimate at over $80 million, and I would like you to establish a private children's school in Dubrovnik named after Katija."

"Pavo, I will make sure that happens," said La Rue as tears formed in her eyes.

"Please, Lauren, there have been enough tears." Ludovic reached over to his table and picked up a memory stick. "This memory stick has all the information you will need to gain access to my funds. Plus, I had Sloan Kettering get me a US lawyer, so there is a duly executed last will and testament. I have named you as my executor."

La Rue nodded and said, "I will make sure your wishes are carried out, Pavo."

"Thank you, Lauren. Thank you very much. I'm afraid this is the last time we will speak."

La Rue put her hand on Pavo's and held it without saying anything.

Pavo looked up at Lauren and said, "Also on the memory stick are all my files. A list of all my clients—and the names, addresses and contact information of every Russian agent I have ever dealt with. The Russians killed me and my Katija, and I want them to pay. Please promise me you will make them pay."

La Rue said, "I will, Pavo. I will."

Pavo closed his eyes, no longer having the energy to continue.

In the investigation that followed, Lisa Collins and Lauren La Rue learned that the Russians had tracked Ludovic to Manhattan and decided he was too valuable a resource to let fall into the hands of the Americans.

But the information Ludovic gave La Rue would cost the Russians for years to come.

The next day at CIA headquarters in Langley, Lisa Collins was meeting with her Middle East section head. On the list of topics to be discussed was Salman Rahman.

Lisa began, "So what is our assessment on Salman Rahman?"

she asked the group assembled, which, in addition to the section head, included her DDI, her new head of operations and the head of counterterrorism.

The ops lead began, "Ma'am we have determined that the attack in Staten Island was his doing. Simply put, he is on a vendetta to avenge his father's death. We believe that includes Lauren La Rue at the top of the list, but we believe it also includes the president as well as some Navy officers."

"He's a twenty-two-year-old millionaire if not a billionaire with a grudge, who's also purported to have an incendiary temper. Not a good combination," said the Middle East section head.

"Is the Secret Service aware of this potential threat to the president?" asked Collins.

"Yes, ma'am, they are," replied her DDI.

"And what about the Navy?" Collins questioned.

"NCIS is aware, ma'am."

"Well, gentlemen, what to do about Mr. Rahman?"

"I believe as long as Salman has a breath left in his body he'll be after La Rue, and once La Rue is dealt with he'll move down his list to the next target," said the Middle East section head.

"Director, he's a clear threat and he needs to be dealt with," added her DDI.

"Besides Salman, how many children did the sheik have?" asked Collins.

"He has two other sons and two daughters. Salman is the oldest. His brothers are thirteen and eleven and his sisters are seventeen and fifteen," said the Middle East lead.

"Great, so this vendetta could possibly go on for the next twenty years, if not more," lamented Collins.

"We don't have psychological workups on the other children, so we can't assess their personality traits," said the counterterrorism lead.

"The best approach is for some tragedy to befall Salman. We'll have deniability and, if done correctly, it won't further inspire his siblings to pursue any kind of revenge," said the DDI.

"What if we approach one of our trusted Saudis, one of the crown princes, and have him deliver a message to Salman that if he doesn't back off it will end badly for him," suggested Collins.

"I don't think that will work, plus keep in mind if later we have to take action it would severely hurt our deniability," replied the DDI correctly.

"All right, gentlemen, I'll get back to you," said Collins. She needed to get the president's input on this matter.

CHAPTER SEVENTEEN

The president, having been a congressman from Brooklyn's Eleventh District, rarely passed on a chance to get back to New York, and he certainly wouldn't miss an opportunity to recognize one of New York's Finest.

On Thursday, April 26, at noon at New York's city hall in Lower Manhattan, the president, along with the governor, mayor, and chief of police, attended a ceremony to honor NYPD sergeant Tom Walsh, the hero of the Staten Island safe-house attack.

Sergeant Walsh was being awarded the New York City Police Department's Medal of Honor. This award was for NYPD personnel who displayed individual acts of gallantry and valor performed with knowledge of the risk involved. It was awarded for acts of heroism, above and beyond the call of duty, which clearly described Walsh's actions on Staten Island.

Still recovering from his wound, Sergeant Walsh slowly approached the platform as the chief of police began to read the citation. Walsh was followed by his wife and two children, and they all stood together and heard the account of Walsh's actions.

With the occasional wipe of a tear from his wife, the family listened as comments were made by the governor, the mayor, and finally the president.

Russell began, "The Eleventh District holds a special place in my heart. Of course, it's where I grew up in Bay Ridge, but it also includes Staten Island. And as every New Yorker knows, Staten Island is a place that many of our police and firemen call home. So, it was no real surprise when trouble—of an international kind—found its way to Staten Island that it would be confronted by members of our great police and fire departments. 'Not in our house' is the line that comes to mind," said the president.

"We know that this city has borne more than its share of grief and violence at the hands of terrorists and those wanting to do us harm. And every time this city is challenged, every time this city is a target of hatred, every time this city is put in the cross hairs of evil—the men and women of this great metropolis respond in a fashion that raises the bar and sets the standard for all of us. The actions of 12 April were no different. Sergeant Walsh, out walking his dog, came across a terrorist attack just a block from his home. Without hesitating, Sergeant Walsh engaged the enemy, an enemy with superior firepower, and defeated them. And he did this at great risk to his personal safety. He is the embodiment of New York's Finest, and I take great pleasure in presenting him with the NYPD's Medal of Honor."

With that President Russell placed the green-ribboned medal around Walsh's neck as they stood for some photos.

Then the president continued, "And now I turn my remarks to those who would do us harm. We will never give in to your violence. And you will never defeat us. Every time this great city and country is tested by your cowardly acts, you witness the strength of our resolve. As a country, we wish nothing more than to end poverty and work with those peace-loving nations around the world to make the world a better, safer, and cleaner place for our children and the future generations.

"But be warned: We will not tolerate violence against our people and our society. We will defend ourselves and our allies. And the spirit, courage, and commitment to duty that you witness time and time again by our citizens is such that it can never be defeated. We welcome those who wish to work with us in friendship. But for those who wish us ill, your future will be one filled with pain and destruction."

As applause broke out, the NYPD band began to play "America the Beautiful."

It was now the morning of Friday, April 27, and the SS *United States*, with flags flying from stem to stern at full dress ship, had just sailed under the Golden Gate Bridge on its way to tie up at San Francisco's James R. Herman Cruise Terminal.

Many of the Apple executives, including CEO Tim Cook, had flown out the day before by helicopter to be on board when the *United States* made her historic entrance to San Francisco Bay.

The *United States* was accompanied by hundreds of pleasure craft and the San Francisco fireboats, which sprayed water into the air to celebrate the inaugural arrival of this great liner.

On hand to enforce order and avoid any mishaps were cutters and rescue boats of the US Coast Guard's Eleventh District, known as D11.

As the *United States* passed the Presidio, an Army artillery regiment fired a seventeen-gun salute, which was appropriate, as Governor Jerry Brown was also on board the *United States*.

Once the *United States* was moored, the plan called for VIPs and Apple employees to tour the ship that Friday, with the public allowed to tour the grand ship on Saturday and Sunday.

That night a gala was held in the spectacularly restored main ballroom with all the power players of Silicon Valley in attendance.

Many commented just how much Steve Jobs would have loved the event. Everyone agreed he would have.

On board the *John C. Stennis*, things were getting back to normal. Admiral Tom "Flatbush" Fraser had seen how his crew reacted under the enormous pressure of an imminent and potentially devastating attack. And while discipline and routine are capstones of the US Navy, Fraser knew he also needed to pay attention to morale.

Fraser spoke to the *Stennis*'s CO, Captain Craig "Chaser" Ryan. "Captain, what about a Steel Beach?" referring to a Navy custom where a ship's crew throws a party on the flight deck. A Steel Beach party gives overworked and stressed crews a day to unwind, enjoy some recreation, and remember the good things in life as they enjoyed a ship-wide barbecue.

"I was thinking the same thing, sir," replied Ryan.

The decision was made. The next day Carrier Group 3 would enjoy a Steel Beach party. Fraser sent orders out to his group to start preparing for the festivities.

He then made arrangements to helo around to each ship in his strike group to thank them individually for their service and enjoy some downtime with each crew.

The *Florida* would miss the party, as it was on a speed run back to Pearl to get its reactor pumps overhauled. PM Jim Hartel was on board the sub.

He had condensed his notes into a series of action items for Torchlight that would address some of the areas of concern that had occurred during the mission.

Top priority was to work with the engineers of Bechtel to improve the filtering systems of the new A1B reactors. Hartel felt that not only could those filters be improved but maintenance should be done from inside the sub, without having to surface or dispatch divers.

Beyond that he had a series of recommendations for SPY-6 that would allow it to better integrate with *Torchlight*. Hartel was also planning his own team's celebration—this one for his people back in Arlington, Virginia. They had achieved their goal, and now it was appropriate to take some time to recognize those who were responsible for Torchlight's innovation and success.

Lauren La Rue walked into the AFB Hospital off Nealy Avenue in Langley, Virginia. She was carrying a bag of burgers from the local BurgerFi.

As she approached Room 112, she checked her hair and then stuck her head into the doorway. "Hey, hero, how about some lunch?"

Chris Dunbar smiled and pushed himself up on his hospital bed. "Perfect timing. I'm starving."

Lauren took the contents out of the bag and spread them on the hospital table. She asked, "So what are the doctors saying?"

Dunbar said, "Well, other than the scar here," he said, pointing to the side of his head, "I'm not going to have any lasting effects from the wounds."

"When will you be able to leave?"

Taking a big bite out of his cheeseburger, he chewed and swallowed, then said, "I think they'll let me go home on Tuesday."

"That's great," said La Rue.

"So, are you going to the big wedding tomorrow?" Dunbar asked.

She nodded yes, as she also had a mouthful of food.

"Who are you going with?"

"Well, the guy I wanted to go with wasn't available, so I'm going stag," La Rue said, smiling at Dunbar.

"Is that right?"

"It is," she said with a knowing smile.

It was a beautiful spring morning as the president and first lady prepared to attend the wedding of Commander Michael "Grumpy" Bartlett to deputy director of the NSA Kristin McMahon. It was a Navy wedding and, as such, was taking place at the US Naval Academy Chapel in Annapolis, Maryland.

"Ken, are you almost ready?" called the president.

"Almost," she replied. A moment later she appeared wearing a light blue Chanel dress that was breathtaking.

Andrew Russell cried out, "What are you doing?"

"What?" replied Kennedy, somewhat alarmed.

"You're going to upstage the bride at her own wedding," the president said, smiling.

"Oh, you," replied the first lady with a smile on her face.

"Kids, we're leaving," said FLOTUS as she checked herself in the mirror one last time.

Andrew Jr., now thirteen, and Katie, eleven, came into the room to say good-bye.

"Mom, you look really nice," said her daughter.

The president paused, then demanded, "And what about me?" He grabbed Katie around the waist and picked her up over his head.

She giggled and squirmed and said, "You look good too."

The president, not relenting, pretended to drop her, saying, "Just good, is that right? Good?"

With Katie screaming and laughing, he spun her around and dropped her on the couch.

Turning to his son, the president said, "Andrew, doesn't your mother look nice?"

Andrew simply nodded, having entered that awkward teenage phase.

Kennedy Russell gave each a quick kiss, then said, "We won't be home until late. Andy, I don't want you playing Xbox all day. Katie, it would be good if you got some work done on your class project."

With that there was a knock on the door from the president's usher, letting him know Marine One was five minutes out.

"Okay, kids, have a good time. You'll be able to watch the wedding on TV if you want," added the president.

The president, working with the White House's Communication Agency and Ron Kirby, had gotten the networks to broadcast a pool feed of the wedding. It wasn't hard to do given the pageantry of the event. Reluctantly, Kristin McMahon and Commander Bartlett had given their approval to airing their wedding.

In attendance were the chief of naval operations, commander of fleet force command, commander naval Air Force, the vice chairman of the Joint Chiefs, the commandant of the Naval Academy, and a variety of other naval officers—enough to fill four rows at the chapel at Annapolis.

Then, of course, there were the members of Commander Bartlett's squadron, the Salty Dogs of VX-23 of NAS Pax River, which was not far from Annapolis.

Not to be outdone by all the US Navy flag officers was the Catholic Church. The main celebrant for the mass was his eminence James Cardinal Gotimer of New York, who'd agreed to officiate at the wedding. And since it was taking place in Maryland, protocol dictated that the archbishop of Baltimore be invited to concelebrate, to which he readily agreed. And to complete the clergical presence, since it was a Navy wedding, the head Navy chaplain, an admiral by rank who happened to also be the bishop of Scranton, also concelebrated at the mass. They were accompanied by a like number of prelates and a cantor.

The small chapel at Annapolis had never hosted so many dignitaries, either military or religious, and the sight was dramatic.

Once everyone was seated, with the groom and groomsmen on the altar, the president of the United States entered through a side door along with his wife. As they entered, the congregation stood until the president and Mrs. Russell were seated.

That was the cue for Commander Mike Bartlett and his best man, Lieutenant Commander Zack Rohrbach, to step forward and take their positions on the altar to the right of the cardinal, who had the archbishop of Baltimore on his right and the Navy chaplain to his immediate left.

Wearing their dress whites, as were all the US Navy officers in attendance, Bartlett and Rohrbach stood looking down the main aisle of the chapel.

The only change to Bartlett's uniform was that his left arm was in a navy-blue sling, as he was still recovering from the injuries he received when he ejected from Switch 15.

Both wore white gloves, and their officer swords hung from their left sides. Their hats were on their seats.

The organ sounded and everyone in the congregation stood and turned. First came the two bridesmaids, escorted by Bartlett's groomsmen, who were also Naval aviators. Next came the maid of honor by herself. Once she was at the altar, Kristin McMahon walked down the aisle accompanied by her father.

Only the British royal family could rival the Catholic Church in terms of pageantry and splendor. The only short-coming was that the chapel at Annapolis was small and could not accommodate all the VIPs interested in attending, but that was probably all for the best, as even more intimacy would have been lost.

Once the ceremony began, it followed the standard format of a Catholic nuptial mass.

It wasn't until after communion that the ceremony took on another level of celebrity.

As the organist began the notes of "Ave Maria," a singer came forward—it was Sting. Arranging for Sting to perform, not just at the wedding but also at the reception, was the handiwork of Kennedy Russell.

A few minutes later Cardinal Gotimer stood and administered the final blessing. The couple kissed and then turned to face the standing congregation for the first time as Commander and Mrs. Michael Bartlett.

According to the program, the organist was supposed to begin Felix Mendelssohn's "Wedding March" from *A Midsummer Night's Dream*, but instead there was silence.

The CNO stood and approached the couple as the cardinal and his concelebrant stepped back.

"Stand fast, Commander," ordered the CNO in a loud and authoritative tone.

Commander Mike Bartlett stood at attention, not sure what was happening.

Then a staff officer with gold braid hanging from his right shoulder approached the CNO carrying a case.

The CNO turned to the congregation and cried, "Call to orders," as a bugle played from the choir loft. The call caused every officer in the congregation to come to attention, while everyone else remained standing.

The president came forward and turned to the congregation, saying, "I would like to ask the bride and groom to indulge me as we conduct some official business."

Kristin McMahon looked puzzled but smiled tentatively, not clear as to what was happening.

"Admiral," said the president, "will you read the citation?"

Saluting the president, the CNO opened his folder and began:

"By order of the secretary of the Navy.

"For conspicuous gallantry and intrepidity as a pilot of VFA-151, Carrier Wing 9, during operations in the East China Sea, 15 April 2018. Commander Bartlett, at great risk to his personal safety, took action that saved the lives of many of his fellow seamen and countrymen. Commander Bartlett demonstrated extraordinary heroism in the face of grave danger and his deliberate and heroic actions deprived the enemy of a devastating victory. By his selfless leadership, courageous actions, and extraordinary devotion to duty, Commander Bartlett reflected great credit upon himself and upheld the highest traditions of the United States Navy."

The staff officer then opened the case and presented its contents to the CNO, who handed it to the president.

The president approached Commander Bartlett but first stopped and said to Kristin with a smile, "I hope you'll forgive me for interrupting your wedding for this."

The president said, "Commander Bartlett, it is with great honor and the thanks of a grateful nation that I award you the Navy Cross."

The president then affixed the medal on Bartlett's left breast, to the right and slightly higher than the other medals Bartlett was wearing, and just below his wings of gold.

The president then took a step back and saluted the commander, who returned the salute smartly.

As Commander Bartlett's arm came to his side, the organist sounded the opening notes to Mendelssohn's "Wedding March" and applause broke out in the chapel.

It wasn't one hundred percent clear if the congregation was applauding the new couple or Commander Bartlett's action that earned him the Navy Cross, but it didn't really matter.

With the wedding ceremony over and the couple off taking photographs, the rest of the approximately 140 guests adjourned to the academy's Midway and Coral Sea Room's North Porch for the cocktail hour before the start of the formal reception. President Russell and the first lady probably took more photographs than Kristin and Commander Bartlett did, which was fine with the president.

It was now time for the receiving line to form. Adhering to White House protocol, the order of the line was the parents of the groom, followed by the bride's parents, then the first lady and President Russell, and then the guests of honor, Kristin and Mike Bartlett.

Now with everyone at their assigned tables in the Coral Sea and Midway Room, the trumpet player of the US Navy's academy band stood and sounded "Attention," which brought the all guests to their feet. With all military personnel now at attention, the band played "Hail to the Chief" as President Russell and the first lady entered. As the president and first lady reached their table, the members of Commander Bartlett's squadron, VX-23, the Salty Dogs, formed an honor guard in two lines opposite each other. On the command "Draw swords," each officer raised his sword in his right hand with the cutting edge facing up. Before entering the Arch of Swords, as it was called, the Bartletts kissed. Then they passed through the arch. The passage was meant to represent the couple's safe transition to their new life. The final tradition occurred as Kristin Bartlett passed the last officer in the line, who dropped his sword and gave her a swat on her backside as the line of officers called, "Welcome to the Navy."

With the bulk of the Navy traditions now out of the way, it was time for the couple's first dance. Kristin McMahon had chosen "Thinking Out Loud" by Ed Sheeran. As the band started to play, with the married couple on the center of the dance floor, a figure walked to the stage. It was Ed Sheeran, also compliments of the efforts of Kennedy Russell.

At the president's table were four other couples—all admirals and their wives: the chief of naval operations, the commander of Fleet Forces Command (COMFLTFORCOM), the vice chairman of the Joint Chiefs, and the commandant of the Naval Academy. In total, there were fifteen stars on the shoulder boards of the admirals just at that table. It was said, "There were more stars at this wedding than on the American flag."

Ed Sheeran did a few more numbers and then introduced Sting, who then took over.

With the reception fully under way and Sting performing, it was time for President Russell and Kennedy Russell's first dance. As the intro notes of "Every Breath You Take" began, Andrew Russell stood and turned to Kennedy and said, "My name's Andrew Russell.

I couldn't help notice you from across the room. I was wondering if you would like to dance."

The first lady with a smile said, "Why not, fly-boy? After all, I did bring Sting."

DEDICATION

It was May 30, 2008, when I first met Captain Brad "Joho" Johanson on the bridge of the USS *John C. Stennis*. He was its commanding officer.

I was invited on board the *Stennis* as part of the US Navy's Distinguished Visitor program as the *Stennis* was conducting carrier qualifications off San Diego in preparation for deployment as part of the US Navy's Seventh Fleet.

Although I knew Captain Johanson for only a short time, I found him to be an inspirational and effective leader who cared a great deal for his officers, crew, and mission. We discussed the tremendous responsibility involved in commanding the *Stennis* and the importance of duty and safety.

We kept in touch after my embark on the *Stennis*, and I learned that Captain Johanson had contracted ALS.

With the support of his wife, Junay, daughter, and two sons, he maintained a positive attitude as ALS took its unyielding toll.

I am pleased to dedicate this novel to Captain Bradley "Joho" Johanson in recognition of his life long career in the US Navy and commitment to duty.

If you have the ability, please consider donating to the Muscular Dystrophy Association to aid in ALS research, in the name of this great American—Captain Bradley Eugene Johanson. I will be donating some of the proceeds from this book to that worthy cause.

Et Al.

In closing, I would like to borrow from P.G. Wodehouse. I want to thank my wife, Jean, my son, Andrew, and my daughter, Katie, without whose constant love and attention this book would've been finished in half the time—but without whom life wouldn't been half as fully lived.

Made in the USA
San Bernardino, CA
13 July 2020